THE
WISDOM TRILOGY

April Ryedale

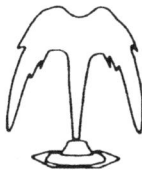

Fountainhead Press Stroud
2002

First published in Great Britain 1ˢᵗ April 2002
by Fountainhead Press Stroud
20 Perry Orchard, Westrip, Stroud

ISBN 0 9532135 4 4 (p/b)
ISBN 0 9532135 5 2 (h/b)

Previous publications:
My Enemy My Friend 1993
Remains to be seen 1998
Wisdom Stranded 1998
Strands of Wisdom 2000
Risking Wisdom 2002

Cover design by John Button based on a bronze Sculpture by
Gertraud Goodwin of Lapwing Studios
Designed and typeset by Bookcraft Ltd, Stroud
Printed and bound by Astral Printing, Stroud
Hard back bound by Tollbridge House, Batheaston

dedicated to
the Spirit of the Planet,
whose play of forces causes us to play,
so work to realise the playful nature
of That 'in whom we live and move
and have our being'.

Foreword

Since completing **The Wisdom Trilogy**, I realise there are three groups of thinkers, whose goodwill toward one another, this epic myth of human evolution, compressed into seven generations of the family of **Wisdom** (as the human race emerging into a consciousness of itself, that will nevermore be quenched) is seeking to enlist. These groups are: firstly, liberal, but disciplined, religious/esoteric thinkers*; second: liberal, but rigorous, empirical scientists; and finally intuitive readers, who feel themselves on the brink of greater understanding, and whose budding thought has therefore much to contribute to the unfolding of consciousness that all humanity is experiencing (considerably bolstered by the shocking events now known as '11th September' and the jolt that has given to comfortable, liberal, western consciousness).

Not myself an empirical scientist, but an intuitive, it has felt appropriate to express my vision of **Wisdom**'s descent into, and ascent from, incarnation, through a rhythmic narrative interspersed by lyrics that range from the start of last century (when colonisation in the South could bring later, northern, civilisations into touch with earlier cultures) to maybe the middle of this we have just begun. I therefore feel required to give no intellectual account of my 'position', beyond referring inquiring readers to the body of thought that distinguishes the **Scientific and Medical Network**, of which I have had the privilege to be a full member for the past 14 years. Their Journal, **Network**, seems to have reached a peak of synchronous thought in its April and August issues of last year, with its *Manifesto for an Integral Consciousness,* followed by Chris Clarke and his wife Isabel's article, *The Primacy of Connectivity: Onwards from the Manifesto,* together with a rich diet of relevant opinion on the needed rapprochement of science and religion, which I promote as conjunction of the transcendent with the immanent divine.

---

* I have especially in mind here **The Lucis Trust**, of whose Arcane School I was an active member for 14 years.

None of this **Network** feast could I spare the energy to savour, as I brought to completion last spring the Trilogy's concluding volume, *Risking Wisdom*, and was thereafter wholly involved in preparing it for publication. Not till September therefore did I discover how my thought had marched with that of the membership, despite (or maybe because of !) my latent ongoing friction with what I experienced as the 'unwitting' patriarchy of most of its leading members. New readers will discover that gender, rather than race, has come to be perceived by me as the deepest split within humanity, and it is partly for this reason that I am here reprinting intact the quite recently written Foreword to *Risking Wisdom*, while absorbing into this one essential insights from those written for the earlier books. I have done this because the theme of androgyny only takes centre stage, as the proper solution of gender conflict, in the final phase *(Life Spreading)* of the whole work. But a fresh understanding of the place in world cosmogonies of the creative Hindu God, **Siva**, caused me to modify my views on this and thus give prominent space to it therein. Similarly, I find in this current issue of *Network* just received, obituaries of the founder of **SMN**, now 'promoted' to serve in other realms. These make it clear, if you read between the lines, that this noble and intriguing man had every androgynous trait that I hold dear. I cannot therefore, as a reasonable, liberal feminist, fail to see that older members, at least, are viewing the **Network** through a prism of gender completeness that transforms its patriarchy – though it may well be leaving intact its paternalism, an allied issue about which every one of us is, I believe, ambivalent (both as to what we really want, and what we may be offering).

This brings me to my central theme: the place and nature of the **Seven Rays** in human understanding of itself and its environment. (See especially the First Scenario of the **Prelude**; the **Seeker** and **Recorder Interlude** between Phases I and II of Book Two; and **Appendix 3**, as well as the final paragraphs of the aforementioned Foreword to Book Three). The channelling of the Tibetan adept by Alice Bailey (who founded the Arcane School I have so long been working with) yielded 18 books, of which more than a quarter form **The Treatise on the Seven Rays**. Essentially these are seven different levels or types of energy, which he firmly numbers One to Seven, and then divides into

v

'two great lines of force': 1-3-5-7, the energy of Will; and 2-4-6, that of Love-Wisdom. Unless the presence of both is expressed in any individual, a lack of balance will be apparent.

Because the underlying assumption (not only of physicists) is that all is energy, of one kind or another – physical/subtle/spiritual – Ray theory is a very far-reaching thesis. Since coming to work with it as a hypothesis, I have found myself preferring to look at all psychological traits through this prism, and to apply it equally to macro events, including those of races and nations, and all the forms in all the 'kingdoms' we have learned to classify (as well as some that lie beyond our ken). This encourages our perception that there is a factor of 'difference' we might term 'quality', which has a permanence that forms shaped by natural selection do not acquire. Such refracted perspectives seem more intrinsic than are most analyses in accounting for the basic differences we find in human beings, who argue from apparently similar premises to totally opposite conclusions, as to what it is best to do in any given set of circumstances. Such is the breeding ground of conflict: the Tibetan actually names Ray Four (the middle ray), **The Ray of Harmony through Conflict**.

We need to understand, however, that at the level of the dense physical, where the subrays of Ray Seven manifest, such cosmic rays are potentially lethal, whether reacting on us or radiated by us – only their randomness seeming to render them harmless. It may thus be due more to our ignorance than to our good intent that we appear innocuous. For we are each in fact a walking arsenal, just as we would be if we carried guns or knives or poison, or phials of anthrax – or used ourselves as suicidal guided missiles...

All this **Wisdom** and her progeny, in their various guises, come to understand. The conception of faults and flaws as inseparable from the facets that make the beauty of a jewel what it is – earth being the jewel on whose facets humans dwell – runs right through all three volumes of this Trilogy.

Of unique relevance to the process whereby the **Wisdom** narrative and the vision behind it were vouchsafed (as coherent images with words to utter them) is a lucid article in this current late December *Network* issue, *The Potential of Emptiness: Vacuum States in Physics and Consciousness*. Its author, Allan Wallace, here describes both these levels in terms of 'true' and 'false' vacuum states, such vital metaphors being shared by both these processes. Perhaps 'relative' (with 'absolute') would be a less unflattering term for describing the creative space out of which I reckon to have written. I recognise this as the 'partial' vacuum that brings about manifestation in consciousness as well as in the actual world. The implications of the 'true' vacuum are of course infinitely wider and deeper than this, and may perhaps be usefully associated with the work done by **Vision** and **Love-lyric** in those corrosive 'border places' they were so much drawn to, in their adventurous teenage zest.

In offering you this culmination of my life understanding, I can but hope that a reciprocal goodwill may flow through those groups of thinkers named above, some of whom may be my natural constituency.

January 2002

For as much as this Work could not have come to birth without the continuing support of Marge Clouts, so neither could it have reached the public domain without the technical help and spiritual understanding of Catherine Crocker.

For further information about the **Scientific and Medical Network** write to:
The Administrative Director
PO Box 11
Moreton-in-Marsh
Gloucestershire
GL56 0SF

telephone: 01306 710072
e-mail: info@scimednet.org

CONTENTS

PRELUDE

TWO POSSIBLE SCENARIOS

I

Long before Time was or could have been was Will-to-Be.
This could not manifest without opposing force: the energy
to induce structure on to wayward might-have-beens, bring
form to shapelessness — become aware of difference.
                                                          Will
shone with such intense agonal brightness —
                                            Rays began
to emanate from the dark/white fulminating core — and play
in ever widening arcs of brilliance.
                                      Aeons passed
as feelings of pure identity attached to some of these —
                                                        until
four of these rays could know themselves and say:
                                                  I am.

As Earth solidified to land and sea —
                                       these
                                            four
                                                quartered
the planet: North
                  South
                       East
                            West —
                                   to form great
fiery, influencing cores: deep, deep beneath the ocean floors —
matched as invisibly in clouds, in wind, in rain, in sky.

II

Once upon a time long, long ago there was Wisdom
…and she was present everywhere with all the desire
and all the intensity
of all there was.

Was it good, this infinite presence of the not-yet-created?
It simply was…
Wisdom alone knew something of its possibilities.

At last in time without time… the Word was spoken,
birthed from uncreation as surely as a mother births a child.

Ceaselessly she loved creation out of uncreation…
She alone knew that the Word arrived
as both gift and burden.

Into the vast unutterable space Wisdom poured herself.

She alone knows something of the possibilities.

These words (used with the permission of Sheffield Academic Press, from their *A to Z of Feminist Theology*) are excerpts from the entry on **Wisdom** by Lucy Tatham).

WISDOM
STRANDED

Unfurling from the felt constraints of **Will**,
Wisdom wandered off and lost herself;
shrank from many places she passed through
(dark after glowing spaces she had known).

But she was free to use her eyes and see
how people lived in what she took to be
　　　　　　　　　　　her father's kingdom.

One day she met a boy who took her in.
He seemed witless, but he shared his shack
and all he had: he brought her food and drink,
and kept her body warm from bitter winds ...

In response her belly grew and grew
all summer through and autumn too.
At last at winter solstice she brought forth
　　　　　　　　　　　a baby — **Wit**.

Witless thought **Wisdom** wonderful:
he delighted in her growing this pumpkin
being in her belly —
　　　　　　　　　　then vigorously,
rhythmically
　　　　　　　　　　　　pushing it out
into the light of day.
　　　　　　　　　　　　All three
cried together for love and joy.
　　　　　　　　　　Then **Witless**
cleaned up everything, while **Wisdom** fed
Wit at her creaming breasts.

He grew to be
a cunning child and sturdy.
Witless made him
a tiny bow and arrow and he could shoot
a lizard off the wall before he walked.
Lying
awake, he had watched them from his crib
and knew which way they'd move and when.
His arrow moved faster.
When they fell
he crawled to pick them up,
and his mother put them in her stewpot
with coriander and crushed garlic.

All three feasted till they fell asleep together.

Witless had no idea he had anything
to do with **Wit** coming into the world.
He felt good providing all that **Wit**
and **Wisdom** needed — specially
when they all lay down with bellies full
by the glowing fire he made so skilfully
out of two sticks —
and a bit of hard rubbing.
Amazing what two sticks could do !

Witless chuckled as his own grew upright —
thinking of the pleasure other efforts made —
how roused and rousing **Wisdom**
could become.

Wit
was playing with small stones he'd found
outside, where he crawled when the door
was open, **Wisdom** busy.
There were four

(which he did not know).
He put them in a line, so all
the spaces looked the same between.
He sat —
                    and liked them.
                                        Then
he took two: one in each fist
and placed them below
the other two, and liked that
even better.
                    He had made
a square by putting two
and two together —
                                        (but
he didn't know that either).

                              Wisdom did
though, when she came and saw.
                                        She laughed
and gathered him and crooned:

                                        *Ah — **Wit**,*
***Wit**, you'll be the death of me !*
                                        He clung
to her and shuddered, not knowing why.

                                        Wit
called his father **Wittle**, which was fitting,
since his father was always
whittling sticks for arrows
or for fires for cooking
what they caught when far from home.

For **Wit** was big enough to keep up now,
and only got a ride on **Wittle**'s back,
when tired and bringing home
best cuts for **Wisdom**.

So the joyful years rolled on
for this lone and tiny family in the forest.

There came at last the day
when **Wit** was old enough
to go hunting on his own
with an almost mansize bow.

As he walked through the forest
following the paths of game,
his hunter's eye
                    spied among the trees ahead
a creature
                    walking upright.

                              Wit had never
seen anyone on two legs
except his parents.
                              This one,
sensing something,
                    turned,
                              startled
to see **Wit** fitting an arrow to his bow.
Though she knew many people on two legs,
she had never seen a bow and arrow.

Alone with her mother near the edge
of town, she seldom went into the woods;
was only there today because perplexed
by what her mother said about a brother.

And now here was a brother
readymade

                              — but doing what ?
Wit met her eye —
                         and dropped his bow.
Light flashed
                                   between them
and for a long minute......
                              each looked past
what the other seemed to see:

Wit saw someone more like his mother
than his father;
                         she the brother
she would never have.
                                        Each
like a rooted tree
                    heard the leaves
                                   whisper:
You can move more than we.

She stepped forward;
                         he stepped back.
A tree root tripped him
and his arrow stabbed
his foot.
                    She saw the blood and ran,
picking a large leaf as she passed
under the tricking plane.
                                             Wit

wondered that anyone so young
should seem so like his mother.
He leant against the tree trunk,
easing inside as its big leaf
pressed and balmed him —

                                   shaken
that an arrow hurt so much.
                                   What

were he and his father doing when they
hunted ?
What was this being doing

here ?

What were you aiming at
when you saw me ?

Her voice like a brook
spilled the stillness
he was lost in.
O no, no!

He lapsed
into silence, at the thought of paining
this hand's owner
like his foot.

What are you called ?
*I'm **Wiz**, short for **Wiz-dom**.*

I'm Wit.
My father calls my mother Wisdom.
I've never seen anyone but them
on two legs —

I was afraid.

Are you now ?

No.

Does it hurt still ?
The bleeding's stopped.

Wit put out
a shy hand to touch the one that stanched.
Not now.

That surprised him.

Pains
lasted longer unless he got up and did
something.

Yet here he sat in deep
contentment.

Wiz wondered whose home

was closer, if this boy's foot were really
harmed.
                        Wit followed her thought
as if she spoke.
                        **It only grazed the bone —
I didn't shoot it.**
                                Wit was
cheerful now and knew
he could have stood, only —
he didn't want to break the spell
of their held hands.
                        But **Wiz** felt brisk —
now the blood was clotting.
                                Can you stand ?
I live near the edge of these woods.
I'll take you home.

                        Wit knew they were miles
from his, so,
                        determined not to lose
contact with this soothing girl,
                                he'd risk
the utterly unknown.
                        Natural hunter,
he'd follow where the spoor was leading.
He stood, still holding the hand
that now rose with him to heart level.
This time their eyes met from so close
they closed.
                        Wit saw a pattern
like his own: two people and a child
and it flashed through him
what could make it real.
                                Wiz saw
what he saw —
and knew why her mother
left her father.

Her body shook
with desire and fear.

                            Wit felt it shoot

through his hand on hers
and reach his hurt foot.

Breathing hard, each opened both eyes
and this time
                really saw
                          a little.

Wit saw a long-haired frightened girl
in a loose blue tunic;
                    Wiz a dark boy

with almost nothing on.
This did not lessen her fear,
nor yet the sap that rose:
both together,
rising sap and fear,
cancelled.
                Her inside drew back.
                            Wit,

quite unaware of the power surging
through his nearly naked body,
closed in on this blue dryad.
(He had often seen them
in the trees, but not for touching).
His hard member pressed her —

and **Wiz** sprang from
this urgent hunter she had healed.

She fled.
                Wit followed to her quick-shut door
to mark her dwelling for his future scrying.

He felt abashed —
as he stood in a double row
of solid houses:
where boys in clothes,
kicking a sort of dead animal
down the street,
were gazing at him
in astonishment.

Wit looked down at himself
and saw
how different he was
from all these others —
who yet were more like him
than **Wiz**.

Seeker: So **Wit** is faced with difference —

                                          by chasing **Wiz**.
             Do you feel a big difference between

                                          the two scenarios
             that announce this tale

                                 of how their story will unfold ?

Recorder: *No more perhaps than which way round a circle you*
             go to re-arrive at the beginning!

Seeker: O — I hope
             our living here on earth does more than that!

                                                        I note
             one of these scenarios speaks of **Will**

                                                 as the core
             all else derives from

                                    while the other

                                                  places all
             the onus (and the gift) on **Wisdom**.

Recorder: *spurred into action*
by the **Word**, *remember* —

Seeker: Agreed — and then we have
Wisdom wandering away from **Will** and getting lost.

Recorder: *Indeed! This story is that* **Word** *in action.*
                                               When
Wisdom *plunges* —

Seeker: But surely that's a different
matter —
          or doesn't difference really matter?
                                        Did you know
that at the turn of this century, a geologist
thought he could solve all the differences
between earth scientists
                                        by proposing
that the continents are moving
                                        and maybe
have been for a hundred million years?

Recorder: (startled)   *No!*
Well, as this is a speeded up telling
of the human story
                              in seven generations
from its first awakening . . .

Seeker: From the slime
or from the light?

Recorder: *Things started from the light*
at just the time they started from the slime

Seeker: when
Wisdom began pouring herself into space —

Recorder: *and time*
began —

Seeker: as cells were forming from bacteria
by chance —

16

and with a little help from polar light.

Recorder: *More than a little!*
That was **Wisdom** *'s light.*

Seeker: Even if she didn't know it —
nor the bacteria
in the slime.

Recorder: *who will after aeons come to form*
the trillion-celled bodies of human beings —
such as
Wiz *and* **Wit**.

Seeker: Some jump!
So where
has that brought us?

Recorder: **Wit**, *bred straight from*
Wisdom, *lost,*
has come out of the forest
darkness — to discover his sense of difference . . .
And you
are telling me now that all the continents are
on the move.
Where to?

Seeker: They're drifting apart
from one another all the time —
but no one
believed the man who said so.
They couldn't see
how such heavy masses could
just come adrift
like that, and then take off.
Solid after all is
solid!

Recorder: *Not to a Light being!*
Nor to a physicist —
today.

17

Seeker: No, but these were down-to-earth Earth
Scientists.
                              What's more, they were discovering
the earth is not just cooling down and shrinking:
radioactivity might even be heating earth again —
so lands could be getting bigger and colliding, as
well as drifting off —
                              for all they knew.

Recorder: *For all any
scientist knew!*
                              *So knowledge was fragmenting
and continents conflicting.*

Seeker: And almost nobody was
ready to believe it really was.

Recorder: *Well, who would!*
Actually the story of **Wit** *and* **Wiz** *takes place
in a vast country south of the Tropics, whose
hinterland is largely unexplored.*
                                                   *Those who
colonised and mapped it call it* **Godwonland**.

Seeker: Does that make a difference ?

Recorder: *I think it might —
especially in view of what you've told me.
The four great Rays who influenced the earth
when only slime was visible*
                                             *will be joined by
three more such rays as human force begins
to make itself felt in actions, feelings, thoughts
— because the progeny of* **Wisdom** *have emerged
from the deep forest to a town in* **Godwonland**.

Seeker: And will they too be invisible ?

Recorder:
But their effects will be

history (or hers)

As causes, yes.

everything we see as

Seeker:

So let it be.

Wiz' mother was known to her immigrant friends as **Sap**, her father having named her **Sapientia** —
                    after her mother died birthing her twin brother, whose head so wedged in the birth canal, he choked and could not be revived.
                    Sap had her child by a man on campus (where her father taught). His name was **Sophist**, so it would have made sense to call this child **Sophia**, in line with a trend in kinship groups to name all offspring by the kin initial.
                    But **Sap** chose to break with this and gave as reason her dislike of **Sophie** as a shortening.
                    But she never seemed to mind her bright daughter being known as **Wiz**.

            Sap was at her loom when **Wiz** appeared
                    breathless and high-coloured. Back to the shut door
            O mother, I've met such a beautiful boy — he frightens me.

            Sap smiled as she turned from the lovely browns and ochres she was weaving:

19

                          Yes,
beauty in a body can be terrifying.
Where did you meet him ?
                         Deep in
the forest where I went, because
of what you said about my father.
I ran away,
                  but he's followed me.

Sap, moving to the window, saw
the back of a nearly naked youth
retreating down their street.

He's gone, but he knows you live
here —
                  he'll be back.

  I know he will:
               he wants a family
and I want him, but —

                Do you want
a girl —
        or boy ?
                Sap was back
at her weaving, having cradled
Wiz' head to reassure.

                    Wiz
again saw **Wit**'s imagined family.
  He wants a son
             I saw him wanting.
  Why ?
        It is what you deeply want
that will decide.
           But I — don't mind.
*I want **Wit**'s son, I want his child.*

Why is it only boys who kill their mothers ?

Sap heaved a deeper sigh than **Wiz** had
ever heard.
                              Her shuttle rested
as she turned once more to face her child.
I don't for certain know they do:
I only know your granfer says
my mother died and so did my twin brother
in the womb I came from.
                              And you have
noticed this among our friends.
*Have you met **Wit**'s mother ?*
                              No, but
*he says her name is also **Wisdom**.*

Sap's eyebrows rose.
                                        Where
do they live ?
                    Wiz shrugged:
                                        deep
in the forest, I suppose.
                              He has no clothes.
Then we'll have to wait —
until he finds some and comes back.

Wit had no trouble tracing his way back
to the place in the forest he'd encountered
Wiz — (and left his bow and saucy arrow)
though he'd seemed to notice nothing as
he'd chased her out.
                              He sat again
under the plane tree wondering:

what was that world out there
she'd come from?
                    Was it his to know —
or must he find a way to lure her
back to his?

                    He felt more changed
by things this day
                    (when he'd caught
nothing) than by the high of killing
and coming back with what they'd shot.
At least he knew where his quarry
for today had gone to ground.
                    Wisdom
was alone when he reached home.

                                        She
knew at once he'd found a girl — and
lost her. Every cell in his body was
alive.
          She waited.
                    **What happened
to your foot?**

He wasn't limping, but the clotted
blood was not from bramble snags.

Wit looked where she did, not
at her.
                    He had forgotten this
was how it all began.
                                        At last
he raised his eyes to hers and let
them say what she already knew:
in one day of hunting he had grown
away from her —
                    and yet his need
was no less great.
                    Wisdom's eyes
were pools deeper than **Wit** had
swum in.

22

They embraced his new
need — and they carried also a new
pain.
                    I wounded myself he said
at last — and laughed.
                            He knew she
knew he had not done so on his own.

And I've brought nothing home
he added with a rare trace of shame.

Your father caught a salmon –
she nodded toward the cooking pot
where the smell of herbs and cooking
fish already soothed his unstrung body.

    Where is Wittle now?
                            I'm not

quite sure –
                        Wisdom shrugged,
but — a shade of something crossed
her face.
                    Wit who had so long ago
put two and two together wondered
now whether they made four or five.

    So he's not coming in to eat?
    Is it ready then for us?

                                        Yes
said **Wisdom** putting clay plates
ready, and dipping a wooden ladle
in the pot she had wisely put raw
chunks of salmon into only when
Wit's footsteps reached the door.

Brought from the river only six hours
back, it was a delicate, much
relished feast.
                        Wit licked
his fingers and his lips:

      Mother,
are there other people
in this forest ?
      I think there must be,
yes, don't you ?
        Her eyes
challenged him.
      Then why
have we never come upon them ?

Maybe they didn't want us to.
We've never needed anyone —
till now.
     Again her eyes plumbed
his.
  Is this salmon his goodbye then ?

Wisdom sighed.
      It might be.

Wit saw at once that if it was,
his mother would need him more —
but there'd be room for **Wiz** —
once he'd won her.
     It was a big,
big jump.
     He'd hoped to talk
with **Wittle** about **Wiz**, and feel
his way to what he thought might
happen.
    Now even that had changed:
only the forest trees —
     and **Wisdom**
were the same.
     And he was not.

So each ruminated in the dark
the newness of the world they found.

Wit knew he would have to put on clothes
to find his way inside the house
in that daunting row **Wiz** lived in —
knew he would have to ask his mother's
help.

      Although she did not wear clothes
like **Wiz**, she did cover up herself —
as he did not.

               He felt
he knew
      she would want to help him win her,
even though —

         Here he could not clothe
his thoughts with words.....

         Mother,
he said, as she brought the clean plates back
from the freshet she had washed them in
outside —
      **I need to wear something —
like Wittle does.**

        Wisdom did not ask why.
As she sought with her mind's eye to 'see'
this girl who had so swiftly stolen
her son's heart,
         she fetched out
Wittle's second best wolf-skin.
         (He had gone
out in his best after bringing her the salmon
earlier.)
        Wit met her eye
with thankful warmth as he took and put it on.

Now he was a man.

                                    Wit and **Wisdom**
spent the evening by the fire together.
                                         Wittle
did not come back.

                              In the morning
Wit set out without his bow.
                                    He had
agonised all night because he longed
to take a trophy of his skill to **Wiz**.
                                         But
the thought of that street and how he'd look —
with a dead and bleeding animal
across his shoulder
                              unnerved him.

So **Wit** was wise and went with empty hands
to refind **Wiz**, persuade her if he could —
to come and live with him and his mother
in the forest.
                                    Boldly
he walked up the street
                         (though feeling craven)
and waited at the door he'd been shut out of.

Sap, who had already seen him coming,
beamed at his confusion as she opened
to him.
                    She wore a rich turquoise gown
with a strange interlocking pattern at the hem.
Her hair fell goldenwhite to her shoulders.
Her face, framed by it, was like **Wiz**', but —
lined a little like his mother's, which was dark.

And where her eyes were pools,

                              these
pierced
              and also mocked —
                         as **Wit**
stood and gaped
              for all his splendid wolfskin.
Wit did not know of course how beautiful
he looked.
              Nor did **Sap** mean to tell him.
But she understood what **Wiz**
                         (who had
vanished when she saw him come) found so
inducing.
              Wit's wits returned.
Are you Wiz' mother ?
                         I am Wit.

Why, so you are, come in
                         said **Sap**.
*I don't think **Wiz** is all that far away.*
                         Nor
would she be while her daughter met again
this vigorous young man.
                         Wit nodded
as his eye and sense took in the house
he stood in —
              so unlike his shack.
                         Bright
with shining windows, where the sun
streamed in to highlight
                         a rich-textured picture
in a heavy wooden frame:
                         pale blue sky
behind a mountain;
                         another below it
upside down.

                              Sap's shuttle
had now reached the foreground: bare rocks
on the lake shore.
                              But **Wit**
had never seen reflected mountains —
let alone a picture or a loom.
                              Sap's eye
followed his gaze —
                    gauging what he made
of what he saw.
                    His eyes were puzzled, but
his face showed pleasure.
                         His body spun,
as it registered **Wiz**' entrance.
                              This time
Sap briskly broke the spell of their eyes
meeting — by looking from one to the other
as they realigned.
                    Wiz wore a violet tunic
and was glad to see **Wit** clad.
                              His wolfskin
certainly became him
                    and his foot seemed
healed.

          But **Wit** knew he could not take her
from this polished place —
                    to his dark hovel.
Wiz saw his face falling as he grasped this…

But **Sap**, impatient to meet the mother of this
boy, asked where he lived.
                              **Deep
in the forest where there's little sun.
I live there with my mother.
                         Father's gone,
I think, but......**

*Why
don't you take us to her?*

gently **Sap**
suggested.
Then we'll see.

She was already
discarding her long gown —
revealing
a workmanlike tunic underneath.

It took
a good while longer to reach the shack
in the forest than **Wit** did on his own,
though he traced a shorter route than
by the plane tree.

Sap asked busily
the names of plants
(as she memorised
the route for her own reasons).

Names
Wit gave were not the Latin ones she
knew them by.

She became especially
excited when she found
Glossopteris —
a species of tree-fern believed extinct
for millions of years.

It grew dark
as the canopy thickened,
but **Wit** was
making for a light that glowed along
a pathway, so well trodden by his still
naked feet,
they could not miss it.

Wiz
and **Sap** presumed it was a lamp.
Yet,
as they drew near, it moved.

                                        A candle
then ?
                    The door opened as they stopped
before it.
                Wisdom had no candle.
                                            Light
flowed from her, glowed in her, lit
the shades of brown and grey and black
she fashioned from strips of bark
and grasses dried.
                            Wit, having lived
with this being all his life, had no idea
she was unusual.
                        Sap's face was rapt.
She and **Wisdom** gazed at one another
with a deep remembrance of a far-off time:

a place of infinite light, a space
where all knowing was, all Life.
                                    The One
of **Will** begetting **Wisdom**,
                            then the pull
toward an arena where this Will be done.

The confluence of **Wit** and **Wiz** would be
the first manifesting
                        of this potency.
                                            So
Sap's racing thinking said;
                        Wisdom's depths
felt, rather, the breath that had impelled her
when she left the Light —
                            to land in this dark
wood where she brought forth
                                this lovely
knowledgeable boy, who now had found

30

and brought to her
                         the felt wisdom
of his love of life.
                         Her own
saw into the future and she quailed —
as she felt their children's children fall away.

Wisdom drew herself back to the present as
she looked at **Wit** and **Wiz** and saw
their tender lying together under law:
the two unrolling ends of a precious scroll
unwrapped for wondering;
                         for sharing
the ancient hidden code,
                         the realigning dance
of destiny, when two people's genes are first
unravelled,
             then dovetailed
                         after choosing
half the pairs —
                         awaiting the right setting
for their growing.
                         Sap was following
Wisdom's images and saw her moment:

                                    Where
is best for **Wit** *and* **Wiz** *to live ?*
                                    They must
dwell wherever the breath can reach
them best.

             These were the first words uttered
since the four had come together.
                         Now they
came inside and sat, at the four compass
points:

Sap in the north and
Wisdom in the south;

                                    Wit in the east
and **Wiz** the west.

                                    They sat
with closed eyes for a long time
and did not speak.

                         Wit broke the silence
first:
     **I've seen I am going to have to learn
another way.**
                    **I think I may just have
understood something I saw yesterday —
in the street outside Wiz' house.**
                                **I saw
boys kicking something thick, and took it
for some kind of animal (it wasn't stone
or tree).**
                    **Maybe a bloated animal skin —
I wasn't noticing.**
                    **But now I sense my feet,
and not my hands,**
                      **are going to be pivotal
in what will bring me joy and livelihood.
I do not yet see how and when this can
replace hunting as what will keep Wiz
and Mother warm and fed —**
                              **but I see
it will somehow if I go ahead, not
fearfully,**
                  **I saw already yesterday,
when the arrow pierced my foot, I must
think again about the killing arrow.**
Wit puzzled,
                looked round the group and saw
smiles on all the women's faces:
                          Wisdom's
inscrutable.

Sap had a knowing look:
she clearly saw Wit's livelihood — at least
until Wiz as mother would feel ready to go
forth to bring home bread.
Wiz herself,
enjoying School and flitting between that
and being perhaps the helpless mother
of this boy's baby —
smiled as she saw
where the arrow pointed,
even anointed
Wit's foot for skills he did not know he had.

Her own meditation had relieved her
somewhat of her fear of dying giving birth
to Witson.
What Wiz said,
never having
looked into the dark like this before, was:
*what a lot of light we seem to have thrown
into the deep darkness of this wood.*
You
seem to see the way the arrow's pointing,
Wit, so maybe the path will open up.
It will,
said Sap with worldwise confidence.

So Wit
and Wiz went walking in the woods.

And Sap
came close and she and Wisdom locked
into each others arms and breathed
earth rhythms until both
felt filled and stilled.

Sap stirred:
*Beloved, now we have found each other
and ourselves,*

*is there anything we two can do
to impel this coming century on its way?*

Wisdom uttered a low, deep laugh:
**What
more can be done?**

**Have you seen
what future awaits the family they'll
raise?**

*I've seen that **Wit** will put football
on the map throughout the South,*

*but I
am more concerned about **Wiz**' safety
giving birth to boys — all other women's
too.*

*Did you have trouble birthing **Wit**?*

**None at all –   though I had no urge
for more.**

Wisdom looked thoughtful as
she pictured **Wittle**'s silent going.
Though he had been on walkabout
before, he had never taken off
without a word —

(nor worn
his smartest wolf-skin).

Had
some urge he could not give
a name to — taken hold?

*Does
Wittle know what makes a baby?*

Sap had been following **Wisdom**'s
unsaid thought.

Now **Wisdom**
looked at her and sighed:

                              He didn't
  – but Wit does, though I've . . .

He does indeed and **Wiz** *is more*
than willing to have his children
— but she is afraid.
                              We know many
mothers who have died because
brains are getting bigger year by
year — and it's mostly boys they
die from.
                              I think girls' brains
convolute — instead of swelling
in the skull.
                              It's not that boys
are brighter, but they are more
confident.
                              Things could get badly
out of balance and destroy
                              the way
of bringing children in — to grow
and learn . . .

              It is going out of balance.
I have seen it.
              Men have doted on us
not knowing the part they play in
making babies.
              Now they do, they
turn away, desiring to make quite
other things.
              The world will change
in ways we've never dreamed.
                              I see
Wit's son a factor in that change I
cannot bear to know.
                              It was **Sap's**
turn to look grave.
                              Wisdom put out
a tender hand:
                              Dear one, Wiz will
not die.

She will have three
children and much to make her
sad – but she will not die in
childbirth.
I think a change
will come:
babies will not want
to stay a moment longer in this
cosy place.
The womb will pinch
and push and make them want to
find the light of day.
I have
only seen this, dear one, since
you came.

Yes said a much eased **Sap**.
*It needs the two of us to bring light
to the foreground.*
*We see from
different viewpoints and we need
to pool our seeing.*
**Now that Wit's
aligned to football, Sap, I do
not think his force will tune to
making babies – however much
they both enjoy enjoying**
each
other's forms.

*I wouldn't be
surprised if* **Wiz'** *first use of her
new energy*
is teaching **Wit** *to read
and write.*
*He'll have to go to school
to learn to play with other boys!
Has he seen a boy in all his life?*

Only Wittle, Wisdom smiled.

When **Wiz** and **Wit** returned, they saw, as
they approached,

                a double glow.
Wiz had never seen her mother look
like this.

      Or had **Sap** only now been fully lit ?

Seeker: Whew!
      But I must check carefully with you
                        which century
      we're throwing light on — since it's really very long
      ago that brain expansion was endangering the lives
      of mothers
                  through their unborn babes —
                              and never
      more by boys than girls.

Recorder: *That's true, I'm sure.*
      Girls' lives were more at risk after they were born —
      and in many places they still are.

Seeker: That I must concede.
      I also understand this family has to bear the burden
      and the gift
                  of human evolution
                            into the present
      and beyond.

Recorder: *This fable sees the coming into time*
      *of **Sap** and **Wisdom**,*
                        each embedded
      in her own culture,
                    as the coming together

of our western ways

in this subtropical
southern continent of **Godwonland** –

at
the very outset,

the lynchpin of our 20th
century,

when meeting with stone age people
came to be a norm.

We stress the wisdom
of the forest people —

freely interpreted
as unconscious elements of being human —

Seeker: Indeed
strenuously denied by colonisers

to exist at all!

Recorder (slyly):   Like the denial of the moving lands
beneath our feet?

Perhaps together we can
offer this befuddled end,

not just of our century,
but our millennium —

a speeded up portrait
of humanity,

as it descends from an inner state
of knowing —

to a vast knowledge from
encyclopaedias,

such a capacity for technofix . . .

Seeker: Yes — I see more clearly now our points of view
could dovetail

and even appreciate this way
of seeing things —

so long as we don't start
switching readers off

by claiming we know
the truth of things.

Recorder: *Don't forget this is a comedy,*
claiming no less divinity than **Dante***.*
                                                        Logos
ludens *lies behind it all:*
                              playful god of a benign
cosmos —
                              as our modern football myth
is there to show.

Seeker: Though that I fear is not to say
all will be fun and games for **Wit**
                                        coming to terms
with school
                              and learning to play football with
his colonising comrades.

Recorder: *You could indeed say that —*
remembering that
                              Wisdom *alone knows*
something of the possibilities . . .

Seeker: . . . of life with the **Word**
as gift and burden —
                    yes.

PHASE II

WIT AND WIZ
BEGIN A FAMILY

Only **Wiz**' flare for sharing
       her understanding,
Wit's will to be the man
       he was becoming,
Sap's careful husbanding
       of time and energy,
allowed the settling of new patterns
              once it was clear that
              where the breath was best
meant **Wit** and **Wiz** together
       under **Sap**'s roof
       and in her care.

Sap herself lived frugally and knew
her weaving skills could only just
support feeding and clothing the two
of them at school.
              She had already
pulled out all the stops for getting
Wit accepted in the local school —
where **Wiz** was the brightest spark.

Apart from shorts and tunics
              Sap had made him,
Wit had to put on a pair of boots.
       His own soles were leather,
but his toes would break if he tried
              a full-blown kick:
he could lift sharply with his instep,
              dribble skilfully
from the balls of his feet, toes clear —
              but hardest was
protecting toes from boys with boots.

It took time to break in his weathered
              feet, feel the same
sensing he had had the first time he saw
              boys kicking, knew

the urge to make the ball go where
               it must — to count.

This mattered more than making
friends.
          He had **Wiz** always and
her generous mother.
                    He also
missed his own — though his new
sense of manhood forbade his
recognising this.

                    So he went,
barefoot and fairly often,
                    to 'keep
an eye' on her and bring her food
smuggled from **Sap**'s larder or
from School.

          He had turned his
back on hunting since the double
revelation
          of his stabbed foot —
almost as though its healing
depended on his being true
                              to
his new vision of himself.
                    Indeed,
he thought, as he sped through
his childhood woods —
                    leaping
fallen trees and plunging through
familiar scrub —
                    the rubbing
boots could never have been borne
— if that wound reopened.

               Wisdom
enjoyed the bright new tunics **Wit**
came in, but found him otherwise
not unlike the son she bore.

She
hardly needed the food he brought
(except to put on the table for his
supper).

With none to cook for, she
could almost live on dew and scents
of woodland flowers.
She knew where
mushrooms grew — and where
they
moved throughout the year.
She
picked berries as the seasons changed:
bilberries, whortleberries, elder — all
grew in clearings where the sun came
through.
Nor was it beyond her skill
to guddle for trout or even
lure a
salmon to the bank.
(Though missing
Wittle's handiness with stone for
killing, she never used hook and line
or set a trap.)
She carefully selected
herbs to make aromatic brews, which
Wit could smell as he approached.

His
first visit after he felt he'd mastered
the esoteric art of writing
and could
read it back and understand,
his pride
bubbled into his talk and **Wisdom** said:

**All right then, write this down
and read it back. Have you paper
and pencil in that bag?**

              Wit
beamed:
    **Of course I have! I always carry
everything I need.**

           Though **Wisdom**
had nothing in the house to write on —
or write with (nor missed them),
                she
made up poems in her mind and could
remember them.
          They pondered themes
that hardly touched the daily details
Sap was busy with.
          So **Wisdom** began
and **Wit** screwed up his face in tight
concentration as his pencil wrote:

    The sun is a danjrus god
    mak no mistak
    and he has messinjas
    hoo kary powa.

She told him when to take
a fresh line and she stopped
at the end of the first four
for him to read it back —
which he did exactly as
he'd heard it.
            Each was
astonished by the other's
hidden powers:
            Wit had
almost no idea what his
mother's poem meant;
while she could not read
what **Wit** had written.
            She
ended with the words:

Mebbee his pashun
is bekuming ovadun.
Kud the werd be
spinning owt of awbit?

Her voice rose as she closed,
so he put a question mark, but
he gave her a sidelong glance
and looked again at the first
verse.
                    He'd worked hard with
Wiz to distinguish **sun** from
son and now he wondered which
his mother meant.

                              She was
smiling one of her most enigmatic
smiles:
              I meant it both ways
Wisdom said,
                              though in fact she
hadn't thought at all of what she
now saw hovering round her son
— but liked the ambivalence of it.

Living alone was suiting **Wisdom**
well.

Wit was having a profound effect
on **Wiz**' growing up.
                    His lithe grace in
the playground with a football (he was
the only dark-skinned boy the School
had yet admitted) took her breath away
— as did his acumen to write and read.

She taught him in that order, knowing
somehow forming letters on the page
was closer to our body's natural doing —

than using eyes to make the words make
sense.
         That followed fast as **Wit**
                           felt he
felt the sense of written words.

                        What
troubled **Wiz** was the others' fierce
dislike, both in the classroom and outside.
She had learned to cope with hidden envy
of herself,
         but winced at how they treated
Wit:
  what delighted her made them so sour
they tried to trip or catch him out;
                  stamped at
his feet when bare; tried to show up his lack
of reading skill in class (for he could so far
read only what he wrote himself).

                   Teachers
knew from **Sap**
         and avoided shaming him, but
other boys (and sometimes girls) complained
he was being favoured,
              even said he smelled —
which surely she would know!
               He didn't —
except when his sweat glands got excited,
either at football or in bed with her
                and that
was beautiful.
           During their long
walk in the woods the day of **Wit**'s inspired
seeing into his future,
          they had sealed their
tryst under the healing plane tree.
            This had
seemed to lift them into higher planes —
               which
now it needed all **Wiz**' wits to keep in mind.

Wit's day of glory came in that
first season.

                        Seniors were
disappearing overseas — to fight
'for the Mother Country', he was
told.
                   With absolutely no idea
what this could mean, **Wit** saw
its advantages when their places
in school teams
                      filled up with boys
from classes further down.

                           Wit's
mana rose when one of the forwards
broke his ankle just the day before
an away fixture with a neighbouring
School, renowned for winning all
its matches.
              The Games master, who
had been watching quietly
                  Wit's speed
at mastering both skills and rules,
                         sent
for him to assess how confident he'd
be at such short notice.
                  Wit's face
was all he needed to decide.

                   Wiz was
there among the School supporters:
this rival school had never faced
a coloured player —
                  least of all a boy
who rose like a dark angel to inject
the ball into the net as though his
brow were a direction-finder with
a pulse of energy to slam it home.

Three times he slammed, from not
expected angles —

                              either from
his forehead or his foot
                              and three
times a usually adroit, but now
confounded goalie
                    let it through.

The tide was turned:
                         both for this
match and for the sporting fortunes
of both Schools.

                    Not again did
classmates mess with **Wit** —
                              though
members of the team looked sideways
at this dark horse who gave no thought
to passing
                    as he sought the best
vantage for his own attack.

                    Since **Wit**
had had no chance to practise with
the team before his summons,
                                   Wiz
found that easy to forgive.
                              After
they had celebrated, they returned
to **Sap**.
                    She, in the easy way
they lived (**Sap** was a forerunner
of the open plan)
                         had come across
Wit's copying out of **Wisdom**'s
poem on the sun as lover.
                              With no
idea who'd written it, but drawn
by its striking images,
                         Sap had
re-copied it in standard spelling.

Listen to this
                    she said,
                                        as they
came in
                    who wrote this, **Wit***?*
I don't really understand it,
but —

                    My mother did said **Wit**
and reddened beneath his umber
skin,
            as **Wiz** and **Sap**
                                        stared
from him to the text and back.
                                             I

wrote it down.
                    I know you did,
but what does it mean? See
here:
                    power to overload
our national grids
                    and blackout cities.

Now what would you understand
a national grid to be?

Wiz and **Wit** looked at each other and
exploded in slightly drunken laughter.

I gather you won your match then,
Wit
    Sap said drily as her eyebrows rose.

Yes, he was wonderful, Ma — but
you never told us, **Wit***, your*
mother was a poet.

                    I didn't know
myself till she asked me to write that
down, when I boasted that I could.

                                        I –
**forgot when this match came up,
though I found it odd enough.**

                              But **Wiz**
was wondering:
                    *Does your mother
   see the future,* **Wit***?*
                         **Sometimes
I think she does.**
                         I know she does
said **Sap**, *but I can't see —*
                                  *I think
   perhaps I can,* **Wiz** interrupted
as she pondered.
                         *Ever since that day
   we all sat in her house to work
   our future out,*
                         *I often see
   images of* **Wit***'s future as a
   star.*
                         *I see a great stadium
   lit as though a hundred moons — or
   even suns — shone in the night so
   football could be played when*
                              *everybody's
   free from work to watch.*
                         *I don't know what 'grid'
   can mean, but*
                         Wisdom *says here
   'electric power' . . .*

                         It was **Wit**'s turn
to feel a flash —
                         like the ball bouncing off
his brow.
                    Of course he breathed, as he
recalled a recent Physics lesson
                                        (**Wiz**
was not allowed into the Lab.)

50

                          Light
can be made if electric current's stored
and carried through copper wire, from
the source to wherever it can be used.

Mother must have seen the world —
with countries, like ours, who have
this power — or will one day.
                          Maybe
she came and lived in our forest — to
get away from too much light.
                          She's —
saying here the sun is dangerous.

  Let's see the whole thing

                     said **Wiz**.

       COSMIC LOVE ?

       The sun is a dangerous god,
              make no mistake –
       and he has messengers
              who carry power.

       They seem so harmless
              on a sunny day:
       great white cumuli
              that lazy roll

       across the breezes of long
              summer days.
       Yet they come charged
              with droplets picked

       from the sun's storms as dogs
              coats pick burrs.
       Imagine millions
              of dogs, a trillion

       burrs charged with electric
              power to overload

our national grids
and black out cities —

throwing for days and nights
on end the basic
switches of our careful,
care-ful lives.
We've known for years of course
that ultra-violet
sunrays pierce our sunbathed
skins to carcinomas.

What to do? Our life
depends on nuclear
sunshine reaching us.
Maybe his passion

is becoming overdone.
Could the Word
be spinning out of orbit?

Wiz was stunned to silence —
while a thousand thoughts
flew through her.

                        When she

spoke, the only thing **Wiz**
said was

                        Isn't she a bit

    sarcastic?

                        Does the sun

    have storms?

                        I wouldn't

be surprised said **Sap**.

                        Most

people do at times.

                        She and I

must meet again and soon.

The next time **Wit** visited his mother,
he not only shared with her his prowess
in the field,
                            he also took with him
a copy of an unpublished fragment by
a **Father Gerard Manley**, which
the English Master found and rescued
from a College Magazine in Wales,
before his posting overseas.
                                                    He
tried the poem on his class of students.

Wit was drawn by it enough — as well
as puzzled by its ardency —
                                            to ask
to copy it as exercise in his personal,
and fast increasing, mastery of skills.

It felt so different in language and in
tone
    from his mother's poem on the sun —
yet both were writing of, or to,
                                        a god
— and love.

                        So he read it to her.
This time he had copied words he saw:

> *Thou mastering me, God,*
> *giver of breath and bread,*
> *world's strand, sway of the sea,*
> *Lord of living and dead —*
>
> *Thou hast bound bones and veins in me,*
>   *fastened me flesh*
> *and after it almost unmade*
>   *what with dread thy doing.*
> *And dost thou touch me afresh?*
>   *Over again I feel*
>   *thy finger and find Thee.*

What do you make of that, Mother?

But **Wisdom**'s usual bonhomie had
frozen.
      A startled **Wit** caught and held
his mother.
         Why did the poem mean
so much more to her than him?
                  Wit
had never seen his mother overdone.
He laid her on her pallet, sprinkled
water from the freshet on her face.

She smiled and hugged and reassured.

When he left, he left behind the poem.
They had not spoken either of this one
or her own.
      Alone, **Wisdom** struggled
to put words to sounds to make them fit.
What she had heard **Wit** read stirred
memories so deep of wandering
               to find
herself, then being here —
             she felt
indeed the touch of the divine Will prod
her heart.

        In the morning, **Wisdom**
could recall each word that **Wit** had read
— just as she always could the lines she
wrote herself
          in inner patternings.

This time she had a written script to
match them to — and did.
         A finger
stirred her will, unbidden.
           Some sounds
— even the first two words — jangled her

as they did when **Wit** referred to masters
from the school, but phrases like
                                    feel
thy finger and find thee
                        tangled with
her soul's spine — like **Wittle**'s fingers
she no longer missed,
                    but fell again to
wondering the why of his departing . . .

Wisdom longed for fuller
understanding:

                she had turned her back
on the overpoweringness of cosmic Will
— to be herself.
                Yet what after all was
Goodwill, of which she felt abundant
founts
            unless it was the Will to Good.

But in her wisdom she knew this must
arise in human kind from goodly giving
— such as she had given **Wit** and **Wittle**
(when he was there) and he assuredly
had given them, when **Wit** was young
and needed it.
                Wisdom wondered
now whether goodwill dried up in
Wittle, as she became more innerly,
more linked to essences, while he
felt still the need for her body's
lovingtenderness.
                            Was
that why he had wandered off —
                            as she
had done from highest Light to this
enchanting forest?

Sap and **Wisdom** each set off on
the same day
                                to seek the other.
Sap followed the route she knew;
Wisdom her intuition.
                                                So
they missed — and thereby found
space to contemplate each other's
milieu, undistracted.
                                        Sap was
amazed **Wisdom** could live so
sparsely;
                        also startled to find
the place lit by her own glow —
not evident in her sunlit home.

This, **Wisdom** was that moment
gazing at —
                        drinking in a coloured
garden: flowering shrubs — a flax
cascading, cream and green, with
spear points scarlet-tipped;
                                                and
citrus fruit trees — grapefruit,
lemons, oranges.
                                Thirsty from
walking in the sun,
                                        Wisdom
picked up a recent windfall, deep
in well-tended grass,
                                and sucked
the heavy juice of grapefruit from
a hole her finger punctured —
                                                once
it was clear she would not find **Sap**
here.
                        Through the large window
she could see much to nourish eyes:
Sap's wallsize weaving of the lake-
reflected mountain, coloured glass,

a light wood table, chairs and low,
wide sills, windows framed with
decorative drapes.
                          But the door
was locked.
                   Wisdom settled
in the grass, leant against a trunk
for shade (a walnut tree), feasted
on her stolen fruit —
                          then slept.
There in the cool of early evening,
Sap, returning, found her:
                          by her
open fingers the scoured rind.
                                Sap
had picked and eaten berries as
she wandered back through the
forest, wondering where **Wisdom**
was.
                After a tender sharing to
revive flagged energy,
                          Sap cut
wholesome bread and mixed a salad,
pouring homemade wine —
                          while
Wisdom pondered every detail
of the weaving:
                          beneath layered
woods and sky and mountain,
                                lake
reflecting every level —
                          to the rich
brown foreground, also layered.

**What a lovely expression, Sap,
you are**
                   **of nature's recreation
of herself in art.**
                          **Levels of
reflection surely are the good
made manifest in nature's works.**

I feel myself cradling the roots –
but you show forth the flowers,
the fruits
        and now I see you know
the crafts of spun wool, which
sheep are glad to spare when sun
torments.
        Wisdom once again had
given **Sap** her opening:
            as they ate,
it was not long before talk flowed to
Wisdom's poem on the sun's passion
— and what **Wiz** and **Wit** had made of it.

Ah! said **Wisdom**.
        **Dear one, you know
that you and I have come here straight
from the Sun's heart.**
        **Without the sun
this planet's life would not continue,
could not be.**
        **Soon it will be time for
all to see:**
        **to learn that power that is
creative also kills –**
        **and that power
dwells in the very particles of being.**

We are all made of sunshine – most
**when we chew and swallow fruits and
roots and stems.**
        **Sun flows through us
– like rain through trees, which draw
water up from roots, through trunks
and branches**
        **till it reaches the canopy
and so the sun –** where out it goes for
everyone.
        **Sap itself, my love, is water;
therefore two fires, two powerful gases
bonded to make them safe for use.**

                              Our
bones and muscles grow because the sun
grows through them.
                       Yet direct sun
scorches skin and tissue . . .

                         But your poem
goes, beloved, so much further: you speak
there of a power we thought was harnessed
for our use — but yet the sun could override.
You call it electric, as though we could take
lightning bolts like Jove and use them —

                              And
we shall, most certainly we shall.
                              And
yet the sun from ninety million miles
will interrupt our powerful light
display –
          as though to show us we are
overstepping, for not acknowledging
our power source.
                       The dog-star,
Sirius, is light-years further than
our sun from us –
                       yet source
perhaps of much of our sun's power.

I dreamt last night that we had found
a way to tap the energy that's trapped
in photographs.
                    This century will see
such leaps of understanding how to tap
the source-
              we shall be drunk with
power.
          Sap, it is possible to be too
wilful –

   Wisdom, *what are you saying? You
don't believe the cosmos punishes! I know
you better —*

No, dear one, no – I don't
of course;
            but you know as well as I
we bring on ourselves the consequence
of what we do,
            whether this be wilful
or unwitting.
            Nature's laws are
necessary structures,
            therefore
strictures on what it's wise to try
within the bounds of space and time.

What I think I see is that each time
we harness nature's powers within
our consciousness,
            then learn to use
what we believe we've understood –

we do not realise we have drawn closer
to us the very source of power within
ourselves.
            The gods are not out there;
they are within.
            And none the less
powerfully abundant – as we know.

Wit and Wiz came back late together
to find their mothers glowing in the dark.

The sense of abundance in their home was
such
            that Wiz that night conceived
— despite intent.

At some level Wiz' body seemed to know;
as though the ancient sisterhood, high
in the dark of every woman's cauldron,
knew one of their number had engaged
to multiply —

60

so sent congratulations
throughout the length and girth of **Wiz'**
'**dom**': to bring about a new contentment,
a protecting of her realm from further
spills.

Consciously, **Wiz** was out of
countenance, never having felt like
this before —

Wit even more so as
he felt her body close against him,
while her mind talked and planned
as ever..

It dawned when her period
failed —

and then **Wiz** knew
that what she wanted most was now
on offer —

no matter what plans
would have to be abandoned.

Sap
sighed and shrugged and went to tell
the School —

where she'd recently
been made a governor.

The Head
was less scandalised than perplexed.
He'd come to set such store by both
of them:

Wit as a one-off phenomenon;
Wiz the surety of future honours.

Sap
pointed out that **Wiz** could sit exams,
before it was obvious she would have
other things to do.

And so the quite
unheard of came to pass:

Wiz
cradled in her untried womb this
new being, gotten less of lust

than
of a heightened atmosphere of trust

that held the house of **Sap** and all
who lay beneath its roof the day
Wisdom came from the forest
to proclaim
                    the force of **Will.**

Recorder: *No simple consequences flow from this.*
                                        Some would say
        a wilful child persuaded her betters that her own
        desires
                        counted for more than quiet
        decorum.

Seeker: What kind of colour should
            we put
                            on this mixed liaison of two
            teenagers,
                            permitted by the Head and one
            new governor of the Town School,
                                                provided
            for the white children of the Colony,
                                                        built
            at the farthest point of recently discovered
            Godwonland
                            whose governors knew they were there
            to rule
                            with the justice only the enlightened
            North was able to dispense?

Recorder: *A fair question*
            of a very literal kind!
                                    Indeed what
            colour would this mixed up kid,
                                    whose elders
            flouted nature's law, betray?
                                    The child
            could be white or black — or in between,
            and whether girl or boy   *be cast outside*
            the tight circles of the civic order.
                                                How
            are your researchers faring on the current state
            of 'Drift'?

Seeker: Still no acceptance, but a man
has picked up the ball and run with it.
                                                    He's sure
the convection currents,
                                                              deep
in the mantle of the earth, so liquid fire,
                                                              are
passing heat up from the radio-active core
— not only to thrust up mountains
                                                    (as believed
before) but also to thrust sideways and apart
the continents
                              at rates he says he can measure
in the North.

Recorder: *But no one else agrees — or evinces
interest?*

Seeker: Not at this point, no.

Recorder: *And this is
just after the First World War?*

Seeker: As in the story,
yes.

But **Wit** was oblivious to these omens.
His childhood free from conflict, he was trusting
of what people did or said —
                                        not even suspecting
his previously bashed up feet were targets.
                                                              He
rejoiced that he was well on the way to fatherhood,
recalling early times with **Wittle** —
                                        even a hazy
memory of shooting lizards for his mother's stews

— not the kind of fare for **Wiz** or **Sap**, so not for
his son either.
                    Mostly anyway **Wit**'s wits
were on his football or his lessons.

           Wiz was
startled when **Sap** came back from School —
to tell her she could stay to take exams.
                     Her
wisdom had descended from her head, and
now lodged deep in her belly and her heart.
Her breasts were getting tenderer by the day
— and growing.

               Now woman all over,
the thought of swotting for exams brought no
competing pleasure.
          Sap understood this,
but she felt a prickling of the skin if **Wiz** had
nothing to fall back on —
                if things with **Wit**
should fall apart as easily as they had come
together.

        Wisdom had not stayed long
enough with **Sap**
            to know before returning
to her forest that her early prognosis
was confounded — **Wiz** already pregnant.

It took **Wit**'s next visit to her, in his proud
new state,
         to break to her the coming change
in status.
        **Ah! So I'm to be a crone
in seven months.**
        I've just completed this:
(**Wit** did not notice what he took from her).
**I seem to see a speeding of events,
the firegod's hand in this.**

        And you say,

Wiz is pleased and more than ready.
You too, clearly, so let me add
my blessings.
                              But what of Sap ?

She seems to have fixed it all at School.
The Head is letting Wiz sit her exams —
before people know what's happening.

Sap's not the same as you —
                                        insists
Wiz should have more than me behind
her, although she knows I'm going
to make my mark.
                              And so I am.

I know that, my son, I always have,
And maybe more than you envisage.
What neither of you knows, though
I have told Sap, is where this child, this —
Witson, will lead you all — or how.
Not that I know exactly how — only that
things will not be easy,
once he's born.
                              Wit brushed all this
aside, as **Wisdom** added
                              Would you like
to take that back to Wiz ?
                              I — wrote it
down.
                    Wit stared.
                                        Yes, you
left behind the poem on God's finger
— also a fair copy,
                         was it Sap's,
                                        of my
other poem, Cosmic Love ?
                                        So now
we both can read and write a little!

**Give Wiz my hugs and kisses with
my love.
Can you read my writing?**

Wit said he could — and left, a little thrown.
He walked back slowly, taking the long route
by the plane tree, where he sat —
                              and looked
at the new poem, to see if he could indeed
make out his mother's hand —
                              so newly
carved out of the forest, where writing
was unknown.
              He could.
                        She could. He read

FRUITS OF LIFE

*What incredible lengths
    a plant will go to
seducing us to eat
    and so secrete
its luscious fruit,
    the housing of
its precious means
    to come again
and grow the same sweet
    fleshy texture
to delight our taste —
    and so absorb
again its sunny nature
    and pass on
its means to fructify.*

Wit liked it and took it home
to read to Wiz.

Wisdom
was no more concerned than
Wiz

                              at the effect this likely
coloured child would have —
in its own community.
                                        Loved
by its parents it would hold
its own.
                              She did not allow
for the vast difference that
growing up with those who
looked askance
                              would make
to this new child's trust.

                                        Sap

did —
                    though she somehow
hoped it would be countered,
confident **Wiz**' brains were
more than half her assets.

                                        Wiz

in the meantime listened to
her child —
                              gorged grapefruit
for her system's reception of
her foetus into all her levels.

This she felt completed when
it quickened —
                              and kicked her
in the ribs thereafter daily.

*Feel him, **Wit**!*
                              Wit's dark
fingers, etched on ivory ribs,
were warm and his eyes were
dancing as he felt his coming
infant's presence there.

                                        Wiz,

with this quickening, felt her
power

                surge to bring together
all her forces.
                                  At last
her schoolwork made some sense —
revealing life as she knew it
here between the sheets.
                                 Indeed
that phrase took on new meaning
as she saw her books:
                            Geography,
History and English literature —
especially Poetry — maybe even
Maths and language — and surely
Natural History
                              were telling her
what was written in the Book of Life.

Recharged, **Wiz** worked to leave
her school possessing a Certificate
that would leave them, as well as her,
more deeply satisfied;
                            she as having
turned another of life's leaves.

Only **Chloe**, **Wiz**' closest friend,
knew why
                          Wiz would
not return after the summer break.
And as her lithe body
swelled and began to droop —
Chloe brought the news that
Wiz had topped the lists
with higher scores than any
won before.
                    Wiz and **Chloe** hugged
this mystery.

When instinct
told her it was time,

Wisdom

came forth again —

and she
and **Sap** together eased for **Wiz**
the coming of their grandchild,
just as they had, unwitting —
eased its conception all those
months before.

Though **Wiz**
was flustered by the strength
of her labouring body — almost
overwhelming —

they and **Wit**

together reassured,

helped her
push, when pushing was the one
thing needful —

a final
violence

as **Witson**'s head
found outer air

and the rest
of his body slithered gently out.

Wiz

held and pacified her baby son,
while **Wit** under their direction,
cut the cord —

deftly
removed the afterbirth and all
bloody messes that attend such
separations

(even as **Wittle**
long ago had done for him).

Wiz,

though excited knew she needed
sleep.

Sap took and washed this

heaving newness, fed it boiled drops
of milk and water, weighed it,
wrapped it in a shawl and laid it,
sleeping, by its mother's bed.

In the morning, **Wit** walked back
with **Wisdom**.
                              Witson
was as white as **Wiz** and **Sap**.

                              Wiz
barely noticed her child's colour,
as he pulled on her nipple, drew
from her sustenance she loved
to give.
          This was a miracle as great
as growing a being in the dark
of her own body:
                    feeling her food,
made in her factory, feed the hungry
— fetched forth by his needing cry.
This tied up everything together —
poetry and biology most of all.
                              Though
it told of plants rather than babies,
Wiz read the poem **Wit** had brought
from **Wisdom** —
                    till she had every
word by heart.
                    Then she went back
to sleep — till **Witson** woke again.

Seeker: So — no problem then!

Recorder: *Don't you believe it!*
          *Watch **Wit**.*

Seeker: But — I
          thought we agreed this was a comedy.

Recorder: *So it is from a divine angle — but*
          *for these next two generations, **Wit***
          *and **Wiz** beget —*
                              it's downhill all the way
          *as **Wisdom**'s progeny descend more and*
          more deeply into our dense planet's life.

Seeker: closer to the convection currents bringing
          the hot magma nearer to the surface
                                        making
          mountains from what had been hillocks,
                                        forcing
          apart
                    deep rifts in the sea-floor
                                        no one could
          imagine to be there.

Recorder: *Ah yes!, I think this might*
          be where
                    the 5th Ray and the 7th . . .

Seeker: Come again?

Recorder: *You'll recall the first time we talked together*
          I said
                    that three more Rays —

Seeker: would manifest as
          human force expressed itself

Recorder: *in actions, thoughts*
          and feelings.

Seeker: So — which is which?

Recorder: *The Fifth*
          is the Ray of mind: of thinking at all levels —
          high
                    or low.

Seeker: What would be low-level thinking then? The slime?

Recorder: *In contrast to the light, well — yes.*

Seeker: So — what about the 7th then?
                    and what's the 6th?

Recorder: *Take it slowly now!*
                    I wished to say the 5th and 7th
        could make common cause
                    as these deep rifts began
        to come to light:
                    for the seventh Ray
                                is the becoming
        visible
                of what has been imagined in the mind.

Seeker: The 5th!

Recorder: *Exactly!*

Seeker: And the 6th?

Recorder: *That's more about what*
        people mean by attitude.

Seeker: Today's sense?

Recorder: *A bit.*

Seeker: Ha!
        That brings us back to **Wit** and **Wiz**, whose destiny
        is to probe the density of being separate —

Recorder: *and thus discover*
        what it is to feel contrariwise.
                            Do you recall
        ***Tweedledum** and **Tweedledee**?*

Seeker: — who had to have
            a battle —

Recorder: *That's it!*
                                    and that is how it's going to be.

Seeker: And only **Wisdom** —

Recorder: *who has poured herself into all*
            the spaces —

Seeker: knows the possibilities.
                                            Which Ray
            is she?

PHASE III

THINGS BECOME TOO BLACK AND WHITE

Though **Wit** felt only joyous tenderness
for **Wiz**' whiteness, which he saw as
a sort of goddess innocence —

                            after
the first flush of **Witson**'s babyhood,
Wit came to feel a stranger to his son
— whose pale presence in the dark, all
those long months,

             had kept **Wiz** from him;
still did so now, through light of day
and night's long dark — as the invisible,
white thread of milk sewed son

                   and mother
in a stitching, not including him.

                       Such
thoughts did not reach **Wit**'s brain,

                    where
he'd have had the wit to look at them.
But, having as an only child, not had
to come to terms with being displaced,
this wasn't part of expectation.

                 Nor yet
had **Wiz**,

           but she was the sewer, the true
epicentre of this stitched up vulcan patch.

Now football Captain of the School
and doing well in all his work,

                Wit threw
himself into School affairs — and matches.

Witson was a really greedy feeder,

                Wiz
possessed of boundless energy —

               and milk
she'd offer gladly every time he stirred
and sounded day or night.

No rules
prevailed for times of lifting.
                                                    Wiz made
her own — and **Sap** did not demur,
                                        no matter
what she may have felt at this display
of lawlessness.
                        There have been worse fads
in baby training:
                        none have produced
a formula for success in rearing children, that
leaves them satisfied — and satisfying.

Seeker: And yet
            there sometimes are such.
                                        Who shall say
            what factors bring
                        contentedness ?

Recorder: *Exactly so!*
            Most animals feed on demand —
                                        and as for birds,
            their fledglings open mouths must be a never-ending
            stimulus for fetching forth.

Seeker: But who is to say what
            causes what
                        once human consciousness
                                        has changed
            the balance from survival to the much more subtle:
            who gets what when ?

Recorder: *It's hard enough with just*
            this trinity. of parents and one child.
                                        Once siblings
            come into it, it's beyond all calculation.

Wiz did not even think to calculate.
Pints poured
                    into her bright, blue-eyed
babe, who prospered like a bay-tree.

                                        Chloe
came to visit, eyebrows raised
                                        to see
his chubbiness and drumlike tum.
                                        She
and **Wit** were both now working toward
exams
            and little was said by him about
the baby left at home.
                            There could
be many reasons for his silence:
                                        What
does Wit feel about his being white?

Wiz looked at her.
                    It wasn't a question she
had given thought to.
                        It's never bothered
him that I am white —
                            or me for that matter
that he's black.
                    That might be different,
Chloe thought — and said.
                                I can't see how
Wiz shrugged.

                        But it set her thinking
after **Chloe** went —
                        knowing how little thought
she gave to **Wit**, now that he had given her
the son she sought.

Sap was so
occupied fulfilling her weaving orders
as well as running the house, they hardly
spoke of what might be lying underneath
the tight routine of getting through
each day successfully.
                                        Wiz

dealt with the daily washing;
                                        Sap

the shopping and providing meals —
for which **Wit** oftener did not return,
as football matches, practices and work
claimed more and more his time.
                                        He

stayed at School to do his homework,
since the house was filled with baby
sounds and bustle.

            Wiz must tune into him
again to know
                  whether he minded that his son
was white —
                  what, if he did, could help
to put things right.
                  Wiz knew she would
in due course want more.
                        They couldn't,
by the laws of chance, be all one colour
— with a father black.
                  Might that be the route
to equilibrium ?
                  It felt trivial to **Wiz**;
                        why not
ask **Sap** ?
            She, near to exasperation, paused
to see the force of **Wiz**' thought:

                                                        disquiet at
a possible falling of the family apart had led
Sap to bring pressure on her daughter's School.
Now **Wiz** seemed to be proposing yet
another helpless creature for her caring.
                                                Sap
put her foot down.
                                This generated unsuspected
waves.
                Pressures were building for the first time
since **Sap** and **Wisdom** accepted their
children's union as destined.
                                For the first time also, **Wiz**
began to open up to **Wit**,
                                        groping to discover
how he might be feeling
                                about **Witson**'s being
white.
                Wit denied hotly any hint
                                        that his son's
skin colour could affect his love.

                                Witson was
the baby of their loins.
                                Wit loved his family,
and like his father
                                (yet also now so unlike)
he would work hard for them as soon as he had
passed his School exams.
                                Everyone was sure he
could get work as a Football Coach.
                                Then no need
to stay
                longer than **Sap**'s roof was welcoming.

Wit would find a place where the breath was
really best, where the wind blew free —
and they could have a bigger family.

Witson

stirred at this and woke to claim his space.
By the time **Wiz** had fed him, **Wit** was fast
asleep.
        Cosily **Wiz** slept too.

Wit woke

with vows renewed.

Not many months elapsed

before he, like **Wiz**, had made his mark
on the Honours Boards –

for 'work and play'.

Yet **Wit** had worked no less to win the matches
he had played as captain, than to pass
cum laude in his School exams.

He easily

found a place to coach in the very School
his own had beaten, when shortages
through War a few years back,

offered him gains

he leapt to take.

He leapt again where the higher

salary was offered.

Now he could make a home

himself, on the sunny side of the hill he had just
climbed — where **Wiz** and **Witson** could live
comfortably, and he could breathe deeply,
radiate his sense of well-being
everywhere he went.

How do
things get written in the **Book of Life,**
                                    Wisdom
woke to wonder after dreaming
                            of vulcan cracks
and subterranean storms.
                            Everything that lives
is on the **Tree** — or in it.
                    But not everything can
know — or have
                a name.
                            Names are written
in the **Book of Life.**
                    But how ?
                            Who by ?
                                    Which
is prior:
            Book of Life
                        or **Tree** ?
                            And which
ensures our knowing going on ?
                            Do we need
a record to survive ?
                    Or just to be ?
                            What could
surviving be,
                if we don't first know we are —
and who ?
                            Renée thought he was
because he thought.
                            But surely
we must BE first —
                    and only afterward awake
to thinking, to awareness that we are,
                            and want
to go on being so (if we do!).

                              Books of course
are mostly made from trees (as **Wit** observes).

But the **Book of life** is surely not of wood —
although the roots and trunk and spread of trees
are truly the truest carriers of life and thought
a being in the world experiences.

                                            Is it
something in the sap of trees, that's more
than water, yet ethereal — that somehow
carries conscious messages
from root to branch to crowning canopy,
broadcasts earth wisdom to a waiting world —
and so creates the first conditioning
for what has been and is to be
remembered ?

Could there be something
in our heads
that's like a very,
very tiny tree ?
A little inner forest
of such dendronites
could work together
to secure our memory —
so long as it is rooted, but —
                              in what ?
                                    Could
there be other kinds of roots than trees ?
Wisdom held her breath as she recalled
the strange contortions of the dream
she'd woken from:
                        the depth below
the deeps — where grinding plates
plunge under/over one another

                                        striking
flint and throwing flaming gases
                                        where
Proteus relaxes and lights up
from his own ocean bottom base.

                                        But
deeper still
                    the restless boiling body
of the iron
                    turns and turns
                                        and turns
the other way,
                    as if a gigantic spoon
were stirring stew
                    in the cauldron of
the planet's fierce inside.

                                        Could there
be
        knowings that could stir this brew
— even determine what its movements
might throw up to influence
                                        our time
and place —
                    like **Dis** emerging to disrupt
Persephone
                    and settle seasons in
their cyclic groove?

                                        Out of nowhere
Wisdom remembered **Wit** at one year
old:
        how he had held and placed four
stones to form a square that gave him
pleasure.
                    She had then seen her son
                    put two and two together.

Why should this pattern return now
as she pondered the possibility that

deeper roots than trees can thrust
may cause changes in our surface
lives
        where people cling to the thin
raft of soil
           we pitch our roofs and
walls and gardens on?

                Do we
construct our immortality:
            throw
bridges across chasms, journey on — till
we have etched our name into
our pathway,
        our planet's present
precarious **Book of Life**,
           our **Tree**
amongst whose blown branches rest
our nests?
          Wisdom fell back
to sleep once more —
           her mind
slipped on these images and was lost
again.

Recorder: *That sounds like a cue for us.*
               *Is **Wisdom***
pre-empting where your geologists' researches have
yet reached?

Seeker:
               She is indeed.
And surely we need to look at what is meant
           by **Wisdom**
knowing all the possibilities.
           What could
this **Wisdom** who has lost herself
in ancient forests know
           of Greek
myth — or **Renee Descartes'** mind?

Recorder: *It is all bulging*
at the seams, I grant you —
                                                        but so
is this twentieth century.
                                                All you've
been telling me of geophysical research —
                                                        and all
I'm recording of the dreams and prophecies
of **Wisdom**
                        tell us of turmoil in our human deeps —
erupting into individual human brains as well as
the consciousness of states and nations —
                                                        both
in the north and here in **Godwonland**.

Seeker: Yes, people
actually are driven mad, when they can't contain
the images they feel assailed by: sights and sounds
and voices they don't know what to make of.
                                                        Yet
Wisdom seems to take it in her stride —
                                                as though
she really knew the problems **Descartes** wrestled
with —
            and that he'd got it wrong!

Recorder: *Perhaps she does*
at her true level,
                        before she poured herself into space
and lost her Light.
                                It's when she's coming
out of dreams she has these convoluted images
and thoughts.
                                As a true primitive
she has more light than most —
                                        but it is sixth ray
astral light and so a bit confused.

85

Seeker: So, that's
why she and **Sap** do best together!
                                                  Since she's known
Sap, she's struggling to make sense of the world **Sap**
lives in.

Recorder: *Exactly!*
                              It's all there somewhere,
            waiting for us to tune in and pick it up.
                                                  Sap *is*
            going to tackle it the hard way ...

Seeker: which maybe
            Wisdom doesn't have to —
                                        if she once knew
            the possibilities.
                              I asked you a while back
            what ray was hers —
                              if, mostly, human beings
            are expressing the 5th and 6th and 7th.

Recorder: *There's more*
            five in her than seven —
                                        but mostly
            I'd say she's expressing
                        the Rays that made the worlds
            behind what we touch and see.

 Though **Sap** was certainly nonplussed,
when **Wit** produced his new agenda —
waving a copy of a contract signed, as he
invited her to see the eyrie he
and his family would soon move into,
                              she,

no more than they,

                        could be dislocated
by a changing scene.

                        While it was not
Sap's way to think so, her name too would
find itself written

                        in **Life's Book**.

Once it dawned on her that she was,
for the first time,

                free

                        of all parental caring,
sap rose in her and resonated,

                        till it reached
what in a tree would be

                        her canopy.

There thousands upon thousands of excited
neurones

                (each structured like a tiny tree
with roots) acted together to emerge in
consciousness, and tell her what the young
could do,

                        she could.

Sap radiated as she laid her plans to further
her education, mapping her route
to a degree she found she could take
by distance learning,

                        sending her papers
all the way by sea —

                        and studying in the local
library

        books procured her from the University
newly opened in the Capital.

Those
servicing all these provisions were
delighted
        to have them made use of by
this enterprising woman, **Sap**:
                first
to recognise her was **Chloe**,
                Wiz'
old school friend.
            Though she had
not done quite as well as **Wiz**,
                Chloe
had qualified for entrance to the new
City University,
            and meanwhile held
a post here in the Library, where **Sap**
came for books and reading volumes
for reference, but not for lending.

At coffee break they would exchange
the latest news of **Wiz'** family:
                she
was pregnant again — expecting twins.

Sap had not been told this, so
                was
doubly thrown.
            Chloe offered
reassurance:
            she's looking radiant,
Sap, like you.
            And Wit is being
attentive, as he was with Witson

before he was born — but what of now?

This admission of disquiet was out before
Sap registered that
                open plan living
within the family
                was a different thing

from scattering it abroad.

                But **Chloe**,
unblinking, held her gaze:
                This was
no easy thing for Wit –
                us all
being white.
             He needs an ally
in the family.

             I know, I know
he does —
        but how are they going to
manage twins and **Witson** on their
own?

        They have help –
            and Wit
is doing well: he gets big bonuses
for matches won,
and they all are
           – as in the days
at our School, before Wit came
and turned it all around.

         Ah, **Sap**
said and sighed.

         Chloe went back
to work.

        Sap soon realised
she could tailor her own courses and
construct a program
        to study science
along with the history of ideas,
        (as had
Wiz' father, **Sophist**);
        also some
of the latest work on how to think, and

what was being said by physicists —
both about atoms
                    and the sphere of stars.

When **Sap** got home one night, dispirited
by what she mostly read, she once again
found **Wisdom** waiting in her garden.

Warm renewal fed them both.
                                              Ah,
***Wisdom**, **Sap** sighed, as they partook
of a frugal meal of fruit and salad —
laced with a coriander dressing, whose
orange/parsley tang grounded, as well
as let them soar:
                    I am driven distracted
by what the scientists today would have
us believe is truth —
                              each from
his little box of fragments gleaned
through microscopes.
                              You might think
biology and physics don't describe
the same planet.
                              Perhaps of course
they don't, but —

                              Ah, my love,
said **Wisdom** with her throaty chuckle,
Maybe it's the only way they can
proceed right now —
                              if they're
to keep a hold on anything.
                              At least
they're digging deep and trying
to find root causes of new things
that come their way.

                    I mean causes
in the substance of our planet –
which is so much more than just
a cooling fireball travelling round
the sun.

          Sap chewed a lettuce leaf with
absent-minded relish of its dressed tang:
*But surely we know root causes aren't
in the planets, but the stars —*

                         **We do,
we do – but to unravel how,
                         do we
not need to find out all we can of
Earth
          and how its own contortions
may affect our understanding?**

*(Perhaps it will take the scientists
half this century
                         to reach the way
we know all life and things connect!)*

**I told you I knew the Wit and Wiz
children
          would move deeper and yet
deeper into the morass.
                         Maybe
by the end of this millennium,
their children's children will
begin to see
                         a more connecting
light.
          How are they all? I –**

Wiz is having twins.
                    *I've only seen
her once since her friend* **Chloe** *told
me in the Library.
                    You know of course . . .*

I know from Wit they've set up
house on the hill.
                        I think that's
where I always saw them, when
Wit brought you both to see me
long ago.

                        Both remembered that
first meeting well.
                        And now,
breathing together once again,
                        restored
their hold on their shared origin of
Light —
        beyond even the Solar System —
where the power and purity of planes
of understanding
                shot them through.

*This is what is so lacking in the
books I read*
                        sighed **Sap**.

As word got round that a young and
personable black
                        was restoring
the football fortunes of a nearby
school —
            strange things happened
in the forest.

                        People hitherto
invisible
            (because denied existence
by those responsible for records of
inhabitants in **Godwonland**)
                        began
in ones and twos to percolate —
                        from

the forest edges
                        to the town,
                                        where
they stood at street corners,
                                        leant
on walls
                or simply sat
                                and waited ...
went on waiting till
                                whites no longer
could pretend they were not there.
                                        Some
even found their way to the ground
where **Wit** was training his new
football team.

                                They sat on fences
watching, raised a cheer
                                when they saw
spectacular goals or saves;
                                        made ribald
noises at missed chances.
                                Old or young,
they were all male — and there to make
a point or maybe more.
                                Years ago
they had withdrawn into the forest, when
white people came and took away the land
they lived off.
                        This was strange for **Wit**,
belonging to an older, hunting culture
and never having come across even one
of these displaced cousins.
                                Though
his team were made uneasy by these ill-clad
watchers,

                    some played better
for the topped up energy induced.

                          One day
when a player fell and hurt himself,
                          a boy
jumped down from the fence to help him.
The white boy shook him off —
                          but **Wit**
could see
      the ankle wouldn't mend that day.

When they had limped him off the pitch,
Wit invited the black boy to try his luck.

He showed a grace of movement and
a flair for connecting with the ball
                          not unlike
Wit's own beginnings.
                    His name, he said,
was **Wilson**.

                    Though his white team did
not take kindly to this sudden shift, they
had no reason they could voice.
                          So **Wit**
decided it was time
                    to talk with his Head
about this new event.

                    Other staff had felt
uneasy that their boundaries were being
breached by coloured strangers no one
admitted to exist —
                    although the town
and taverns were now full of them.

At a Governors' Meeting members were
divided
      as to whether more harm or good
would come

94

by offering School places
to those who were that age and might be
taught to read and write.
Who knew how
many more might ooze from the forest —
to upset the School regime ?

The Head
could only point to the effect
of **Wit**'s
presence years ago, when he appeared
in the opposing team.
This drew
the comment that
one outstanding
player was a very different thing —
from a ragged bunch of ill-assorted
blacks.
Wit was the very man to sort
them out.

Both his own past experience
of pain,
and recent successes on the field
and off,
had bred in **Wit** an inner sureness.
Husband, and father of a growing family,
Wit knew he knew how to turn a rabble
to a team.
And now he had enough to form
a second.
Let the Head find desks
and books and clothes; the Town Council
sort out moral claims, decide who
lived where and whether drink and lack
of work would lead to riots.

             Wit would
discipline his two competing teams,
discover whether
             blacks and whites
together could endeavour —
             to make
this once again the best of Schools.

Before long a ramshackle shanty
township sprouted
             leeward
of the Main Street —
             far enough
from the little household on the hill
and not too close to **Sap**'s home either.

But, as the time drew near for **Wiz'**
twins,
             a brawl was brewing in the
central tavern.
             Several heads
and limbs (both black and white)
were dressed in the Cottage Hospital —
where **Wiz** came weekly for a checkup,

brought by **Wit** —
             driving a brand new
Ford with skill and some abandon.
             Wit's
mouth fell open, as he reversed, to see
Wittle emerging, bandaged, through
the door —
             his once best wolf-skin
somewhat the worse for wear.

             The two
were still standing off from one another:
both pairs of eyes revealed the pain
of these last sharp, unshared years,
as well as long, loving ones together —

when **Wiz** came out, full-bellied, her
white hand holding her white son's, his
chunky shoes clattering down the steps.

Wittle and **Wiz** had never met
and **Witson** looked as if he didn't
want to now.
                    Robust with the milk
of his first year and more
                    (when **Wiz**
decided to encourage a new pregnancy
by weaning him)
                    Witson was already
warding off the double displacement
on the way —
                    so hardly inclined
to welcome this straggly stranger
                                        Wit
was urging him to recognise:
                                What's
a granfer?
                    Witson sourly asked.

Wittle grinned amiably and **Wit**
firmly picked up his son and said
This is and he's yours. Don't you
forget.
                    How are you, Wiz? What
did they say?

                            Wiz explained
they wanted her in next day —
                                        until
the birth which could be any time.
                                    Sap
was expecting to take care of **Witson**
while **Wiz** was in recovery.

                            But **Wit**,
remembering his father's early care, and
softened to his warm, familiar presence,
now demurred.

Wiz swallowed
and her overloaded heart missed beats —
as she tried to imagine this black man
fitting into her neat house up the hill,
where she had white domestic help.

Wit's
work prevented his presence by the day,
but he expected a much fuller part in helping
with these twins

than he had ever had
with **Witson**.

Now the thought
of healing all by leaving his son in **Wittle**'s
care each day

was gaining strength.

Wiz
knew **Witson** wouldn't wear it — but she
refrained from saying so out loud.

Meanwhile
they all stood rivetted:

Wittle was never
a man of many words —

yet so much was so
unknown.

Wit picked up fast
on **Wittle**'s silent speech — and, though
he knew nothing of **Wit**'s astounding change
in lifestyle —

Wittle nodded
as though what he saw made sense, and he
even answered **Wit**'s unspoken question:

*You and your mother had no further
need,* his eyes revealed, *so I moved on* —
he shrugged with a small eyebrow lift.

But where to, who with ?

98

*You see us
all around –   now that you've made
your name.*
*The women are still in
the forest.*
Isn't Wisdom?
This
unspoken sharing had the speed and
spontaneity of dreaming.

Even so
it was too long for **Witson**.
Wiz
was fascinated by this lightning
exchange of vital information.
All
climbed into the little Ford:
Wittle
with some difficulty settled into
the back with his hurt arm.
Wiz
needed the space in front for her son
and billowing belly.

*They needed
me to help them hunt for food.*
*Some
of them were starving.*
*I sometimes
watched you go to visit Wisdom.
Once we understood you had made
good in the white man's world, we
knew the time had come.*
Wittle
murmured into the back of **Wit**'s
neck, as he drove up the hill and
home.
**It has, it has! It's time
for everything –**
**do you know
that Wiz is having twins?**

Wittle broke into a broad grin
Wiz
could see in the centre mirror:
You knew!
she said, squirming round to see him
in the back.
Gently **Wittle** gazed
into the eyes of the mother of his three
grandchildren.
Yes — and I know
they will be born tomorrow.

And
they were.
Two black girls:
the one
emerging first weighed nearly twice as
much as the second, **Wiz** called **Wanda**.

*What shall we call this first one, **Wit** ?*
Windel!
Wit was rapt — as he saw
in this tough black babe his fellow soul.

Wit went home to **Witson**, **Wittle**
and the live-in help, leaving his wife
to feed their new black twins.
Wanda
took a good while longer to make fast
her grip on life than **Windel**.
Though each
fed from a different breast, **Windel**
emptied hers, while **Wanda** drifted
into sleep, so **Wiz** let **Windel** finish
that one too (for her own comfort).

Wanda,

therefore must be bottlefed, because Sister
wouldn't let **Wiz** take the babies home
till both regained at least their birth weights.

Sap blinked when she visited and saw them:
Wanda, a little slender snake, who wriggled
on her mother's chest, drank a few sips, then
closed her eyes,
                              while **Windel**
supped and smacked her lips and smiled
her beautiful black smile and gazed
into her mother's face.

Witson

could get anything from **Jane** he wanted.
                                        She,
glad for her own reasons to live in and cook
and clean for **Wiz**, looked somewhat
askance at **Wit**;
                        more so at his dishevelled
father, now to take charge of **Witson** —
who surveyed him with all the acumen
of a bright, white, not yet two year old,
who knew how and who to please to get
his way.

          Wittle, out in the guest sleeper,
woke with sun up —
                              his arm stiff.

Groaning as he sat up, he saw
                                        sky
orange and turquoise , where the hills
rolled maybe to the sea:

                              all heard of,
never seen
              from under his dark forest
canopy.
       But now a new thing and he must
be alert
       as he had not been to let himself
be mauled.
       Finding **Wit** and coming here
could turn things round, although it was
not clear how any of it would work out.
Wittle felt right that change was there.
He chuckled that **Wit** didn't as yet know
that **Wilson** was his brother — though
he was picked for the football team.

This small **Witson** meanwhile was his
charge.
       He heard **Wit** get the car out, put
Wiz' baggage in: a quick exchange and
they were gone.
                       The scene was set
for tussle.

                  Wittle relieved himself
in the yard and went indoors.
                              Smelt
pig cooking.
              Jane was frying an egg
in bacon fat for **Witson**,
                       heating up
coffee for whoever;
                       did not smile or
even turn to him.
              Witson stared.

Wittle, gently affable, looked round
for food he knew.
              Settled for bread
and two bananas.

When **Wit** got back that night he found
the house wary and a little quiet.
                              Shared
at once his joy at the births of his new
black baby girls.
                    Wittle nodded sagely.

**One of them's really tiny, Dad –
Wiz has made a bond with her
already.**
                    **But the first one out's
a scorcher. We call her Windel.
We call this house WINDSWELL.
Do you like it, Dad?**

                              Wittle smiled.
*It's pretty different from the forest,
but we knew it would be.*
                              How's Wilson?

You know him? He's fine.
                              How's
Witson then?

                    *Jane bedded him when
he fell asleep.*
                    She had not reappeared
since taking **Witson** up.

                              **That arm –
how is it, Dad?**

                              *It'll mend, lad.
Tell me more of Wilson.*

                              **He's good –
he plays a bit like me!**

                              Does he now!
grinned **Wittle**. *Maybe he should! He
is your brother.*

             Wit's jaw tightened.
But you only left here –
            he's 12.

Wittle dropped his eyes, went back
to eye and thought talk . . .

             Wit sighed
as his last childhood innocence fell
away.
       **So what are you all hoping
this town will give you?**
            A place
in the sun, Wit,
      a place in the sun.

Sap was sitting in the Library two
days after visiting **Wiz** and the new
enchanting babies.
           Chloe came up
suggesting coffee:
           her face,
as they imbibed, concealing worry.

At **Sap**'s inquiring eyebrow, **Chloe**
said:
       up at the University now
all the talk's of blacks appearing
– not just here –
        and the white
authorities are starting to resist.
They're forming plans to make it
hard for blacks to move about.
         Saying
they must have passes –   only be
allowed work that whites won't do.

Sap was aghast:
       her mind had not been

moving in this groove
                              and nor had **Wiz'**.
When they'd told her hastily that **Witson**
would after all be staying at home with **Jane**
(because **Wit**'s father had appeared), **Sap**
only noted that would leave her free
for the work her mind was set on,
                                        heard
nothing further till the birth — when **Wiz**
was once more occupied with babydom.

                                        Now
Sap was gripped with horror as she saw
a not so distant future which could blast.

When **Wit** reached school one morning
following his daughters' births,
                              the Head met
him with a worried frown: word was —
things would no longer be as **Wit**'s new
team would need.
                        The Town's scheme
to absorb and try to educate these blacks
was stopped.
                        Harsh laws were in the making.
Once enacted, everything for his family,
and even **Wit**'s appointment to the School —
would be affected, **Wit** could see …

                                        It took
a little longer for this news to reach the nurses
taking care of **Wiz**.
                              When it did,
they panicked:
                        ***Nonsense**, the Sister said.
**Of course it won't affect these babies.
Don't upset their mother or her milk**

will go —
                and one of them is doing well.

Things did not move against their town as fast
as feared:
                Wit duly brought **Wiz** and her new
babies home,
                where a silent truce was holding.

Witson behaved with cool decorum,
                            allied with
Jane whenever he felt outnumbered by the four
black members of the house,
                            where **Windel** thrived
while **Wanda** dwindled
                            and their mother felt near
panic.
                    Latent anxiety lay everywhere:
Wit trained his teams,
                    not knowing if they would
ever play in matches.
                        He never acknowledged
Wilson brother openly,
                        though he saw the likeness
and knew that **Wilson** knew.

                        Further deferment
when War broke out again across the North,
where shortages of man-power made the less
unruly welcome.
                    Many blacks went overseas
as volunteers, seduced by promised livelihood.
Nearly as many would not have life for long.

Wittle, who could turn his hand to much,
served in the tavern, playing the accordion
Saturday nights.

Because of uncertainty, Sap went
to visit **Wisdom** after dark
                    guided by a glowing flicker:
her own toward the forest heart, thereafter **Wisdom**'s.

The women in the forest showed at times, so **Wisdom**
knew of **Wittle**'s part in things;
                    also (as **Sap** did not)
of the boy, **Wilson**.
                    She had met his mother.

Wisdom took these facts calmly, as the day years
back, when **Wit** met **Wiz**
                    and **Wittle** went.
                              Her deep
concern was understanding larger forces playing
on them all.
                    What **Sap** had come to tell her felt a fit
with premonitions of upheaval all across the planet;
that vital movements stirred the earth to waking.

That would leave nothing in the world unchanged —
indeed would blow apart the family of **Wit** and **Wiz**.

Sap, it is more than Witson I see now.
                              He is
a casualty of dark force erupting.
                              War across
the northern hemisphere is seeking to bring
to birth a new perception —
                    and Witson has
two sisters now, you say.
                    This will not yet bring
harmony.
                    But what can
*you and I do, **Wisdom**, if the Law breaks*
up this family ?
                    ***Wiz** doesn't believe it can.*

*She's fighting for **Wanda**'s life*
*while **Windel***
thrives as though black babies were the very
heart of things —
*as, for **Wit**, she surely is.*

Beloved Sap, we must wait while the forces
clarify.
Then each of us be ready
— for whatever ...

Witson
held his own (with **Jane** content to be his valet),
but felt displaced by these squirming serpents
crawling everywhere
and that included easy-going
Wittle.

Wit's joy was watching **Windel**,
bathing,
putting her to bed and dressing her each morning
after her rich feed —
while **Wiz** coaxed **Wanda**'s
wandering lips with a warm bottle teat, when she
at last emerged from sleep.

Windel surely knew
to make the most of **Wit**'s attention;
would catch
his eye from her cradle when he came in
and he
would swoop and toss her high and catch her,
every
cell in her gurgling to his touch.

                              Wiz found this
vexing, but was glad for **Wit** to be so useful
there at night
                    (as **Wittle** was by day for heavy jobs
inside or out).

                    Witson watched from the sidelines
as the bond tightened between his dark sister
and the father he had not been near to.

                              All the while
dark clouds gathered at the edge of things.
                                        Just as
surreptitious ethnic slaughter
                              took place across
the North,
          so the white government of **Godwonland**
laid plans to rid itself of an opposing force
                                        it thought
it had laid to rest years since, when farmers,
prospectors, diamond miners came — to wrest
the land's resources for their own
                              both at the surface
and very deep beneath.
                    Witson's other granfer,
Sophist, would be proud of the lines of argument
being forged
          to build the platform for the coming
laws of severance.

Seeker: Contemporaneous with this plan for severing
              black from white at the earth's surface —
                                                  (in this
              southern continent of **Godwonland**),
                                        once that

Second World War was over

                    research into 'Drift'
redoubled, and from that time on

                    the way began
to open for scientists of all disciplines

                    to pool
their projects and their understanding.

Geophysicists, in particular, inquiring freely
into the nature of Earth's magnetism,

                    delved
into the history of the earth's magnetic field —
to find the relation of its wandering poles

                    to
magnetised rocks
         as real evidence

                    continents
might indeed be drifting.

                    Only by inventing new
and complex instruments,

                    could they persuade
the science community that this was fact —

                    thus
setting standards of accepted accuracy

                    that gave
the force of law.

Recorder: *What irony!*
*Like **Sophist**'s laws in **Godwonland**, which united*
successfully the white minority against

                    the blacks,
the scientists came together to agree
the Earth they lived on

                    was itself fragmenting!
I don't think even Sophist saw

                    that piece
of accepted law

                    as an argument he could use
for segregation.

Seeker: He couldn't then.

                                   It took
quite a few more years for the majority
                                   to
change their tune
                    and start to alter Science
text books.
                    When they did they called it Plate
Tectonics —

Recorder: the means of shoving continents
together —

Seeker: or forcing them apart!

Recorder: That's
Rays five and seven for you —
                                   born
of the conflict Ray four generates.

Seeker: Why?

Recorder: That, only **Wisdom** seems to know —

Seeker: And she is one of the first three — as I
understand.

Recorder: Essentially **Wisdom** is the 2nd Ray —

Seeker: and **Will**'s the first?

Recorder (nodding):   The 3rd's the **Word**.
Four is the Ray that must balance the two sets of three:
if **Will** and **Wisdom** and the **Word**
                                   set
the whole thing in motion —

Seeker: and human beings
make a go of it
                    with actions, feelings and attempts
to think —

111

Recorder: *then the fourth Ray becomes*
a strange attractor seeking harmony,
                                                    which cannot
happen until every pair of opposites
has played its part in this complexity,
allowing thus chaotic consequences
to emerge and disappear from conscious thought, as
other seemingly more vital causes

Seeker: rise to the surface
of our consciousness —
                                                              like
the convection currents,
                                                    turning both ways
and spewing up the magma
                                                        till the plates
grind one against another —
                                                              inducing
lateral faults.
                                          But how does all this relate
to **Sophist**'s wiliness ?

Recorder: *He and the scientists are*
clearly both
                                          seeking to use the printed word —
as if that made it Law!

Seeker: While we understand

Recorder: *that only **Wisdom** knew the possibilities —*

Seeker: of the printed Word as Law —

S/R (together):   *both gift and burden.*

By the time **Sophist**'s law was passed, **Witson**
had been going to school two years,
and the twins were due to follow him next term.
Witson sighed politely when they said
Windel and **Wanda** would be going to school
the other side of town, where **Wit** would be
headmaster.

For **Witson** this would certainly
be easier —

and that was the driving force
of every argument: better for everyone —
the government of **Godwonland**, especially.
Much time and care had been expended
working out the nature of the schooling
all black children would receive:

yes, of course
they would be taught to read and write, do sums
correctly —

even learn to play football, if
they had (as here) an ace, who could teach
them when he wasn't doing all else a Head's
required to.

In such conditions it would be
a wonder if any child learned anything.

For this
School was to be housed in the shanty town —
that mushroomed when the blacks had first
emerged — a while before the twins were born.

Witson's inner sigh was huge relief.
Windel's feelings were too mixed to know:
to have her dad as Head was wonderful
— and she would not miss her brother,
who made white, if any, friends.

Looking after
Wanda was her second nature:
*What a little
mother* people said, convinced the small twin
survived because of **Windel**'s care.
(**Wiz** knew
better.
Wanda seemed willing to go along
with whatever others said.)

But when **Windel** saw
the actual School they were to go to —
(she had
been often with her dad to his school, where
Witson was)
deep within her she resolved to fight
who and whatever placed her in the horrid
squalor of this building.
She looked at her father
and he looked at her.
Wit was sure he had an ally
he could trust for life.
He had also **Wilson**,
seventeen, as his assistant — and **Wittle** was
appointed caretaker (wearing tunics made by
Wiz).
Windel had learned to read and write
at home, could draw and sing with confidence
(often duets with her father's pleasing tenor).
Wanda found reading hard: her mind roved
everywhere: more like tree-spirit than a human
child, she felt even less at home in class, where
high, narrow windows let in only slits of sky.
For
Windel, busy teaching the others to read — to
help her uncle, **Wilson**, — there was no time

114

to notice this.

            Sap was appalled to discover
the educational conditions of her two grand
daughters.

              True they had all had time
to think out in advance what they would do
once the blow fell, but —

                    on paper it had all
seemed much less harsh than they originally
feared.

          That was where **Sophist**'s very clever
propaganda
               fooled everybody.

                  It put such stress
on Tribal Education, the liberal North believed
the South had found

                  creative solutions
to the problems of two cultures sharing the same
land.

          Those, like **Wit**, who had experienced
both,
      knew better.

                  Wiz and **Sap**
worked quietly behind the scenes, enlisting what
support they could among the few, who seemed
willing to oppose the government.

                    Too few
understood the actual deceptive gap between
government statements
              and its real provision.

Even fewer wanted anything except their own
securing of what they'd worked so hard for —
coming, as they had, to **Godwonland**,
only because assured the land was empty —
as indeed it looked when they arrived.

                                                            Trekking
for weeks for fertile soil, and now established,
they'd side with any moves that might incite
blacks to rioting in the shanty townships —
thus excusing
                         sending in armed troops
to 'shoot the lot'.
                              This came very close
to happening where **Wit** and **Wittle** had
to protect their school.
                              In the murderous
melee that ensued, **Wit** was arrested
for the part they said he played.
Wanda was lost and **Wittle** went to find
her, leaving **Wilson** to take care
of **Windel**, who sensibly hid
until things quietened.

                              Of course even this
frightening incident did not of itself ignite
the fuse that would set the whole South
ablaze.

                         But it set a pattern that would
spread,
                         as yet another strange attractor
came into play in ways not seen.

                                                            This
would induce apparent chaos, that
would presently resolve itself
into a new layer
of complexity.

116

Wiz panicked when no **Wit**
brought back the twins, though **Witson**
was returned from School by neighbours
worried to see him waiting all alone.
The Shanty School was phoneless,
Windswell out of earshot of fired shots —
though **Witson** thought he'd heard some.

Late in the evening, **Wit**, released on bail,
returned with the two girls unharmed —
plus **Wilson** and their granfer, **Wittle**,
(who had somehow known
where to look for **Wanda**).

But the township could not settle,
so **Wit** insisted both should stay
on the School premises overnight —
to protect what little was of worth,
for building their new culture.

                                                    While
Wit was driving them both back (despite
their protests they could walk)
                                        Wiz
tried to learn from the two girls
what really happened.
                                        Both
shivered in a hot bath:
                        she sponged their fears
to quiet,
        but could not from their words extract
a sense she could make sense of.
                                Had **Wanda**
run off in terror when she saw her father led
away in handcuffs ?
                        If so, where was **Windel** ?
Wiz did not want to probe too hard,

for **Windel** was as shocked as **Wanda**, who
said less.

> *Well you see*

said **Windel**,
taking a deep breath.

> *There was shooting*
> *everywhere and Daddie said take care,*
> *so me and Wanda hid.*

But **Wanda**
shook her head and whispered:

> *they were*
> *dead — I saw them, so I went away.*

> *But how*
> *did* **Wittle** *find you ?*

> *I don't know.*

> *And how*
> *did* **Wilson** *know that you were safe ?*

Wiz
wanted, but forbore, to ask her other daughter.

Softly she put them both to bed instead —
neither,

> for once,

> swallowing more than
a morsel and a soothing drink.

> Not till
midnight, when **Wit** finally got back,
could **Wiz** discover quite how serious
was **Wit**'s brush with the Police.

> Now
he was known to them as trouble.

> What
strange attractor was at work in this ?

                                        Dropping off
next day a silent **Witson**,
                                        Wit went on alone to
his own damaged building and diminished
pupil roll.
                        Wilson and **Wittle** had cleared up
as best they could
                                        messes left by bodies shot
at random.
                                        Two at least had died —
their punctured bodies carried away by grieving
parents.
                                        No one could understand
how things had started.
                                        Treating their dead
or dying was their first concern:
                                                        mothers
— newly come from the forest
                                        to this slaughter.

Wisdom was dozing in her sapling shack, woven
by **Wittle** thirty years before — in this deep forest,
where silence
                        penetrated
                                        more than light.

Feeling a strange nausea that signalled birth —
conception, rather —
                                        in her coming to know,
Wisdom felt a tremor, very slight,
                                                        and saw
on the woven wall above her head
                                        a resonant shimmer.

Only being in these depths alone,

could register
so small a boding of what was to come.

Not she
its epicentre.

Where ?

Sap,
telephoned by **Wiz,** had learned everything
that could be known of the disaster.

Now
she was holding forth at the Town Meeting:
How can we stand silent while death
is being dealt our young ?

Two are dead.
They could have been my own.

Not for
nothing did **Sap**'s voice ring through the hall
(though few within were roused to action by
her call).

The frequencies she tuned to
tapped into others, touched yet more,
till messages, vibrating whispers passed:
by air and earth, along rock surfaces,
through trees and soil and water —
till they met and matched with fire.

Sap did not know her words were taken up.

Nor had the town

any more intent than
yesterday

to change its ways.

Who
shall say

by what subterranean
routes

120

                  of rending and
colliding
                answers come?

              Sap's flame
reached other flames —
            and, as the months
went by,
         more and more shanty schools
in **Godwonland**
            expressed resistance
to the unjust laws.

           The more they did so,
the more crushed they were.
               Fear froze
the government into vicious violence —
                  till
the young blacks refused to go to school
at all —
         and punished those who did.

Wiz and **Wit** could not be unaware —
that only dragging moments lay between
them and enforced separation
                into black
and white.
           Wit and the twins
would have to move
         to the makeshift home
of **Wilson** and **Wittle** in the township.

Seen as a bold experiment
               in interracial
living,
         their family life could not be
judged successful.
           Wit and **Wiz**
looked wistfully at one another —
              and,

remembering the plane tree, tried to
hold,
      each from the other,
               the tear
that welled and would not brush away.

Perhaps they saw more clearly —
through those drops —
          what each had
truly come to mean
            for the other.

Neither spoke.
          Wiz turned —
to put to bed her twins for the last
time —
       certainly in that windswept
house on the hill.

          Witson bade
his father a correct goodnight.
              Wit
made no move to hug his only son.

Wiz and **Sap** sat sombrely
          nursing mugs
of coffee in the Library,
       where **Chloe**
(long since gone away, to read English
at the City university)
        had joined them,
knowing their most recent pain.
           She
shared what she could glean of official
clamping on the rights of blacks —
          and
those of whites for visiting black areas.

Wiz had to wrestle the authorities —

to get a pass to see the twins and **Wit**.
Wanda was more than ever nebulous;
Windel so belligerent, **Wiz** feared
for all of them:
                                Wit and **Windel**
had become
                        a mysterious high-powered
unit of dissent
                        it seemed only **Wilson**
could restrain.
                                He was now
the football star —
                        while **Wit**
                                        focussed
on clandestine acts of resistance, well
beyond the law.
                        His smouldering anger
that he could not play in teams with
whites, as destined —
                                vented itself
in devising ways of sabotaging white,
commercial projects.
                                Wiz felt
sure that **Windel**'s energy redoubled
Wit's.

                        Witson also was
becoming as intransigent a white as
any in the State.
                        By no means all
at School felt like him.

                                In fact
said **Wiz**
                *now that I'm back at our old
School (teaching biology part-time) — I'm
thinking of transferring him as well —*

But the Head's more liberal there –
Chloe objected.

I know he is,
but he's also much more tolerant
of different views.

I think he'd keep
an eye —

Witson *just shrugged*
at parting from his friends.

Have
you still got Jane?

asked **Chloe**.
Wiz shook her head.

It didn't make
sense. She easily found another
live-in job — she's always been
happiest as second fiddle.

So
they gossiped about **Jane**

to cover
from themselves their deeper pain.

Though **Wit** had not visited **Wisdom**
since she felt the tremor and divined
its source,

she knew it linked
with others and that each

could bring
catastrophe.

She guessed the twins
removed to **Wittle**

in that over-
crowded no-man's land between

Sap's
home and the forest,

knew her own
time of forest peace was soon to end;
began to see the future phasing in —
as more than one kind of vulcan
happening:

Wisdom had long known

a seam of gold
                     passed underneath
her thus desirable home.

                          It did not
surprise her therefore when she heard
men and machines approaching her
seclusion.
                     She was prepared to go.

By the time the twins were ten, **Wit**,
                                   who
had by then inevitably been
consigned to prison,
                          had already served
two years in solitary
                          on an island so
remote —
                     no one would think to plan
escape, and few could hope to visit.

Windel was beside herself at this
abandonment.
                          She could endure
life's crudeness in the shanty town —
if
     she could have her father's presence
once a day.
                     Denied this, **Windel** ran
amok:
                     At first pestering **Wilson**
to find ways of visiting he could no way
deliver,
                     she turned to more vindictive
actions in the township —
                                   joining in
vicious necklacings of boys who went
to School.
                     This got her listed.
                                   It was

therefore the twins' tenth birthday before **Wilson**
managed to secure three passes for them to try
to make their way by land and sea — to visit
Wit.

That night **Wanda** went missing
once for all.

Not even **Wittle**
could think where to look for her.

Wanda
lost herself trying to reach her mother.

Wisdom
found her just as she herself emerged at the very
edge of the forest.

Wanda twined herself
round **Wisdom** soundlessly,

though both knew
it was not she this snakeling sought.

Little one,
they'll never let you stay with her.

Your
mother would have to hide you,

and they'd
put her too in prison.

I am the only one
they'd let you live with

and I have no home.

Wanda had seldom seen her grandmother,
but now she looked deep into the dark pools
of **Wisdom**'s eyes —

and saw herself
reflected there:

two tiny human faces,
lit by the moon and **Wisdom**'s glow.

We're ten today

she said.

I went away.

Windel *wants to visit father.*
                                         Where
are you going ?
                    Ah! said **Wisdom**.
                                  Now
I think I know.
                    Why don't we
start walking and see how far we get
before the world begins to change
and everything seems simpler than
it is today.
                    You're ten and I am 56 —
or is it 560,
                    as it sometimes feels!
That would make me 100
                    Wanda said.
Let's see how far we can get before I'm
as old as you!
                    We could try
said **Wisdom** smiling,
                    let's begin.

When the Prospectors arrived at
Wisdom's shack, they found a small pile of
Papers with a curious rock on top.
                    These they swept up
together to inspect.
                    The papers were marked
for **Sap** —
                    but who was she ?
                                  Shrugging
they filed them in a pending drawer.

                                  It would
be ten more years
                    and the gold seam worked
out —

before they would come to light
again on a yet more fateful day of realigning.

Witson was a credit to his School:
found
his way smartly into the State Police —
as a cadet.
At twenty-two,
he was put in charge of a detachment,
deliberately sent to hassle a small gang
who hung round **Windel**
(the restless
remnants of **Wit**'s second football team).

Orders passed down to him from above,
Witson had no idea of the true target
of this disguised assignment —
even when
he positioned his men in the shanty town
he had actually never visited.
Windel
was a very angry activist —
but kept
in the background and was hard to catch.

HQ Intelligence were confident
Witson
hated blacks enough to follow through,
even when he couldn't fail to know —
the real objective of the operation;
not
that **Witson** wanted especially
to get
even with his younger sister.
He had
never deeply looked at what he felt. He
merely projected his unconscious
darkness
on what was in his way.
He

would as easily crush ants.
                                            But also
would admire the relentless tenacity
of an ant column on the march —
                                            its
intent and orderly procession.

                                    Here
he saw only rowdy mess,
                        a pointless
absence of control that roused a deep
desire to bring to order.

                        Fire in the air
first –
        and if that doesn't fetch them,
let them have it.
                        Now – Fire!
A moment's silence.
                        Then the resumed
racket.
                        Again! Fire!

This time the burst was longer.
                                    So
was the ensuing silence.
                        Witson
and his men went in.
                        Every one
of the black boys was dead.

                        Windel,
enraged,
                appeared from the back
premises and faced her brother.
                                    Guns
swivelled:
        Hold your fire!
                                    yelled
Witson.
        Windel was less restrained.

She also held a levelled gun —
                              and fired.

Wiz was called to her son's bedside
about the time
                    Windel, of course,
was charged and bail refused.

                         No one
was ever charged for the black boys'
deaths.

               A slug was removed from
Witson's groin that night.

                              Wiz
could not face her empty home.
                                    She
went to **Sap** —
                    to find her poring
over the Papers
                    left in the disused
Prospectors' Offices —
                         whose fresh
incumbent knew and valued **Sap**.
                                    He
brought **Wisdom**'s Papers to her
the very day
               Windel shot her brother
in her rage
               and his men arrested her.

The Paper these two mothers took most
comfort from
                    was a poem **Wisdom**
titled *Fault-Lines*:

FAULT-LINES

If you can see mountain ranges as
zones of collision or compression, where
the interfaces of a fractured plateau
have left one falling
                or the other thrust up
to induce sheer cliffs that rain can run down,
carving gorges opening into valley pastures —
    then you know
    the beauty and the majesty
of nature is her faults:
    her broken bones
re-clothed in ferns and trees and washed
by waterfalls,
           fast-flowing streams
                    bisecting
alpine meadows daubed with gentians and
the nests of opportunist birds in niches —
taking chances.
                It seems there are three kinds
of faults: 'normal' — where one section falls
away, as though submitting to a higher
power; 'thrust' — where the other fracture
looms to overwhelm, in splitting; while
a third and lateral fault is known as 'wrench':
forcing to left or right the land it splinters.

Mixed, as most faults are, a twist is set
on the rock faces lying contorted underneath
the cladding vegetation we stride over —
exulting in its sheer dramatic form.

We do not dream that far beneath
these lovely surfaces lie
magma currents miles, deep miles
below —
setting off tremors in the crust
for lava flow
    to burst through funnels
and erupt in flaming basalt —

somewhere
under the ocean, maybe —
we may never
know.

What do or can we know
of chance or need?
Of which cause faults —
or what faults cause?
We only know we live with fault-lines —
that those faults are life.

As **Wiz** read
these words, she knew she had come at last
into her own wisdom.
Knew she could ask,
but could not answer yet:

**Is love the wielding of the force behind
the worlds?**
This **Wiz** saw can only be so, if —
potentially at least —
the name of everyone
is written in the **Book of Life** — just as everyone's
a twig upon the **Tree** —
rooted below the fractured
interface
deep in the doubling currents that convect —
to turn the Wheel of Life this way,
then that —
twisting the roots to make us cry again:
**Is love
the wielding of the force behind the worlds?**

Recorder: *Only Wisdom in the spaces knows*
that possibility —

Seeker: And where is she ?

STRANDS
OF
WISDOM

dedicated to my children
LAURA, SAMUEL & CHRISTOPHER
here — in London — or scattered through the cosmos —
and to theirs:
RACHEL, EMILY, DAVID, CHLOE,
currently in London, Scotland, France
and even on the wings of planes.

PHASE ONE

WIT EMERGES FROM
HIS ISLAND PRISON

Wit was at his wit's end:
                                        he had
finished one more stint
                                        of splitting
rocks he would never see the use of —
an almost daily process
                                        down the years
he'd already served
                                        of his life sentence
for what the State
                                        called terrorism.
Doing his time cheerfully,
                                        at first,
he persuaded his guards
                                        to let him form
a football team.
                                It had to play against
itself —
                        until he could scrape another one
together,
                but
                                he could thus keep in trim
his body and the team's —
                                        and,
so far as the prison regimen allowed —
his mind
                from fracturing
                                        like the rocks
he split ...
                        But now a deep malaise
was overtaking
                                the will and wit he'd
always had to trust in.
                                Wit thought
he had accepted long ago
                                he could never
hope to see his wife again.
                                Windel,
his special daughter,
                        (a wince as he thought

how special still)
he did see sometimes —
since she had dourly served
her lesser
sentence for injuring
her white brother,
Witson,
Wit's firstborn,
himself now
father of two little children
by the white nurse,
who helped him recover
from his wounding
in the groin
(by a wholly unrepentant
Windel).
As **Wit** aged in this place
(his fight for fairness between black
and white,
had driven him into),
he no longer felt
racial conflict was the world's big issue —
as
in **Godwonland** it had become.
As a boy
from the forest meeting **Wiz**,
he gave
no thought to this
and nor did she —
or
they could not have risked
the bringing
forth
of such a brood.
These very children,
now full-grown,
carried,
like diseased
blood or bone,
seeds of race hatred.

Could it be sensitivity to this —
                              had
stunted **Wanda**'s growth —
                              perhaps
even sent her mad?
                    For she had gone
for ever on the day that **Wilson**
                              was to
have brought both twins to visit him
                              here
for the first time
                    on their tenth birthday.
As this
      clinging memory of loss,
                              along
with his mother's,
                    for she had vanished too,
never having been
                    to see him,
although not proscribed —
                    as all this
flung clouds of hornets
                    through **Wit**'s
consciousness,
                    to sting more painfully
than any hitherto
                    allowed to penetrate —
Wit saw
                    right there before him
in his cell —
                    Wanda and his mother
striving together up a hill
                    in a land
it seemed of scents and sounds and warmth.

Wit blinked and the vision went.
                    He blinked
again.
      Strange things
                    happen to men in solitary
  — which was why

he kept his body fit.
Surviving prison could depend on this.

Yet
what might he think

he was surviving for?
A life-sentence,

for a black, meant

that.

Wit at first believed a change would come.
But nothing

he could learn from guards
suggested any movement

all those years
by workers who opposed

the racial laws.
Sheer weariness

was wearing out **Wit**'s bones.
Even letters

now and then from **Wiz**

(who
signed them **Wiz-dom**),

nor her mother's,
could reveal if anything was afoot.

Nor
could **Wilson**'s visits,

in front of guards,
allow more than a flickering eye

which hid
despair.

Where

could **Wit** turn
for nourishment?

Again that vision

of the two:
Wanda still seemed small

and slender.
Wit tried to focus on her face.

The twins
were eight when he was first in —

prison;

Windel twenty when —
                            she and **Witson** —
(**Wit** could not look at that ...)
                                        Three
more years gone by since then,
                            so **Wanda**
must be 23.
                    How old his mother then?
What were they doing together —
                                        so
purposeful,
                    as they bent to the hill
they climbed?
                    Where was it?
                                        Where
were they?
                    Wit called out
                            in anguish.
Wisdom turned.
                    He saw her face —
but
    could not meet her eye.
                            She seemed
to wait
        as though she heard —
                            but could
she see?
        Mother!
                    Wit — I hear you,
    but I cannot see — where are you?
                            Here
in my island prison
                            where I've
been for fifteen years.
                            Where
are you and Wanda going?
                            Why
did you leave
            your forest home
                    you love?

13

There has been no home there
                                   for us
for years.
                 Wanda and I
                                   have been
walking up this hill
                                   into our future,
since they made my home a gold-mine.

Does Windel visit you?
                                   Seldom,
but she's not in prison now —
                                   not at
least as I am
                                   and must stay ...

The vacuum funnel that
                                   for a few
moments
                          brought connection,
                                   broke —
and **Wisdom**'s words of comfort
                                   crackled
on wind
                   that she and **Wanda**
                                   often faced.

Though **Wit** saw and heard no more,
                                   his heart
had quickened:
                          he had seen an open space
and people in it
                          dear to him.
                                   Wherever
they were and set their face,
                                   they seemed
in better spirits than his own.

Seeker: This
has lost me.

Recorder: *Why?*

Seeker: Well, whatever
level of reality this is,
                                                              why is
Wit
              suddenly able
                                                   to be in touch
with them like this?

Recorder: *I'd say*
it's because he's
                        better in touch
                                          with himself,
his own pain
                    at last —
                                so, reaching out, he
touches what he values.

Seeker: Does his mother
mean more to him
                        than **Wiz-dom**?

Recorder: *No,*
I don't think so —
                        *but **Wiz-dom**'s even deeper*
into pain
              *than **Wit**.*
                             and that's an interface
too tender to be touched.
                                It's that denial
*that has kept **Wit** going*
                        until now ...

Seeker: when
maybe he half knows
                                    he's moving into
life's second half —

                                                    with all its inner changes.

Recorder: *Searching enough to find,*
                                        but not so expectant
                        as to block things off —

Seeker: thus allowing
                        this momentous opening.
                                                   Yes, I think I can
                        accept that as a way
                                        Wit,
                                                   in his stress,
                        might have been able to perceive.

Wiz-dom was sitting
                        breathing very deep,
as she had first learned years ago,
                                        when
the four of them —
                        she and her mother,
Wit and his —
                        had sat at the compass points
in **Wisdom**'s forest shack
                                   to decide where
she and **Wit** would live
                                   and how.
That day
                        had been for **Wiz**
the start of her long journey
                                   into wisdom —
despite
             Oh such misjudgings
                                   on the way.
Wiz-dom saw the part
                        her over-confidence
had played
             in earthing,
                        like polar magnets,
the repulsion

16

                              between her firstborn
and the stronger of her twins;
                              saw also
neither she nor **Wit**
                              was wholly cause.
Beyond that she saw
                              the fractures
at the fault-lines
                              which had sundered
her family at its seams,
                              had brought
to light,
            at this potent
                              micro-nuclear
level,
                  the chance to find facets
a polisher of gems
                              would give his life
to finish.
                  How much easier to see
than for any of them
                              to make good.
As her mind's eye roved
                              from **Wit**'s long
and distant prisoning
                              to the boy
with the bow
                  in his free, wild state
in the forest,
            Wiz-dom sighed so heavily
she almost reached across
                              the boundary
between them now,
                  (even as **Wit** had
broken through
                  to his mother and **Wanda**).
This time it did not happen,
                              but the fog
was thinning,
                  the connecting web
increasing its power

                                        to link all
living things
                                   that learn to live
their loneness,
                                       so can delight
to know themselves at one.

                                       Wit's pain
gave sudden utterance
                                         as he woke:

>   *Spring is unwearying*
>   *as though insane.*
>   *It will not take NO*
>   *for an answer — but*
>   *keeps on coming, like*
>   *a punch-drunk*
>   *boxer, who can't gauge*
>   *the odds.*
>
>   *Spring rolls in like waves,*
>   *like oceans —*
>   *each tangy rainbow drop*
>   *a copper gleam*
>   *of bifurcated leaf*
>   *emerging from*
>   *rotten, lacerated bark*
>   *that smarts*
>   *from winter's biting ice.*
>
>   *Spring comes with messages*
>   *we can't ignore,*
>   *electric summons from*
>   *another shore —*
>   *crying where there's nothing*
>   *there is more.*

As **Wit** wrote down these words
                              and read them back,
Wiz-dom heard them too.

This was the first
sound of her man's voice
                              for eighteen years —
since the Laws
                    sent him and the twins away.
It rushed blood through her
                              till a blush
spread to her forties face
                              and flushed
the spring
                    that **Wit** astonishingly felt
across all distances
                              to make her glad.
The web
                    that both connected
and divided
                    became transparent
till each saw the other's face
                              — not seen
for far too long.
                              And now the tears
not shed that day of parting,
                              trickled
incontinently,
                    tickled cheeks that tingled.
Empty fingers, flexed to brush away,
                              could not
disentagle from
                    involuntary engorgement
— till,
          as in a mirror, both
                              spontaneously
came.

                    The subterranean relief
that reached,
                    from the buffeted island
                              where
Wit and his companions

19

                              smashed stone,
to open again
              his wife's heart
                          and his —
would trigger changes
                      waited for so long,
few any more expected them.
                          Of these few,
Wiz-dom was now one.
                      The question
she had asked so painfully
                      after she and **Sap**
had read
          Wisdom's poem, **Fault-Lines**:
                                          Is
love the wielding of the force behind
the worlds?
                      Wiz-dom found answered
in her body's joy.
                      Those with inner sight
like her could follow
                          the path
that energy, released,
                  would take.
                                  Sap
and she,
              though treading different routes,
each perceived wisdom
                  in the other's moves.
And both had seen **Wisdom** all these years,
toiling with **Wanda**
                  toward their chosen
summit.
          This inner link had kept them sane
throughout.
              It helped **Wiz-dom**
understand
              that invisible route
                              Sap's
overt gestures took
                  (and had since

the painful Town Meeting years before,
which none responded to).
                                    Yet her stand
induced a fiery way
                        beneath the level
of the everyday —
                        till the south blazed
and government clamped down.
                                    Today,
the reverse of that momentum
                        gathered force.
Sap picked up
                        the new vitality in **Wiz**,
who seemed to know
                        Wit had taken heart,
and was
            like his mother,
                            writing poems.
Neither knew
                        Wit had also seen
his mother and **Wanda**
                        trudging upward.
A great triangle
                        of redeeming energy
in fact was forging
                        around these power
points
            with the searching dynamic
of great intersecting rays.

Seeker: That
            is a very powerful image —
                                    like searchlights
            in war-time
                                lighting up the sky at night!
            But otherwise,
                        I have to say
                                    I am confused
            as to what any of us means
                                        by higher
            or lower,

21

                          ascent
                                   or descent
                                              in human evolution.

Recorder: *That's not surprising!*
                                              It's maybe the central
                          paradox of all existence.

Seeker (breaking in):   Even Darwin
                          called evolution
                                              the descent
                          of man.

Recorder: *Exactly!*
                                              If we didn't
                          come into incarnation
                                              here on earth,
                          we could never know
                                     how precious
                                              individual
                          difference
                                     really is.
                                              Without this
                          we could not have choice —
                                              our human glory
                          and our downfall.
                                     We have to learn to handle
                          its astonishing power,
                                     without running amok

Seeker: or becoming dried up apricots,

Recorder: *because*
                          we fear to ripen
                                     and fall off the tree.

Among an indifferent batch of dog-eared books,
                          Wit's guards had,
                                     after much

persuading,
                let him have
                                (along with
a pencil
                and the paper he had used —
to write down words,
                                which lifted so
his spirits and his lifetime mate's)
                                        was
a well-thumbed volume
                                on the basics
of astrology,
                which **Wit** had never
                                thought
before to ponder on.
                        As he perused
its tattered pages,
                he began
                        to hear echoes
of his inner impulse,
                                saw quirks
in the patterned points of light
                                the night sky
opened up —
                        hidden when the day
was ridden by the sun,
                                scorching rocks
he and his fellows smashed —
                                and only seen
briefly between
                                canteen and cell.
These night
                        and day visions seemed
to him
        two
                totally opposing views of life.
Wit had never seen
                        his mother's poem,
Fault-Lines,
                did not know
                        how it had

comforted both **Sap** and **Wiz**
                              the night of
sundering
                of his son
                            and daughter,
because it spoke so movingly
                              of flaws
as lying beneath the beauty of the garment
Nature wears —
                        almost as though
that beauty
                needed those faults to underpin;
offering foothold
                        and safe anchoring:
two seeming opposites
                        that formed a whole.

Now,
                as the full moon rose,
back in his cell,
                Wit took up the book,
and riffled its pages:
                        it fell open
at the pair of opposite signs,
                        Gemini and
Sagittarius:
                the twins in air,
                            the archer
with his firepower;
                each, he saw,
                            the sign
before
        the solstice:
                        winter
                            or summer.
Which,
                would depend on the half-world
you
        lived in.
                If,
                    like Wit,

                                        you were
born in the world's South,
                        then **Gemini** —
which was now)
                        fell in the month before
the winter solstice,
                        June,
                                        the time
of his own birth
                        under the sign of **Cancer**.
Its opposite,
                Capricorn, following the arrow
shot
                by **Sagittarius**,
                                plunges deeper
into **Earth**
                        and rises
                                higher than any
other
                starry influence.
                                        In the North,
they called that Christmas-time,
                                        caroused
on hot food and drink
                                into the icy night.
But **Cancer**,
                its opposite,
                                was special too —
If **Wit**
                could fathom why.
                                He felt in awe
of the significance
                                these signs might
really have —
                        if he could know their cosmic
power to plumb
                        depths and
                                pull out stops —
as though
                hearts were organs,
                                not just for

pumping blood,
                              but playing on,
for opening:
                        the **Gemini** full moon
was pumping now
                                        air
through his heart and lungs,
                                    jarred
by the jaded years of splitting rocks.
                                    Wit
let his calloused fingers
                                    loosen.
The book.
                    slid to the floor
                              as he slid
into sleep
            and meanings
                        into focus:
                                    Wit
dreamed the whole planet
                        was a gem
                              and so
was he ...
                        In the early morning
light he woke
                        and before the guards
clattered them all awake, he wrote:

GEMINI

Which then is crystallised when I
experience the gem in I?
The painful person I'm distracted by
within these crushing walls
where images of splitting stones
seem all I'll be remembered by?

Or
my expanded Self that soars,
breaks barriers of space to fly
to my polar opposite, the bowman

26

making fiery targets out of my
mercurial, yet bejewelled, thoughts.

They say
Gemini, the twins who lord the sky
before the Crab emerges from the water,
are the means whereby
                    Love's Wisdom's
poured to earth — and shall transform
each pair of opposites that shapes
our fluid destiny.

                    Thus the battering Ram
and pair of balancing Scales;
                    the Bull
of illumination and the Sting;
                    Twins
from heaven and the flying Arrow;
the Crab who crawls sideways from
the sea to mountain foot — the proud
Unicorn has scaled.; the wilful Lion
and the Man who carries water;
the Virgin Mother and the Fish
her son baked at the lake's edge.

                    To all
these helpless, alternating pairs
                    Gemini
pours its subtle energy
                    to form
a dynamic triangle in airs
                    potent to pass
through planets to our own –
                    wipe out despairs.

This is the work the Gem-in-I performs:
enabling thus my eyes to transit storms;
sit in my brow, the storm's eye — my
facetted jewel reflecting, refracting
the light that frees all I's.

                              All that day
after bringing forth his poem
                        on the zodiac
opposites,
            as **Wit** split rocks,
                              he found
himself wondering
                        that he had
felt compelled
                  to write of spring
                              which was
half a world away
                              while he
struggled with
                        autumnal blankness:
dried up earth
                        before the solstice rain
began to sprout the winter grain.
                                          Wit
heaved his iron mallet
                              to destroy
the sterile matter
                        that obstructed him.
Aware
            he could call
                        on all the planet's
power
            to aid his comrades
                              overthrow
the tyranny
                  of reaction to
                        his father's stand
at the forest's edge —
                              as he swung
the heavy tool,
                        Wit sang —
and all the others took it up —
                        and chanted.
Whereas **Wit**'s voice
                        had always been
a pleasing tenor,

                    now
                              he startled himself
and all who heard.
                              His voice rang
the range of utterance:
                              from deepest bass
to a high C
                    so pure,
                              he touched it
like a bird
                              and then flew down.

Guards were so flummoxed
                              by this change
they felt unsure
                              whether it boded good
or ill
          for containing
                              the locked up force
to keep them and the island
                              safe.
                                        Thus
marching home
                    to evening meal
                              and lockup,
Wit and the men
                              kept up their singing
far into the night.
                              Then they fell silent.
The quality of that
                    was so unlike —
                              anything
the guards had known,
                              it unnerved them
more than rioting and clamour.
                              Word
reached the State Department
                              a mysterious force
was coursing through
                              the inmates
on the penal island —

                                                  29

                                        focussed in the sudden
and continuous
                        singing
                                    of the black terrorist
Wit
                    and taken up
                                            by every
other prisoner.
                                The Governor sought
advice,
                    but recommended
                                        Wit's early,
if not instantaneous
                                removal.
                                                    Since
the Government
                                    were anxious
about world reaction
                                    to their now seen-
through policies,
                        they devised a plan
                                                    to turn
to the South's advantage
                                    this black singer's
new-found skill.
                                At a single stroke,
they could remove him
                                    and improve
their stock
                        by making him a star.
                                                    So long
as their publicity
                                    were strong enough,
this could reverse
                                    the untoward impression
overseas
                                    that blacks were ill-treated
and their skills unseen.
                                Therefore, so long
as **Wit**
                        was,

30

                              without obtrusion,
kept under armed guard —
                              and TV cameras
strategically placed,
                              this black prodigy
could be
            transported
                              to the Central Stadium
to sing
                  before the largest   audience
of, preferably,
                  whites,
                              with enough blacks
to give the right impression
                                    to the world.
Wit,
                  who could now perceive the wiles
behind these tactics
                              at high levels,
felt confident his singing,
                              (like his football
prowess years before)
                                    could draw
from everyone
                        who really listened,
the power to bring to bear
                                    energies
to overthrow
                  oppressive human laws.

There then began
                        a stranger interlude
than known
                        since segregation.
Wit,
                  informed of his new status,
was required
                        to be removed altogether
from the prison regimen —
                                    to clear

                                                      31

his air passages of silicates
                              and train
his vocal chords
                    to utter
                              whatever songs
should be decided.
                         Transfer took place
at the winter solstice,
                         Wit's own birthday
in the sign of **Cancer**,
                         whose higher keynote
(his book showed him)
                    was:
                                   I build
a lighted house
                    and therein dwell.
                                   Though
still on the island,
                    in a hut on the shore
                                        two
guards in charge,
                    he dwelt
                              in better light
than the cell he left.

                         He could see the sea,
as it pounded rocks
                    he need not pulverise.
The rhythmic sound of it,
                    splash and spray of it,
coming, going —
                    quenched every bone of **Wit**;
pulled his sinews,
                    filled his tissues,
                                        till
he felt he could reach
                    and pull down clouds
— quench arid spaces,
                              rotten places,
spill into flowforms
                    water magic fills.

Wit

found
      he need not even swim
                to feel thus
stanched.
      At once
           permission for this was
offered —
        and accepted.
              Both guards
were glad of this relaxed assignment:
              no way
could **Wit** escape
        and had he tried,
           no task
explaining
      why he died.
           That was not now
the aim:
      for Wit,
           as ambassador
for the goodwill
        of northern nations,
was become
           a central asset
for the Government of **Godwonland**.

           So,
when the Manager
          Wit was given
to prepare him
        for his concerts,
turned out
        as mercurial as the sea —
Wit felt
      poured through,
         making his being
an instrument of power —
        to reach and change
whoever heard him
        and all who would be

33

reached
    by those who heard.
                    The one
thing needful
        was the purist sound
Wit could conjure
        through his vocal chords:
to penetrate the inner
          ears of listeners,
over the air
        and in the Stadium.
Words he would sing
         were secondary
to notes he'd sound,
        though he would
compose
        songs to convey
the power of freedom
        every Godwonlander
believed his country stood for.

          His manager
brought him
      a guitar
          to strum
as he ruminated
      how —
        his world
now seemed to him
        and how
he could express
      feelings of helplessness
and yet of power —
      both for his countrymen
and the listening North;
      thoughts that could
bring
      all humans everywhere —
to bend their subtle sinews
        to the end
of freeing those who flee

34

                              from being pressed.
Together
          Wit
                    and his new mentor,
                                   Herm,
devised their program
                         for his Concerts.
These
          would be broadcasts
                              relayed from
the island —
                    except the one vast Stadium
Show
        on World TV.
                              Three songs stood out
and would be
                    circulated
                                   continent-wide
performed
                    on every radio station,
                                        till
a mounting crescendo
                         of **Wit**'s words
and sound
                    penetrated hearts and minds
throughout the breadth
                         of **Godwonland**.
The first of these
                         Wit named

PURGATORY

Not being understood is purgatory:
     it tears heart muscles,
bleeds the system till hot air's
     excluded — and the flow
restored to functioning.
     Never say
that hell's a place you can't
     escape from.
There is ever space for searching,

finding nooks
and pathways, crannies you can
creep through
to the light — to shed it on
whoever's
with you, equally invisible
in the dark.

The second they agreed to call

CONSUMERS ALL

If God is a consuming fire,
then what are we —
when we consume like locusts
plant and tree?

Man has turned to desert
forest land —
so what was carbon is now sand.
What's the strategy?

For aeons this has been the way
evolving man
has left his scorching mark.

Is this bright spark
who has nearly now consumed his carbon base
becoming silicon?

Of the third
       only the first two verses

                   were
submitted for the programs

               to be
circulated.

          Government preened itself
on its liberal stance

             in letting through
the second stanza of this song:

SERVING LIFE SENTENCES

Which of us is not
*   serving a life sentence?*
Most of us come into being
*   to work our way through life*
from forest, farm or factory.

People pronounce sentence
*   on us — we on them,*
as to what is — or not
*   felt satisfactory.*

The authorities felt confident

        the music,

not the words,

      people remember.

Wiz-dom picked up these changes

        long

before they were announced:

      therefore,

when she and **Sap**

      saw posters blu-tacked

in the Library

      of programs to be broadcast

all over **Godwonland**,

      Wit as lead singer,

to climax at the summer solstice

      in the big

Stadium in the Capital —

      it quickened,

rather than shook,

      her wakened heart.

Much effort must be made

      to secure tickets

for this high festival

      in December.

      Wiz

recalled the first poem

      Wit's mother wrote,

on dangers from the sun:
                                  how they pieced
together
              her prophetic meaning,
                                          before
electric power
                              lit stadiums.
This would be mid-summer night
                                  and **Wit**,
playing
              not football, but
                              with his voice
as huge a crowd.
                      She trembled
                                  wondering
how his pure tenor
                          could hope to fill the night,
even with microphones.
                      Then **Wisdom**'s
chuckle:
              **All is taken care of —
                              never fear**.

Meanwhile
                  a rather different tale unfolded,
for **Witson**, who,
                  recovered
                              from his wound,
limped from a pain
                          not felt by doctors
to be 'there'.
                  Violet, his wife,
who gave up nursing
                              to become
the mother of his children,
                                  was inclined
to accept,
              if **Witson** winced,
                          he suffered pain.
He did.
              Indeed he was more changed

by **Windel**'s shot

                        than his cool air

would have led

                anyone

                        to think

he could be.

              Realising how he had been

fooled by his own bosses,

                    yet had drawn

back

          from shedding his sister's blood —

to be nearly castrated

                by her sudden shot,

caught **Witson**

            between a rock

                  and a place

too hard to stay.

                    He found

increasing comfort

              in the family visits,

made in a ritual sort of way,

                  to **Sap**

on Sunday afternoons.

              These he saw

as taking his children —

              William three

and **Viola**, not yet two —

             to keep in touch

with their great grandmother,

              now family

head

          (or so he felt reason to believe).

Violet was acquiescent:

             her father a hard-

worked Minister,

             he and her mother too

involved with parish duties

           for such visits.

She liked **Sap**'s strength,

             delighted in

the ordered beauty of her home

              and garden,
and responded
          to her brusque warmth
with **William**,
        her tenderness with **Viola**,
whose strings already resonated
               more
than **Wanda**'s had
        at five.
            Both children
looked full whites —
          and **Violet**
gave little thought
        to what their colour might
have been,
     though well aware,
           of the aunt
responsible
      for **Witson**'s limp.
             That side
of things
        was a cupboard she was glad
to leave not only closed,
         but locking in
its skeletons.

           Sap did not
reveal to this new family
          her work behind
the scenes
     for **Wit**'s release.
             Nor
did **Witson** comment
        on the prominent
posters,
      of his imprisoned father's
concerts.
     Did he know?
          Sap could not
fail to wonder,
       but feeling the tension,
did not voice.

Witson was never quite
sure why
            he felt so disinclined
                            to visit
his mother with his family
                    like this.
As **Wiz-dom**'s firstborn,
                    he knew
he had a special place.
                        Yet
lurking distaste
                replaced the bond
of birthright
                sealed in milk,
                            later
events would wipe.
                    Sometimes,
                        Witson
visited his wife's father,
                        who held views
culled from the Bible
                        that extolled
the moral virtues
                    of segregated living.
Though valuing control so highly,
                        Witson
no longer felt at ease
                    employed by
the State Police.
                    But he needed
a living.
            What better
                        than one ordained
to teach race purity?
                    With the backing
of this new
            father-in-God,
                        even his training
could be free.
            Witson's early readiness

41

to sum up odds
and make a choice,
had
not deserted him.
What had
was a much deeper confidence.
Witson
had been reprimanded
for killing
the blacks,
yet knew
his superiors
fumed
that he had not included **Windel**.
This crushed his trust
in seen authority.
As months and years went by
and **William**
became a tiresome toddler,
there birthed
in **Witson**
a desire
to placate what powers
might be:
he called **Violet**'s father 'Sir',
when they met,
though offered **Ned**
as more natural
these modern times.
Once **Ned** caught on,
he took the needed
steps
for **Witson** to begin
his 'sacred calling'.

What took place exactly
that climactic night
of the Summer Solstice —
which happened also
to be **Capricorn** Full Moon —
in that bright

42

shining Stadium
                    where **Wit** sang,
                                        was
never unambiguously
                    reported.
                                Some said
an increase in sunspots
                    must have been
responsible.
                        Others heard
a low rumble
            as the many-thousand-throated
crowd took up the chant.
                            We do know
that as **Wit**'s singing ended,
                        to thunderous
applause
                and calls for encore —
Wit
        not only repeated
                    the first two verses of

SERVING LIFE SENTENCES

*Which of us is not
        serving a life sentence?
most of us come into being
        to work our way through life,
from forest, farm or factory.*

*People pronounce sentence
        on us — we on them
as to what is — or not
        felt satisfactory.*

but launched into a third,
                    not heard before:

*Do we know — or not
        the words to choose
to form the sentence
        that releases all*

from thraldom
        to sentences
not meant at all
        to help the planet's
life advance?

        Pronounce the sentence,
sound the Word.
        Let everywhere
the sound be heard
        to succour
humans, animals and plants.

                                        As **Wit**
went into his lowest register,
                                the chant
was taken up all over the Stadium,
                                        until —
a full-throated roar of human power
welled up,
                light flashed
                                and everything
went black.
                                The full moon
had yet to rise.
                        Only
                                by torchlight
or interior knowing
                                could people find
their way
                out of the stadium
                                and home.
All this was seen and heard
                                on World TV
to the final flash
                        and blackout.
                                Nothing
could ever be
                                the same again
in **Godwonland**.

INTERLUDE

Seeker: So what did really happen then —

                                            in terms
of those four Rays
                      the First Scenario speaks of,
as well as the greater
                           and remoter three
you tell us lie way behind
                           our minds
and body feelings?

Recorder: *Before I try to do that,*
I should explain
                   that talking about the Rays
is like
            trying to tell a fish
                    what water is.

Seeker: You mean
             it's so close all round,
                     s/he doesn't
know
          it's there —

Recorder: *or how it is affecting hir.*
I feel I'm telling hir
                s/he's swimming
in H two O.

Seeker: And that of course
s/he doesn't need to know.
                  But maybe
humans

at this juncture do.
Maybe they
need to understand
the elements they move through —

Recorder: *and which move through them.*
All matter,

Einstein showed,
is energy at work
and moving at a rate —

Seeker: it's not beyond the wit
of 'man' —

Recorder: *to calculate.*
Right!
So, moving away from water
for the moment,
to its two fiery components,
we have exploding

Seeker: Light!

Recorder (nodding): *And if we multiply*
the speed
it moves at

Seeker: by itself,
we have the relation
between mass
and energy.

Recorder: $E = MC^2$
Exactly!
And when we say
'light',
we mean precisely that!
You said it yourself.

Seeker: You mean
light is —

46

                                                Consciousness?

Recorder (nodding): *So **Einstein**'s special theory*
                                     of relativity

Seeker: is throwing light
                                   on the relation

Recorder: *between energy and consciousness.*

Seeker: But physicists
         don't use the term
                   energy
                        to mean more
         than physical —

Recorder: *More's the pity!*
                         That's where
       they miss out —
                    like fish in water.

Seeker: Perhaps they're afraid of gasping,
                         like fish
         out of water
              if they do!

Recorder: *No doubt they would*
       at first.
            We do,
               when shifting consciousness
      to 'higher ground'.
             Really high,
                  the air gets rarified —

Seeker: But
         the fish swimming ignorantly in hir pool
                      is just

Recorder: *as prone*
             to using force
                   and being influenced,

Seeker: but doesn't have
                          or feel
                                    the need to know it.

Recorder: *While **Wit**,*
                          as a human,
                                    did,
                                              once things
                were tough enough
                                    for him to want a grasp

Seeker: on everything
                          he felt
                                    controlling him.

Recorder: *Thrown back on his resources,*
                                    he strained

Seeker: for what
                          affected what.

Recorder: *The light in him*
                began to pierce the dark
                                    and he tuned in
                to aspects of
                          his own major rays.

Seeker: And what were those?

Recorder: *Well,*
                                    he was born
                *in the sign of **Cancer**,*
                                    which is Ray 4,

                where harmony comes
                                    only after
                                              conflict.
                His energy's basic keynote is:
                                    Let isolation
                be the rule —
                                    and yet the crowd exists.

48

Seeker: That seems fitting enough
to being in prison —

Recorder: *and also*
to being brought out of it —
to face the crowd,
when the opposite sign —
of **Capricorn** *—*
held sway.

Seeker: What ray is that?

Recorder: *Essentially Ray 3,*
because so singularly ruled
by **Saturn***.*

Seeker: What exactly do you mean
by 'ruled'?

Recorder: *I mean*
influenced by
its dominant force
as understood
throughout the practice of astrology.

Seeker (incredulous): Are you
putting this forward
as a serious
scientific proposition?

Recorder: *In as much*
as anything is so founded —
Yes.

Seeker (gulping): How would you argue it?

Recorder: *As in psychology.*

It's what we find —
over large samples.

Seeker (swallowing more calmly):   I see —
                                    yes,
                                        I think I do
    Perhaps.

Recorder: *It's not*
                        rule of thumb, you know.

    You have to feel your way.

Seeker: So what do you feel
    was happening to **Wit**
                    that caused
                            what seemed
        to happen?

Recorder: *Well, I think this powerful*
                                    3rd ray
            influence
                    (and remember
                            ***Wit** is basically*
        3rd Ray himself —
                    as
                        the Word made manifest)
            will have made it easier
                            for the line of force
        that drives from Will:
                        that is to say —
                            Rays One,
            through Three and Five
                    to Seven —
                            to bring about
        results that could be seen.
                        ***Capricorn**,*
                            *like **Earth**,*
        is ruled by Ray Three:
                    Creative Intelligence,
                            the Word.
        Also,
                touching Earth
                        at its most dense point,

it will reflect
the Seventh Ray —
of visible effects
you see and know.

Seeker: But — were there any?
Except the lights fusing —
which,
as **Wisdom**'s poem*
said
could well have been
the work of sunspots.

Recorder: I think we could infer
the happenstance
of that event
(which allowed the possibility
of **Wit**'s escaping in the dark
and finding **Wiz**)
suggests the presence
of the other line of force:
Love-Wisdom.

Here the Recorder paused
and like another teacher
long before,
made markings in the sand
both sat on.
1-3-5-7
he scratched;
then a line beneath
2-4-6
placed to fit
the spaces.
Then
he linked them back
into one unbroken sequence
with a snakelike curve: $\left(\begin{smallmatrix}1\\2\end{smallmatrix}\right)-\left(\begin{smallmatrix}3\\4\end{smallmatrix}\right)-\left(\begin{smallmatrix}5\\6\end{smallmatrix}\right)-\left(\begin{smallmatrix}7\end{smallmatrix}\right)$ and carried on —

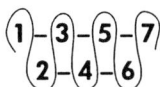

* see **Wisdom Stranded**

(as the **Seeker** let out
           a long, understanding
                                sigh).
Ray Two,
      Love-Wisdom,
                  with the other even numbers
four and six,
               intertwine
                        with the odd
numbers of the Seven,
                    (the four thrusting Rays)
to induce relating —
                  the way we humans
                                   do.

Seeker: Aha!
                  Could one say
                              this conjunction
      of ray forces,
                  which includes
                        Wit's high intent,

      gave opportunity —
                     but did not cause
                                 the action?

Recorder: *You could indeed —*
                        a pleasing case of synchrony.
            How such things happen
                              could be due
            to a special relation —
                           across the lines of force —
            Ray 2
                  is said to have
                              with the power of Ray 5
            to think things into being.

Seeker: Ah now!
                           With the help
      no doubt
             of Rays 6 and 7

                                        to make things actual.
          So a lot more force
                                        is going to be required
          to bring real change
                                        to **Godwonland**.

Recorder: *It is.*
                          But the Seventh Ray
                                        is coming in stronger
                year by year
                                        *as we move into **Aquarius***
                *and out of **Pisces**,*
                                        now altogether crystallised.

Seeker: Don't we need
                          the Sixth Ray now then?

Recorder: *Of course.*
                But not the way
                          it has become.
                                        After 2000 years
                its attitudes are rigid.
                                        Look at fundamentalist
                behavior,
                          whether in religion
                                        or in politics

Seeker: or race!
          Got it!
              So —
                          what races then are blacks and whites?

Recorder (sighing): *I feared we'd have to tangle*
                                        with this one.
                It's delicate to move through;
                                        maybe the best way
                is this:
                          modern whites
                                        tend to be dominant
                in the 3rd and 5th Rays
                                        of reasoning and …

Seeker: rational behavior.
But that's exactly what
white racism is not!

Recorder: *I know,*
I know!
But that's
because
in becoming rational,

Seeker: they've screened out
instinct —
or left it in the dark
to come out
festering.

Recorder: *For some it does,*
when life gets hard.
But most,
being 'new' to reason,
are inclined

Seeker: to feel superior, 'because':
while reason
by itself,
is only half a trick.
Does that mean
blacks are on another ray?

Recorder: *No, it doesn't.*
Almost all of to-day's races
are the fifth.
But each
of the seven root races,
we understand,
gives rise to a clutch
of sub-races
over time —
as if a hand grew fingers
one by one
to play a chord!

European whites
are said to be
the fifth of these —
and some of the sixth
are coming into being
even now.

Seeker: So, there's more than one handful, then!

Recorder: *Yes,*
seven again:
one on each ray.

Seeker: So what are most?
And what is **Wit**?

Recorder: *His warm relating*
would suggest
a major ray
on the second line of force.
I'd guess
the 4th subrace
of the 5th rootrace.
A hunter once,
***Wit** shows all the adaptability*
of Ray Three,
Creative Word,
but he balances
both lines of force
attractively:

Seeker: which I take
to be the goal.

Recorder: *Yes!*
***Witson**, you see,*
has the cool calculation
of the northern white,
whose stirling
third and fifth ray
qualities

are not offset
                by second ray
                              or even fourth.
Indeed they may be aggravated
                              by a sixth ray
emotional body
                all the stronger
                          for having been
repressed.

Seeker: Yet he did refrain from shooting **Windel,**
which is more than can be said
                       for her!

Recorder: *True —*
but, regrettably,
                refraining —
                            is what
a well-brought up
                white child
                          is best at.
This careful training
                trains out
                          all our joy.

Seeker (thoughtfully): Yes —
                   I do know what you mean.
Now is this Ray thing
                       the only way
we can explain
                      how subtle energies
work through us?
                      Your strong emphasis
on the two opposing
                      lines of force
(which seem to mean
                 being driven
                      by Ray One
or allowed
         by Ray Two)
                      remind me

of the **Tao** opposites
of Yang and Yin.

Recorder: *Yes,*
the same understanding
is at work in this:
to bring into consciousness
both sides of an equation
— and so balance opposites.
Wit *saw this*
in his **Gemini** *dream*
of Zodiac polarities.
The cosmos really seems to work
this way.

Seeker: But
there are twelve signs,
not seven.

Recorder: *Once*
there were only eight,
they say;
maybe
there's a truth for every age.
For this one
the 3 and 4 of 7
form a link:
3+4 is 7;
3 x 4 is 12.
Through the year
the twelve signs
cover all four
elements:
air, earth, fire and water —
three times each
in different modes:
cardinal,
fixed
and mutable,
all different expressions
of our being's rhythm.

Seeker: So, there certainly are
more ways than one —
of tuning into
pairs of opposites!

Recorder: And every one
involves
sensing subtle differences
in fields of energy.
Like the fish
we swim
in a sea of energies.

Seeker: But who
gives names to these?
Who or what
is the real origin
of the nature
and behavior
of Rays?

Recorder: Ah now!
I reckon we'll need
to reach the end
of this epic story
to form a worthwhile view
on that!

Seeker: I suppose I invited that.
So, could we say
everyone
and maybe every thing
is a complex mix of interacting qualities
we choose
numbers to describe and pinpoint,
then label them
the one we feel predominates?
Isn't that
the very worst kind of stereotyping?

Recorder: It would be
    if we were crude
                        rather than subtle
                                        in our way
    of doing this.
                            And don't forget
    the subtlest thing of all:
                        you cannot truly move
    from one to seven
                        unless you come to terms
    with the relating numbers
                        2/4/6.
                                If you try,
    things are at once
                        thrown out of balance.
    All hell breaks loose
                        and floods
                                wash things away.

Seeker: That makes me think
                            of attempts
                                    to straighten
    rivers:
                    dams burst
                                and water sweeps
    through cities —
                        while the rivers
                                just go back
    to their own beds
                        and follow again
                                their true,
    meandering,
                    self-purifying
                                course —

Recorder: as will start happening
                        in **Godwonland** —
    because of the morbid racial laws
                            and all that flowed
    from them.
                    Things will now move

                                          *to **Riverstrand**,*
          the University —

Seeker: where we shall
                                          no doubt discover
          what strands of wisdom

                                          are sensitive
          to natural waterflow.

Recorder: *We surely will discover*
          we dam up rivers
                    (indeed all forces)
                                          at our peril,
          because we have not learned
                              what causes drought
          or when
                    winds will carry clouds that burst
          in thunderstorms —
                         to overspill
                                   watersheds
          we thought we had controlled.
                                   Whether
          *life lived at **Riverstrand***
                         can yield
                                   this wisdom,
          remains
                    to be
                                   uncovered.

PHASE TWO

WAKE'S DILEMMA

Chloe sat ruminating at her desk
                              the day
following her return
                        From the 'Event'

(as the Solstice Concert
                        would be called).
Morning sun
                slid down her
                              auburn hair
and freckled arm,
                        as her thought
unpeeled
                layer after layer
                              till it reached
memories of school
                        with **Wit** and **Wiz**:
then forward
                        to the birth of **Witson** — so
unexpectedly completely white;
                              meetings
at the Library with **Sap**,
                        as quite slowly
Godwonland
                        roused itself to sever
whites
                from blacks;
                              her time reading
English at the City University;
                              then
training in Librarianship —
                        to specialise
in the theory
                        and the fascinating practice
of actually
                classifying knowledge.
                              Chloe
constructed her own system,
                              tying it in
to evolutionary interpretations

                                    of our claims
to know.
                She still used the Dewey decimal
notation system,
                        since it offered
                                    infinite sub-
dividing possibilities
                                in whatever field.
Her innovative logic,
                        though controversial,
caught on
                        with liberal educationists.
And so it came about that **Chloe** landed
the post of Chief Librarian at **Riverstrand**
(the most prestigious University
                                        in all
of **Godwonland**)
                            while **Wit** languished
in his island prison,
                        Wiz endured the ache
of her race-ridden young —
                                and the continent
was suborned
                            from its true purpose
by its government.

                                            Sap,
in choosing to bring up **Wiz** alone,
                                            never
actually pronounced
                            her father's name.
Chloe thus
                had no idea
                            when meeting
with charismatic **Sand** and **Snake**,
                                    that both
were half-siblings
                    of her school-friend,
                                            Wiz.
When **Sap** had left him,
                        dry and wondering,

Sophist had been fascinated,
                              for a while,
by **Sidewinder**,
                    who appeared from nowhere,
giving him two more children
                              before
the forest
          once more swallowed her.
                                    These,
whom **Sophist**
                 alternately pampered
                                      and
neglected,
          became virtually Campus
runabouts.

              Having been a student there,
when **Wiz** was born,
                  Sophist had never left
this nourishing tree:
                      scheming his way
from branch to branch,
                       he reached its apex
on the broadening base
                       of the economic
standing in the world
                      of **Godwonland**.
Sophist was now
                 Vice-Chancellor
                             of **Riverstrand**.
Though **Sap**
               had long achieved her 'First'
(in History
            and Philosophy of Science);
then worked toward a Doctorate
                               in Political
Science —
          to gain more powerful entry
to the world of men —
                      she had never
been certain of the part

                              Sophist had
played
                  in getting on the Statute Books
the racist laws.
                        Nor did she realise
his complex social place
                        at the edge of **Wiz'**
life and hers.
                  (What **Sophist** did
                              or did not
know
            of his first wife's work
                              to undo his,
was also hidden).

                              By the time
Chloe came on campus,
                        Snake and **Sand**
had not only gained their first degrees,
                              but
won provisional posts
                        among the Staff.
Snake had majored in Anthropology
                              (doing
her Field Studies
                  in her mother's culture),
while **Sand**
                  burrowed into Architecture,

revelling in smashed traditions,
                              classical
or modern.
                  He built the first Eco-House
in **Godwonland**
                  on the campus edge,
                              where
Chloe moved in with him —
                        once she knew
which of these two beings was
                        the gender
to procure her progeny.

                                          65

Both a rich coffee
colour,
the young produced by her
and **Sand** were not:
their daughter, **Carol**,
was as fair as **Chloe**;
Silicon,
a delicate *café au lait*,
more like seasoned
timber than the circuits
his nimble fingers
mastered —
before miniscule chips
became the way to go.
That these
would leave
a chaos time-bomb ticking
by the millennium
was not then knowable.

Another lay nearer:
Chloe had
that night
offered to harbour **Wit** and **Wiz**
to work
in camra
in her department)
until what squalls
the Solstice happening
gave rise to
subsided when
Security
failed to apprehend
the vanished **Wit**,
whose guards
lost touch
with him and **Herm**
in the dark chaos
following the chant of power.

                              As **Chloe**'s
quiet rumination reached this point,
                              she
looked up through her window
                              at the cows,
whose munching mouths
                              accepted so readily
the taking in
              and passing on
                              of nourishment
from chewing grass.
                              All the way,
down to the riverbank
                              (this community
of learning was named after)
                              the pasture
stretched —
              its rich milk
                              recycled alike
for staff and students:
                    seldom
                              for the calves
these cows gave birth to.
                              Chloe sighed.
How democratic really was
                              democracy?
What might happen next
                    in **Godwonland**?
Here in **Riverstrand**
                              opposite twists
of power abuse
              were frequent:
                              a serious
scandal was averted
              only by high-handed
intervention,
              when her bond-sister,
                              Snake,
had become pregnant by
              a black football ace,
whose team came there to play.

                                        Through
her father's pressure
                    (out of sight)
                                        Snake
received maintenance
                    for their daughter,
Wake,
        not often visited by her father
                                        even
before the days of segregation.
                                        Chloe
had never met him,
                    but **Silicon** and **Wake**
grew up together —
                    while **Carol**
                                        seemed
to make her friends elsewhere.

                                Sap had begun
to feel her age.
                    When therefore **Chloe**
rang from **Riverstrand:**
                        she had two tickets
for the Solstice Concert
                        if **Wiz** would like
to go there with her,
                            Sap was glad
to stay at home.
                    She had still to make ready
for **Witson**'s Sunday visit —
                        maybe his last
before the family move
                        wherever **Ned**
and his ecclesia
                    could find a place.
                                        Sap
on the Saturday night
                        watched the Concert
on her television:
                    elated by **Wit**'s singing,

but exhausted,
                    she drowsed —
                              and woke,
startled
                    to find her TV had gone blank.
Knowing **Witson**'s family
                              would not have
watched,
          Sap said nothing
                              when they came.
Will and **Vi**
                    jabbered about moving house.
Witson and **Violet** explained:
                              Ned had been
told there was a vacancy
                              somewhere up-
country
          in a small Seminary, where —
                              Witson's
convictions could be tested
                              and there would
be space
                    (a cottage in the College grounds)
for all the family.
                    The academic year
began in January —
                    so
                              they would be off
next week.
                    Where he would next be sent
would be decided
                              when he had shown
his mettle,
          in Theology,
                              Bible Studies,
Greek
          and pastoral work.
                    His training would
be paid for by the State.
                    Leaving the Police
with fair emoluments,

he could afford
                    to have
his family with him —
                    if they let their house,
                                        as
Violet said.
            While **Sap**, exhausted,
                                rested
after lunch,
            the four went for a walk
                                toward
the forest
            at the end of town.
                        Will and **Vi**
ran on ahead,
            not knowing
                        they were heading
for the spot
            where **Wisdom**
                        years before
had stumbled across **Wanda**,
                        running, lost.

Will pulled **Vi** backward
                                just in time
as a crack —
                        in the raw earth opened
at their feet,
                                loose
soil trickling
            down the naked edge,
                        stretching
miles and miles
            as **Will** put it,
                        when they
returned to a drowsy
                        unbelieving **Sap**.
The crack
            divided the forest from the town
and must have begun to open
                        hours since,

as though a giant ploughman furrowed it:
not deep as yet but widening.
                                        Sap half
choked on this:
                        though **Witson** had never
been to **Wisdom**'s shack —
                                and she had left
years ago,
                        it held such memories for her,
she felt her own ties loosening
                                        from Earth.

We were lucky
                        the children didn't fall
right in
                        was **Violet**'s only comment.
   I might've been dis,
                                dis-
                                        persed down it
Viola squealed
                        with awed delight.
No you wouldn't, silly
                                (Will disdained
to comment on his sister's choice of words).
I'd've pulled you out
                        by one of your fat
legs.
                Vi, giggling,
                        pinched **Will**'s calf.
But it was well
                        they came upon the gulley
on its first day out.

                        Chloe was still gazing
at the ruminating cows,
                                doubting a little
the wisdom of her offer
                        to harbour **Wiz** and **Wit**,
yet what else —
                        when **Silicon** and **Wake**,

(who had watched the Concert on TV

                                      but

stayed awake

          and slept thereafter)

                           trooped in

with mugs of steaming coffee.

                          So —

Mum?

     Silicon draped a leg round the chair
Wake had dropped into:

                 all three savoured

the rich aroma.

              Chloe was not yet ready:
How did it look on TV?

            It just blanked out,
as the chant was reaching boiling point,
after Wit

         put out that —

              call to action.

I thought

         it was the censors —

              but Wake

doesn't.

           What do you think, Wake?

I think —

           Wit *and the chanting —*
touched the cosmos —

            and ...

               Did Wit

get away?

          Yes

               Chloe

nodded slowly.

          He and Wiz

              are now

together and —

         But the Police'll go straight —

to Wiz

         to look for him!

              That's why

I've suggested they come here,

                              once Sap
understands what's happening.
                         Wake
breathed:
                         This could be it
this really could.
                    Chloe, *you're wonderful.*
(**Snake** was so much away on Field studies,
Wake felt more mothered here.)

                              But how
are we going to hide them?
                              Sil
brusquely interrupted.

                         There's lots
of things I could do with help over ...

                              They
could have my bed at home —
                         if I move in
with Sil —

          or mine here
                         if I move in
with Wake.
               They'll be less visible here
than in Snake's quarters.

                    And you'd be
a whole lot more
                    where it might be best
you weren't
               retorted his mother.
                         They might
be best off
               in the sleeper here together —
though it's not
                    so comfortable for two
for long
                    and it might be long.

They'll want to be like peas

                                  in a pod,
Mum,

                     after all this time —

After all this time
                  they'll need their space
to come together at all,

               said **Chloe** drily.
Sand was away,

             taking Carol with him
on a midsummer conference in Fiji.

                   Soon
she would be going overseas —

                to study
ecology in a British University.

                  So
there would in fact be room

                eventually
for **Wiz** and **Wit** —

             but **Carol**'s room
was not available now;

             nor did **Chloe** want
to push at the edge

             of **Wake** and **Sil**'s
relating —

       O come on, Mum,

                     no
problem,

       as you know!

               How dark is Wit?

Black coffee.

        Chloe put hers down.

                     Then
you're a glass of milk

             with spraying drops
of orange juice

        flashed **Wake**

            with wicked

accuracy.
Chloe burst out laughing.
The phone rang.
Wake,
aware of being as
dark as both her parents,
realised **Chloe**'s
face
was changing as she listened:
Shall
I come over right away —
and bring you
both back here?
So long as no one's
watching.
You'll be at Sap's of course.
I'll come at once.
Chewing a sandwich,
Chloe took her leave again
of this
virtually
not untwineable pair —
to drive back
to her home town,
where before dawn
she had dropped
so recently united
Wit and **Wiz,**
as near as was safe
to **Wiz'** own home.
But this time
she drove to **Sap**'s house
on the forest edge of town.
Wit met her
at the door.
How is she, **Wit**?
Slipping in
and out of consciousness —
saying little.
Wiz won't leave her:
she's in shock —

herself
                    after all that's happened.
(So am I.)
                        Are you sure you can
manage all this?
                    We can't just walk away.

They'll come looking for you here,
                                as soon
as they find
                        you don't return
to Windswell.
                    Tomorrow at the latest.

It seemed that soon after
                            Witson left
with his family
                        (the lunch dishes
were still stacked)
                        Sap collapsed:
she had reached her bed
                        and lain down.
There **Wiz** found her when —
                    she came to say
she and **Wit** ...
            What did **Sap** know
                    of last night's
happenings?
                And what had passed between
Wiz' son
            and mother?
                    Why did **Witson**
choose this time
                to bring his family here —
as though his father,
                    (his name plastered
over the town,
            to honour him),
                        did not exist?
Wiz felt frenzied
                in her helplessness ...

76

Chloe beckoned
                    from the doorway
Can you and Wit
                    help her into the car?
Wiz shook her head.
                    I don't think she'll come.
I think she's dying,
                    Chloe,
                                        and she'd rather
do that here.
                    She won't know
how unsafe it is for us.
                    She can't know
Wit *is here.*
                    As Wiz spoke
Sap closed her eyes
                    and drew
her last,
          long,
                    quite unrattled
                                        breath.
Wiz-dom saw
                    her mother's face
                                        serene.
A sighing, grateful silence.
                    She'll be
with Wisdom and **Wanda**
                    next time
we look in
                    forgetting 'we'
                                        meant her
and **Sap**.
          Chloe
                    looked mystified —

They wrapped
          Sap's body in a groundsheet,
gently
          tied it carefully to the roofrack
and all four drove back
                    to **Riverstrand**

with as much of Wiz' baggage
                              as the boot
would hold.
              Nothing at all
                              of **Wit**'s.

Seeker: So each of them has some
                              of the jig-saw pieces,
                while **Sap**'s

Recorder: *have now*
                                    died with her.

Seeker: And **Wiz-dom** can't
                              have a proper funeral
                for her mother —

Recorder: *since she's not supposed*
                to be there anyway —

Seeker: while **Sophist**
                has no idea
                              either his daughter —

Recorder: *(or his 'wife')*
                are on the premises.

Seeker: Still less
                              the wanted terrorist,
                Wit —

Recorder: *whose uncanny powers*
                have just upset
                                    the applecart
                for him
                              in **Godwonland**.

                                    In fact
the immediate outcome of the concert
                              seemed

78

the spontaneous unravelling
                              of **Sophist**'s
carefully constructed Laws.
                              People simply
forgot to carry passes —
                              and nobody
at all clamped down on them.
                              Wit
still felt fazed —
                  and badly missing **Herm**,
his constant companion through his training.
It was not yet two days
                       since the climactic
blackout —
            so like that first poem
his mother had dictated:

    ... charged with electric power
    to overload our national grid
    and blackout cities.

which he and **Wiz** and **Sap**
                              had wrestled
to make sense of.
                  Now
                       he and the son
of **Wiz**' friend, **Chloe**,
                            had dug a hasty grave
in alien territory
                  to dispose of **Sap** —
and he was free,
                perhaps for days only,
where he could not feel at home.

                              Dazed,
the little group
                that stood in the lemon grove
for **Sap**'s committal
                       (in the old tarpaulin,
just as they'd brought her:
                           they could not risk

attention buying a coffin)

included **Wake**,
because she 'happened' to be there.

It was
she

who smothered a cry

as they planted
a lemon tree

in the filled-in earth.

Wiz-dom
glanced up sharply:

What did you see?

I —
I thought I saw a tall, fair woman

greet
a shorter, dark one.

Another much younger,
slender —

looked on with joy ...
Wit and **Wiz-dom**

clung to one another.

Chloe gazed,
recalling **Wiz'** words

as **Sap** expired.
Only **Sil** was mystified.

Wake nodded at him
vigorously.

Now she knew this family.

Wiz,
wiping tears away,

came towards her.

Wake
and **Sil** would soon be told

the scattered tale
of all three children

Wit and **Wiz**

had given
life to —

the slim girl of **Wake**'s sensing
being one.

Chloe was right:
                    there was much
for the fugitives
              behind the scenes!
                                Sil had
long been clamouring
                    to put on computer
the Library charging system,
                          while **Chloe**
doubted his staying power
                      to see it through.
With two
        quick-witted brains
                        as extra hands,
he would try
            persuading her again.

Not unaware
            how anxious **Chloe** was
(returning the night **Sap** died
                          to fetch
back **Wit** and **Wiz**),
                        Wake and **Sil**
had felt no reason
                  to refrain
from intimate enjoyment
                      of a space
uncluttered,
            where,
                    for two successive
nights,
        Wake was at her most receptive.

They do say:
              as one goes,
                            another comes.
(**Wiz'** nose wrinkled
                      to banish a tickle
she would not accept
                    as from
a pricking tear gland)

when,
two weeks in
to their clandestine stay,
Chloe unburdened:
Wake was 'late'
and could be carrying
her own first grandchild.

Who is Wake,
really, though?
Wiz
would like to see more
of her
than time in the Library allowed.

Ah now!
said Chloe with a complex sigh.
Who is Wake, indeed?
No one I know
has met her father —
though it's said
he used to come
to see her.
Her mother
is Sand's sister,
Snake,
but neither
knows their mother,
although Snake
does field studies with her kin.

But what
about their father?
How do they come to be
part of all this?
Wiz waved her arms
to take in all the campus
from their Ecohouse
near the river bank
to the forest
that formed

82

another boundary.
                              I've never asked
about your bond with **Sand***.*
                              This house alone
tells me he must be special.
                                        No, well
said **Chloe** mumbling.
                              It wasn't a thing
to chat about —
                              with Wit in prison.

Well, tell me now!
                              At least for the moment,
I've my man again —
                              while yours seems
hardly here.
                    Chloe dithered:
                                        how to tell
her oldest friend —
                              the Vice-Chancellor
was her father-in-law,
                              a fact felt generally
to be lived down.
                         Provoked by her silence,
Wiz drew breath —
                              when **Chloe** blurted
Did you know
                    Sand and Snake's father
is Sophist,
                              the Vice-Chancellor?
Wiz-dom gaped.
                              But neither knew
he had also fathered **Wiz** herself
                                        a few
years earlier.
                         Nor yet that he was,
till now,
                    the power behind all
                                        found
most oppressive
                    throughout **Godwonland**.

So — how will he take it,

      *if **Wake** is —*

casually pregnant

     by her closest cousin?

How can he take it?

      How did he

get Sand and Snake?

     Not that he's ever

acknowledged he's their father —

       but

the Staff aren't fools.

      It's known,

just not alluded to.

     Sand and Silicon

think it's hugely funny.

      I don't care —

though I have wished Sil

      more circumspect.

I see

   said **Wiz-dom soberly.**

       The campus

atmosphere

    was feeling odder

      by the day,

like a wave

   that climbs and combs

      and will

not topple.

   Many,

     staff as well as students,

had been at the Concert —

      doubtless some

who used the Library.

     Though out of sight,

Wit and **Wiz**

     must have been noticeable

as they came and went.

     Yet no one

challenged them

and no one spoke.

Radio and TV,
                    as though there had been
no Concert,
                    filled the airwaves
                                        with bland
summer leisure;
                              they would look again
at things political,
                    maybe
                              when holiday
recess was over.

                                        In fact
the energy of **Godwonland**
                              had changed,
as if a spell were cast.
                                        Only
in **Riverstrand**
                    an undercurrent:
                                        as **Wake**'s
'lateness'
          grew into a month —
                              she began
to dream strange dreams;
                              a point within
registered,
          like a relay system,
                              messages.
Wake's **mind** was waking to impressions
that could hardly
                    yet
                              be foetal
wakening.
          But she felt them in her midriff.
And when she saw or heard,
                              (or thought
she saw and heard)
                    phrases that seemed
messages,

they came as though
her solar plexus spoke —
                              so seemed
uttered by the babe she knew
                              she carried:
fruit of her joy
                    in opening to **Silicon**.
He,
            though enchanted by the thought
of coming fatherhood,
                        frowned at **Wake**'s
muddled murmurs
                    of words and messages
uttered from her womb.

                                        Sand
back from Fiji
                        knew the score —
accepting,
            as did **Chloe**,
                                the urge
the young exhibited
                    for making life.
But,
        when a worried **Sil** approached him
with tales of voices
                    from **Wake**'s womb,
Sand was aghast.

                        *But what words
does she hear?*
                    asked **Chloe** reasonably,
when this disturbing item
                    of hallucination
was retailed that night.
                        Beware of Sophist
was the core message
                        Wake
                            felt shareable,
when **Chloe**
            delicately broached this.

Since the family
                    hardly took him seriously,
this was startling,
                    especially
                              as fears
round **Wit**'s escape
                    were lessening —
time, it seemed
                    healing the race wound.

Though **Wake** made light
                    of the men's anxiety,
she shrank —
                    that they had talked
and not to her,
                    felt labelled as,
at the very least,
                    disturbed.
                              She knew
what she thought she heard —
                              not
what it meant
          or might;
                              just as
she'd known
                    what she thought she'd seen
at **Sap**'s commital …
                    Ah!
                              Was that
what this was, then?
                              But why?
Why should this joyously united pair,
                              Wiz'
and **Wit**'s mothers
                    and their longlost child,
send her warning messages,
                              through
her babe,
          of her notorious grandfather —
unless …
                    the incarnating babe itself

were **Wanda**

                    knowing she must return
to win her earth experience

                           through
another womb?

                Wiz-dom,

                        Wake felt,
was the only person

                    she could share this
sudden insight with.

                She only

                    would not
call her mad.

          For, mad she knew

                 she seemed:
though **Sap** had

                clearly died —
and **Wake** had 'seen' her reunited,

                   both
with **Wit**'s mother

           and her granddaughter,
Wanda,

        yet these two

                had not
been known to die,

           but had been 'seen'
struggling over many years

             to climb a hill.
What could this 'say' —

           to academic
staffs?

        Even her lover and his father?
How did **Wanda**'s mother

          see

           the nature
of the cosmos?

        What was 'reality'
if this could happen?

                Complex
was **Wiz**' response

88

                    when **Wake** at last
caught up with her
                    in the campus hair salon
(after a heavy day
                    transforming the Library
with **Wit** and **Sil**).
                              We can't talk here.
So,
                    when they were both blown dry
and spruce,
                    they wandered down
through the cow pasture
                    to the river's edge
and sat,
                    feet in the warm summer water,
as the air cooled round them
                    and the sun
blazed up a little —
                    to dip and vanish
behind the nearest hillock.
                              Tell me again
slowly, **Wake**,
                    I did know from **Sil***'s mother*
that you might be pregnant —
                    but what
you're saying now,
                    if I get you right,
is …
                    that I'm hearing voices,
                              through
my stomach
                    — as though,
                              the babe itself
were speaking to me,
                    which it couldn't —
but it is.
                    What
                              does it say?
It tells us —
                    me —
                              I don't know who —

to beware of **Sophist**,

                             which is ridiculous

because —

                             we all think **he** is.

Wiz looked questioning:

                          Chloe said that too,

but he's a powerful man.

                             Is that why

you do it?

                So you don't feel overwhelmed

by your illustrious forebear — ?

                             If he is:

he wasn't all that illustrious

                             when I

was born,

              Snake says,

                      but he still got

my football father …

               Wake started —

                      to pay her

for my keep.

             Do you know him?

                       I don't know,

yet,

    but it rang loud bells.

                     What's his name?

Well, I called him Dad

               when he came here,

which he hasn't —

               He wouldn't be allowed

on campus now

               if he's who I think.

Is he like **Wit**?

       Yes.

Then they're half-
brothers.
At least I think so,
and his name is
Wilson.
Wit hasn't said much about him —
I don't think he can know this.
It does
seem **Sophist** had a hand in everything.
Why
are you being warned just now —
why you,
I mean.
It's **Wit** in danger.
Both heads
jerked up —
as they saw together
the image
Wake had seen at **Sap**'s commital.
But now
the slender one had vanished.
The other two
looked directly
at both **Wake** and **Wiz-dom**

My God, **Wake**!
said **Wiz** in sudden awe.
I don't know how to say —

You needn't.
It's because I've wondered this,
I wanted
you to know.
Wiz-dom folded **Wake**'s
swelling body to her.
But
I still don't see
how it's posible.
Wanda
didn't die,
did she?

91

Well, yes and no

        sighed

Wiz-dom,

    unclasping **Wake**,

        She never

really managed — on her own.

        But will she

have any better chance right now?

        Wiz-dom,

there's something else:

        although there are

all these warnings

        about **Sophist**,

everything else I'm picking up

        suggests

things are different

        since the concert.

Nobody is hounding **Wit**.

        I wondered that

myself

    Wiz whispered.

        It feels different,

but I don't see how we can assume —

The voice says we can

        said **Wake**.

        Only

Sophist *can endanger us.*

        So — who is

saying so?

    I am

        said the voice of **Sap**

with calm distinctness.

        And, apart from

anything else,

        he is your father, **Wiz-dom**.

This was too much for both of them,

        hard

to say

    which the more shocked.

                              No
more was said.
                    Wiz-dom and **Wake**
leant on each other as they walked back up
the pasture in the fading light,
                              too dazed for
either to pick up
                    they were aunt
                              and niece —
and that **Wake**'s new baby,
                              when it came,
would be
                    Sophist's great grandchild
no matter who
                              had fathered **Snake**
and **Sand**.
                    Wiz-dom needed
to be on her own.
                              It felt harder here
to meditate
                    than alone at **Windswell**,
Wit in prison.
                              The raft of safety
Chloe's goodness offered
                              rocked
on a sea she feared,
                              left her
with no bearings
                              she knew how
to follow.
                    Granted her mother
left her father
                    too long ago,
                              for her
to know why
                    or even who he was.
But what was the source of danger now
                                        if
Wit was not searched for
                              by the State?
Wiz-dom had to feel her way

through this,
before she could share with **Wit**
horizons
Wake's disclosings opened up.
Wit,
who had always found action comforting,
was finding **Sil**'s demanding task
a fine
distraction from the fear
of being caught.

The blow when it fell
was subtly different
from anything they thought
they must avoid.
Wake felt reassured
about her sanity
by all the acceptance
Wiz-dom gave
of what she'd had to hide.
The trouble was
she hadn't,
at the beginning
from her lover.

She had been canny enough
to suggest to **Sil**
they call the baby
Strand,
whether it were
girl or boy,
to which
(also a campus child)
he happily concurred.
But the damage
was already done.
Seed sown in **Sand**,
when **Sil** first told him
of **Wake**'s voices,
spilled more than a little
into campus soil.

So,
        when **Chloe** told him innocently
                                Wiz
thought the new baby
                        was a reborn **Wanda**,
Sand seemed to feel
                        the honour of Science
was at stake.
                        Not that Architecture
was considered science
                        by scientists —
but even humanists like **Sand**,
                                who built
Ecohouses
                        rather than traditional
office blocks
                        teaching students to acclaim
postmoderns
                        fell back on the 'best'
empirical foundations —
                        when the point at issue
was the psychic state
                        of his son's partner,
abetted by his wife's best friend.

                                What
unutterable nonsense
                        are you talking?
said this son of **Sophist**.
                        So it came about that
where race mix began
                        to leave things calmer,
difference of sex outlook
                                stirred up
the passions
                        of suave academic staff
at **Godwonland**'s
                        impeccable university
of **Riverstrand**.
                        The atmospheric wave,
hovering

                        when danger pressed on **Wit**,
came crashing on to campus,
                              as the issue
focused on the sanity
                          of **Wake**.

Seeker: Hang on a minute:
                                    this is the sixties, surely!

Recorder (nodding): *when everything to do with*
                                        madness
                  was suddenly in the melting pot

Seeker: with eminent men
                proclaiming there was no such thing —

Recorder: *just cultural*
                  ways of seeing.
                              So, it would seem a time

Seeker: when flexible,
                        liberal attitudes
                                    would come down

Recorder: *on the side of* **Wake**,
                                so hearing voices

Seeker: would be shrugged off
                                as whimsy.

Recorder: *Just so.*
                          But the more that tends to happen,
                  the more capricious
                              the power behind the scenes.

Seeker: And **Sophist**
                        will wield that
                              where he can —

Recorder: *Having just been thwarted of his prey*
                              by **Wit**.

Wake sat quite comfortably
                                        to knowing
her source of livelihood
                                    was others.
                                                    Funds
seemed to be forthcoming,
                                        for what needs
she noticed.
                        Open to
                                        'unitive experience'
(a dreary phrase
                                    to spell out spells
we'd die for),
                        Wake did not feel the need
to force distinctions
                                    between giver,
                                                            gift
and who was given to.
                                            Accepting
easily
            the sunny side
                                    of people's natures
natures
            (not least **Chloe** and her silky son's)
Wake
                            was more awake to loveliness
than painful people —
                                        though aware
of absences,
                    she had to fill with presence —
and did now.
                                        Wanda,
who had trudged
                            what we call years
towards and up
                            a hill into her future
(watching **Wisdom**
                                    growing younger
as she herself
                    grew up),
                                had come to see

and seeing
                come to know,
                                a time would fruit
when she would seed again
                                the turmoil
of the earth experience.
                                In saying
to **Wisdom**
                (as she had at ten)
                                the two
could go on walking
                                till she was as old
as **Wisdom**,
                Wanda was nearer right
                                than
reasoning would allow.
                                While **Wisdom** shed
her years of being burdened
                                by the Word
made flesh,
                Wanda grew into readiness
to receive its gift:
                                this time not sidelined
by a gifted, overbearing twin
                                (as **Windel**
even in the womb
                                most surely was),
but springing from the body ecstasy
                                of **Sil**
and **Wake**,
                hungry to bring to life
                                new life.
Snug in the wet warmth
                                of **Wake**'s inside,
Wanda,
                who would become
                                        Strand
in the outer world
                                (where life was changed
in subtler ways,
                                than sloughed off

shanty towns) —
                                    began to talk
to her new mother,
                        Wake.
                                    Tinier
than she had ever known herself
                                    and now
without **Windel**'s strong protection,
                                    she who
had been **Wanda**
                        gasped
                                    at the vast empty
space
            she floated in;
                        felt safer,
                                    when
she clamped
                        to a soft spot in the womb
wall,
        and scrabbled to dig in there —
                                    to feed
and breathe
                        through her new belly tube.
It had been
            early in this first trimester
                                    Wake
had heard messages
                        sent out by **Sap**
and relayed by this unsure embryo,
                                    quite
unaware of the vibrations
                        passing through her
to the ear of **Wake**
                        — turned upside down
by multiple sensations,
                        voices,
                                    wonderings —
and less support from **Sil**,
                                    than she felt
used to.
            So she turned

to the more
certain sense
of this no-longer-**Wanda**
she now harboured.
Wake heard
her baby say:
I am coming to know
by being
inside you now;
coming to life,
coming to live,
coming to learn,
coming to love you, mother.
Do you love me?
Wake breathed her loving
to her not yet born.
Her tears dripped
to her swelling belly
as she half-recalled
her own perfunctory babyhood:
how
she had clung to **Sil**
because he was there
and **Chloe** let her.
I am a thread of living
energy
the voice within her sang.
A strand
it added,
as it picked up **Wake**'s
joyous
awareness of the meaning
put already
on this new
weaving in the making.
I come to learn by weaving in
and out
of all conditions I may meet.
You are
the first
the best and worst.

100

                    And you are now.
I am here
          but cannot stay.
                    When I am big,
here will be tight
                    and I will have to leave
to live.
          You will push
                    and I will pull
and it will not feel wonderful.
                    I seem
to know this.
          I do not know how.

Though **Wake** recalled nothing
                    of her birth
and **Snake** had said nothing —
                    except
that her father
          was not there —
                    Wake
felt sure of what her baby said.
                    Moreover,
Sil was so wedded
          to work in the Library
with **Wit** and **Wiz**,
          she could not see him
or **Wiz**
          being there
                    for her labouring
to bring forth **Strand**.
                    During the weeks
to quickening and beyond,
                    the thread
who would be **Strand**
                    said less and less,
as she bent her being to the task
                    of turning
inside out
          her layers:
                    to let them shift

from globs of cells —
                              to structured organs
of her foetal self,
                              whose head and heart and
differentiate limbs,
                              whose lungs and liver,
spleen and kidneys
                              would in their fullness
burst
          breathless
                              from her sacral bag —
as the first spring days
                              unfolded from Virgo
in south-of-Capricorn
                              September.
                                                  Not
Silicon's absence,
                              but his father's
chance meeting
                              with the campus 'shrink',
stirred up the hornet's nest
                              that would
put pressure upon **Wake**
                              beyond the point
her psyche could accommodate.
                              Because so
sure
          her 'voices' were not there
                                        (or if
they were,
          she surely must be mad),
                              and 'sure'
with all the sureness of the male,
                              for whom
only the seen,
          so certain,
                              can be real —
Sand and **Silicon**
                              and the cocksure shrink
bore down upon the place
                                        Wake

102

and her babe-filled belly
                                    occupied.
Wake shrank
                        as their collective energy
ravished the dual space
                                    she dwelt in:
fragile soap-bubble,
                            colours lifting
as lips blow —
                        to send it quivering
with the spiral warmth
                            of the incoming soul
to form a vessel
                    for this new minted being.

This invisible process
                                    these three
well-meaning males
                        crashed into,
                                    brash
hikers heedless
                        of the dawn-dewed web,
new-spun,
                their opening of the gate
                                    breaks
from its moorings —
                        to leave its spider
creator dangling
                        from its unmoored centre,
belaying silk from her creative belly,
                                            till
the blast
                that wrecked her fresh new work
is past.
            So **Wake** withdrew
                            to her sanctum
as they came.

                    They came with nothing but
    a deep concern
                    for **Wake** and her baby's

welfare:
                        indeed **Sil** was startled,
when his father
            interrupted
                        the ongoing task —
to say his medical colleague,
                                    much
esteemed,
            was willing to bring his expertise
to bear
                        upon the unusual condition
of his son's partner.
                                    They
found
            a slip of a girl with frightened eyes
and mountain belly
                        who closed against
them,
            as they closed on her.
                                    Sil winced
for her
            and for himself.
                                    Sand too,
caught
            by his own nature,
                        went for Chloe.
She,
            having not closed down the Library
during the great updating
                        operation,
remained apprehensive —
                                    until **Sil**
would pronounce the work
                        accomplished.
She and **Wiz**
                        had not had time alone,
since **Wake** disclosed
                        the babe's identity.
Poised between
                        the possibilities,
she felt no need

104

to affirm
                    or to deny
the baby would/
                  would not
                          be **Wanda**.
How could anybody know?
                          Sand
found her in the kitchen making tea.
                              When
he told her who
                  was there
                        and why,
                              Chloe
rounded on him
                      with a face of bleach:
Where is he now?

                    In there with Wake.
Chloe bit her lip
                  and turned away.
                              She would
not
        be sucked into this family's counter-
clockwise swirls.
                      Surely this shrink
would not harm **Wake** —
                          however he chose
to interpret
                  her strange voices.
                              She added
another teabag to the pot,
                          picked up the tray
and swept into the livingroom.
                              Wake,
eyes closed,
                  lay motionless,
                              facing
the sliders and the open view.
                              Silicon
stood awkwardly;
                      the psychiatrist,

covering with truculence
                              his abashment,
announced to the sky beyond:
                                        I'd like
to take her in for observation.
                                        Have I
your permission?
                        Why?
                                        chimed
Sil and **Chloe**.
                        Well
                                        returned
the shrink,
                glancing sideways for support
from **Sand**,
                                she does appear ...
to have ... er ...
                        lost all contact with —
reality.
                        Right now she seems in trance,
and prior to that, I understand,
                                        she made
claims of hearing voices
                                telling her things
improper to believe.
                                Taking
these things together,
                        I would be failing
you all in acting otherwise.
                                Chloe's
heart sank
                as the men did not demur.

You played me false
                        shrieked **Windel**,
(who now had two children
                                of her own
by **Wilson**),
                        when word came through
that **Wake**,

                           his much neglected child
at **Riverstrand**,
                           was not only in a home
for the disturbed,
                           but in late pregnancy
to her childhood playmate,
                                    Silicon,
son of **Wake**'s uncle
                  Sand,
                                    Snake's
brother.
                  Wilson,
                           who came and went
with cheerful ease —
                           as had his father,
Wittle —
                  did not deny his partner's charge.
But it had all been so long before ...
                                               he
shacked with **Windel**
                                    in the shanty town
and brought forth twins,
                                    he had not
thought to tell her
                           of this earlier time
with **Snake**.
                           Wick and **Wind**,
as sharp and lithe as any,
                           were for the present
all-absorbing.
                  So **Wilson** smiled,
                                    as he hoisted
to his shoulder,
                  Wick,
                           who gripped his head
and grinned.
                  She had her mother's brilliant
black eyes
                  and knew how to use them
as effectively.
                  What are you going to do,

then?
                        demanded **Windel**.
Wilson shrugged
                        as he moved off
into the messy middle of the town.
                        It had not
lain heavily with **Wilson**
                        that **Windel**,
                                when
Witson brought his squad to take her,
                                killing
all her friends instead,
                        did not hesitate
to shoot her brother
                        out of pure revenge.
Nor,
        in his easy-going way,
                        did he see
this moment
                as another,
                        maybe poised
for passion
                by his possessive partner.

                                        Life
in the township was no longer
                                punctured
by sallies from the armed Police.
                                        But
living conditions
                        were no way improved.
Windel had no idea
                        her father was free
and unpursued.
                No Concert Notice had been
posted there
                and none was taken of events
so far removed
                from day to day existence.
Blacks from the forest could be left to rot —
in their own mess.

Yet now came word —
that **Wilson** had a daughter,
                        old enough
to be
        in several sorts of trouble.
                                Windel
felt in double turmoil
                            as she turned
to pick up **Wind**
                        and go in their dingy hut
to try
                        to find him food.

PHASE THREE

STRANDS OF INQUIRY

So **Strand**,
                    for not the best of reasons,
was born
            in the laundry
                        of a Mental Home,
attended by no one
                        but a startled cat —
who went in there for warmth
                            and stayed
to lick
            with concern
                        the slimy bundle,
premature, but
                alive
                        and mewing —
                                    like
her own litters.

                        Staff came running as
they heard **Wake**'s groans
                                    (her
first sounds uttered since
                        her admission
days before).
                    They rescued her baby
from a hillock
                of damp washing
                                    (now
no longer
                waiting to be hung)
                                    shooed
from the scene
                    the feline midwife —
and bore the baby
                    to a place of safety,
deeming her mother
                        hardly that.

Wake in that moment
                    faced

                                        the void:
abandoned
               by those who knew her
                                        best,
now snatched from
                              by strangers
with false, soothing words
                                   who led her
where
               her bleeding emptiness could be
washed down drains
                         and thus with speed
forgotten.
                              They dried
and put her back to bed
                              with hot sweet tea
that made her retch;
                         then gave her pills
to bring her
                         'sweet' oblivion.
When **Wake** woke in darkness,
                              flat in belly,
she did not know
                    if **Wanda**
                              was alive
or dead —
               nor where.
                              Her chest
felt tight:
               her breasts
                              weeping
for the work they swelled to do.

                              Strand,
in a far-off place,
                    was given milky drops
of water,
               saline drips
                    through alien tubes,

cold air —

through a nostril bunged
                              with plastic.
There
        Wiz and **Chloe**,
                              late enough,
found both of them
                              and had them
brought to one place
                     to be again together.

Wake wept as they hugged and kissed her,
placed her dripping nipple
                              into **Strand**'s
urgent mouth.
              whose gums
                              gripped,
hung on
              and sucked.
                              Well!
You wouldn't think that was **Wanda** —
                                    Wiz
gasped wide-eyed.
              She is, though
                              came
the familiar voice
              of disembodied
                              Sap.
  I warned you to beware of Sophist —

                              But,
Mother,
        what's he to do with this?

                     A whole lot
  more than meets the eye
                     for you.
                              Now
Wisdom *and I can see*
                     from up this hill,
  both of us have almost X-ray eyes
                              to scan

113

influencing powers and presences,

                                      not

all of which

                 bring energies to bless.

                                    I

understand a great deal more now,

                            Wiz,

than when I left your father —

                             though,

even then,

                  I rightly intuited it was best

for all …

                         As voices

and the sound of feet approached,

                            Sap

stopped.

        So!

               said the now white-coated

'shrink'

        with an entering flourish,

                    And who

are you?

           pinpointing

                Wiz-dom

                        with

his steely eyes.

                    Wake's aunt:

The Vice-Chancellor

                  is my father.

Surely this trick was hers.

              Ah!

                  said

the doctor softly —

            Then you'll know

his views on protocol.

                So long

as Sand's daughter

          is here

               and in

our care,

she need have no medication
for her state of mind.
That will be
best —
for her to feed this baby safely.
I see she can do that for herself —
it has
not come all that early.

Her name is

Strand
said **Wake**

as she lifted
the baby to her shoulder,

patting her
gently to encourage wind

and placing
her deftly
to her other breast.

Of course
I shall not take drugs.

Whatever
for?

For a thoroughly unstable
mental state
rejoined the shrink,
flicking the wrist-bands

of his cuff-linked
shirt.

Would you mind offering
us evidence of that?
asked **Wiz**
with honeyed voice.

It is mostly
hearsay
admitted the psychiatrist,
pursing his lips judicially,

I brought
her in for observation
                    because
of allegations made.
                              Until
today,
          I have not heard Wake speak,
itself unusual
                    to say the least.
However,
          the name she gives her baby
is indeed
                    what its father agreed
it should be called.

          She is also **Wanda** —
Wake and **Wiz-dom**
                    said together.

Ah-ha!
          so more than one of us may
be subject to —
                    wanderings of the mind.

   All of us maybe
                    said the distinctly
audible voice of **Sap**.
                    The psychiatrist
jumped
          and turned.
                    So, which of us
is a ventriloquist, then?
                    he suavely asked,
now alert to 'serious' possession.

          As **Chloe**
opened her mouth for the first time,
                    a fresh
commotion sounded
                    and the door
swung open to reveal

                              Wilson
(his younger daughter perched,
                              her legs
wound tightly round his neck),
                              a bevy
of shocked nurses
                              unable to prevent
his bursting in.
                    Strand
                              slirrupped
to a standstill
                    as the overcrowded room
became too much:
                              her eyeballs rolled
and she broke into the mewing
                              that had so
concerned the cat.
                    Dad
                              squealed
Wake,
         clutching her three-day baby to her,
    who is that?
                    Wiz-dom
                              head
spinning,
                knew at once.
                              The eyes
of this toddler
                borne aloft
                              had to make
her
         Windel's daughter.
                              Though
she had guessed
                    Wake's father,
she had not
                imagined this.
                              Great aunt
to **Wake**'s newborn,
                Wiz was, it seemed,
grandmother

to this unknown
two-year-old.

Meet Wick
said **Wilson**,
unwinding
his daughter
to the floor.
He
only remembered meeting **Wiz-dom** once:
the night
the shanty-school
was under fire;
Windel and **Wanda**
only five —
two killed
and **Wit**
arrested briefly.
Meeting
Wiz' eyes now,
Wilson knew
Wit
was free
and close.
The Mental Home
was not so many miles
from **Riverstrand**.

The white-coated shrink,
no longer centre-
stage,
grew restless —
but **Sap**
had not
yet finished with him:
So which of them
do you think is a ventriloquist?
Wick and
Wilson
peered round the room
astonished.

118

How is your father, Wilson?
                                        came
a voice
                only one in that room knew —
unless the new baby.
                                The psychiatrist
blanched —
                for he could hear them both.

   Why don't you gather
                                some inquirers,
   Frederick?
                said the voice
                                most of them
knew as **Sap**'s.
                The shrink,
                                who never
used his given name,
                                was dumb-founded
enough
        to begin fearing for his own mind's
health.
                Only his mother
                                would have called
him this.
                Who in this room
                                could possibly
have access
                to the Records
                                of the Home?
None licitly —
                so, who would pilfer?
                                        Frink
looked helplessly at **Chloe**,
                                whose partner,
Sand, had first alerted him
                                to this discordant
mêlée.
                She looked as bewildered as he felt.
She was:
                nine months before,

                                                        119

she had been
present at **Sap**'s burial.
Now **Sap**'s own voice
presumed to turn the tables
on the dictum
pronouncing **Wake**
mentally disturbed —
while **Wiz'** family
was increasing by the hour.

Wick has a brother
Wilson said.

We're
twins
said **Wick**
gleefully looking
round the crowded room.
He's **Wind**.
We left him with mother
in the shanty town.

Is that where they found you?
the shrink
inquired,
(concerned for the hygiene
of his well-appointed Home).

Yes.
Wilson
felt **Wick** tug at his sleeve,
and **Chloe**
helped them both to find a loo.
Wake
was exhausted
and so this Bedlam
gathering dispersed.

The upshot
of this crossing of the ways
was that

the psychiatrist,
                        in need of reliable help
in house and garden,
                        did not find
it difficult to persuade
                Wilson
                        to ask
his partner, **Windel**
                        to uproot her
family
                so they could come to live,
as Housekeeper/Caretaker —
                        here
at his Mental Home.
                Though a Consultant-
Psychiatrist on the Campus,
                        this was
his centre of operations,
                        where patients'
children received schooling —
                        and not
all were white.

                Surely,
                Wilson thought,
when **Windel** heard
                        that **Wit** was out
of prison
                and at **Riverstrand**,
                        she would
leap at the chance
                        to leave the township
for a clean existence
                        in a place like this.
Before returning to her,
                        Wilson talked
with **Wiz-dom**,
                who revealed
                        how **Wit**
and she
        had come to be

at **Riverstrand**.
Wilson had discovered
on his way
with **Wick**,
that life beyond the shanty town
was different,
in some mysterious way —
only
non-enforcement of the Passes
seemed to make real.
Any other
sort of change
he saw
was up to them.

When he got back
to **Wind** and **Windel**,
she first tore strips off him
for going off
with **Wick**
without a word.
I know
where Wit is
Wilson calmly said.

We all do
Windel stormily began,
then
stopped as she saw
what **Wilson**
knew.
I saw a new baby,
Wick
told her startled mother and her brother.
She's our cousin
Daddie says
she added
conspiratorially
to **Wind**.
Though **Windel**'s feelings
about

the proposition
     Frink had put,
         were
painfully mixed,
       knowledge that **Wit**
was well and free
     and would be
          not
far away
      was overwhelming.
They left next day.

        Sap's
suggestion of inquiry
       had been lost
on the confounded **Dr Frink** —
         but
it was taken up
    by **Wiz** and **Chloe**
        when
they returned to campus
       and retailed
to **Sand**
    and **Wit**
       the various
unscheduled happenings
       at the Home.
Each of them
     had the unpalateable
to digest:
    Sand had a grand daughter,
who was claimed to be
       Wit's own
lost daughter;
    while
      the other twin
had made **Wit**
      grandfather
to his half-brother's twins.
      How could
such hot material

                                be handled
                                          in a place like
Riverstrand —
                                          except by inquiring into
the nature of the claims
                                          of these, already
ambiguously
                                cross-referenced,
                                                    relations?
But how deep
                                must such inquiry go?

Wake, meanwhile,
                                left to rear her baby
in a mental home,
                                would be attended by
an unlikely assortment
                                of her relatives —
never before set eyes on:
                                her father's
other family.
                                Even **Sap**
                                          expressed
consternation
                     that **Windel**
                                would come
so close
           to new **Wanda**
                                now called **Strand**.
But **Wiz-dom**
                     took deep breaths
                                and sought
to see
           the over-all connecting pattern:
the library work was
                                just about complete.
So she and **Wit**
                                (who no longer feared
pursuit)
           could,

                    if **Chloe** and **Sand**'s
                                        extended
hospitality
              allowed,
                            research and provide
some relevant data
                                  for a context
that would make some sense
                                  of what would
otherwise
              be written off
                            at least as multiple
hallucination
                    if not
                            downright lunacy.

Frink already had the edge
                                  by freeing
Wake from drugs,
                      while feeding **Strand** —
so long as she was here
                            in virtual custody.
This was oppressive use
                            of social power —
begging the question
                            of alternate ways
of understanding
                      what we see and hear:
it assumed
              seeing is believing,
                            hearing not.

As **Wake** began quietly
                            taking stock
of her position
                      in this private cubicle,
her baby cradled next to her,
                            and more
trees seen from her window
                            than from
Silicon's room

in **Chloe**'s house
near the
river delta —
a truth began to dawn
at last:
she had neither earned,
nor yet
inherited
the means to live;
and now
was the helpless mother
of a precious baby,
whose very identity
was in dispute —
to the powers
that housed and fed her.
Yet
she and **Strand** felt close enough
to form
a oneness in this quiet place.
As this thought
surfaced,
Wake's eye was caught
by the sage
nodding of a rounded face:
an owl,
gripping a branch outside her window,
looked
as though following her train of thought
to say
and about time too.
But, which bit
of her thinking
triggered this,
Wake wondered.
The owl gazed
disdainfully
and flew.

Strand stirred in her sleep
and thrust a tiny

126

fist
　　　　to punch the air.
　　　　　　　　　　　As **Wake** turned
to pick her daughter up,
　　　　　　　　　　　　　the door,
kept ajar,
　　　　　　　　　was pushed from outside.
The cat
　　　　came purposefully in,
　　　　　　　　　　　　dangling
a new-born kitten from its jaws;
　　　　　　　　　　　　dropped it
in a dark corner
　　　　　　　　furthest from the draught
and left.
　　　　　　　　　By the time **Wake**
was feeding **Strand**,
　　　　　　　　four kittens nestled
in the corner
　　　　　　near the window,
　　　　　　　　　　where **Wake**'s
travel bag
　　　　　　gave some protection.
　　　　　　　　　　　　　Wake
could only just remember
　　　　　　　　　　　her night
of birthing.
　　　　　　Maybe the cat
　　　　　　　　　　recalled the smell
of **Strand**
　　　　　　and sought it
　　　　　　　　　when her own need
pressed.
　　　　If **Strand** felt this incursion,
　　　　　　　　　　　it did not
disturb her own
　　　　　　　absorbing
　　　　　　　　　from her mother,
as the cat
　　　　　suckled her brood
　　　　　　　　and purred.

127

Into this gentle dynamo of living,
                              thrust
the inquisitive head
                    of **Wick**,
                              not two feet
from the floor.
                    Aha!
                              its broad grin said.
Wake, quick to secure an ally,
                              drew her in.
Wick, who had watched the cat
                              from the end
of the long passage,
                    now became a willing
conspirator with **Wake**
                    to hide
                              from staff
the presence
                    of this feline family.

She went for **Wind**:
                              between them,
daily,
          these adept accomplices found ways
to divert authority's attention
                              from
this cat existence:
                    eight blue eyes now
open.
          Their opportunist mother
                              trusted,
when the twins
                    stuffed each of her kittens
in their pockets
                    to go in opposite directions
as the hoover
                    moaned and
                              scoured
its way
          through corners,
                    just vacated.

Delight at this outwitting
                    kept **Wake**'s mind
from dwelling much on **Windel**'s presence,
where this reconstructed strand of **Wanda**
crawled with the kittens on the floor,
                                      when
Wick and **Wind** pronounced it safe.
                                   The new
Housekeeper's duties
                    busied her enough
to keep her from this haven
                        prisoning **Wake**.
Even her Caretaker father
                        had only once
looked in
                    since their arrival.

The wider world of radio and TV
                            watched
and listened to
                    by those at **Riverstrand**,
had come to life again with news:
                                America
was offering to make life safe
                            for all
in the south
                by means of
                            M. A. D.

How about that then!
                    Wiz,
                            with the special
sarcasm
        she reserved
                    for the ruling world
of men,
        declared to **Wit**.
                            What is that
supposed to mean?

129

Mutually assured
destruction,
          I believe.
                    It seems to be
a ruse cooked up
                    between Russians
and Americans
          to ensure
                    neither of them
ever uses
                    their stock-piled nuclear
weapons.
                    I suppose it does have
a sort of insane
          sanity.
                              How
does it work out in practice then?
                    It seems
the Americans
                    offer to patrol our ports
here —
                    with nuclear warships —
so keeping
          communists out
                              as enemies
of colonists.
                    I picked this up in prison,
but it's now
          gone stages further.
                              What
if there should be
                    a nuclear accident?
Ah!
          said **Wit**.
                    Of course they say
there won't.
                    Mad
                              indeed!
said **Wiz-dom**.
          mad as **Frink**.

130

                              Wit,
she continued thoughtfully,
                         Now we've done
with **Chloe's** cataloguing,
                         what do you think
of her remarkable classifying system?
                              Ah!
you have me there.
                         I hardly took it in.
It's meant
                    to follow lines of evolution,
isn't it?
                    And they are still evolving,
I presume.
                    They must be,
                                        so —
the whole thing
                         raises issues of inquiry
as to what is ...
                         a proper starting point
for saying what's true
                                        or real.
Chloe's system
                    rests on a huge assumption
Riverstrand must have swallowed whole —
to make her Chief Librarian.
                              Maybe
that's why she didn't remonstrate —
                                        when
the shrink proposed to take Wake in.
If all is chance and natural selection,
what can we do but go with it?

                              A_s

Strand and the kittens
                         prospered,
it occurred to **Wake**
                         to take advantage
of her seeming sentence:
                         so long as

131

she had milk for **Strand**,
                              her place
in this warm secluded atmosphere,
                              without
the invasion of mind-numbing drugs,
                                        was
quite secure.
                              (The nodding
of the watchful owl
                    again affirmed).

                                        But,
so, equally,
            must she be free
                              of psychic
disturbance from her fellow inmates —
                                        who
flitted,
      drugged,
                down corridors
                              to toilets,
seeming not to see her
                              or to know.
Wake wondered
                    how many others might
be there
        for no better reason
                              than herself.
But for now,
            Strand's wellbeing
                              was her first
concern.
        So **Wake** made no attempt to brave
the communal rooms,
                    nor share in therapy
groups,
        though told
                    she would be welcome.

Strand was **Wake**'s world:
                              a dusky pink,

with eyes as blue and clear
                          as skies
                                    the sun
has cleared of vapour,
                          leaving space
for anything.
              Wake's eyes
                          were brown
and nothing
              in her or **Silicon**'s inheritance
could draw forth this blue —
                                    unless
the unacknowledged play
                          of **Sophist**
from
          two generations back.
                          Wake sighed;
      Is this the influence
                          I must beware of?
Strand looked at her and smiled
                          and shook
her head.

          The kittens had grown to cats,
                                    who
stalked the woods
                    for the same prey
                                    the owl
would swoop on
                    and scoop up
                                    just as they
pounced.
              They would look on with wonder
and go hungry
                    home.
                          Wick and **Wind**
did not go hungry now.

                          Wake wondered
if,
          when she weaned the baby,

Frink

might leave her free of drugs —
                                    provided
she undertook to stay.
                                    She put this
to **Wiz** and **Chloe**
                        when they came.
Their efforts at inquiry
                        had, so far,
                                    yielded
no frame of reference
                        that would brook
reconsidering a case,
                                    where no
material change was evident —
                                    and drugs
so patently rejected.
                        Stalemate prevailed
(as in the larger world,
                        where nuclear war-
ships sailed
            in southern ports
                                    to keep
the eastern hemisphere at bay,
                                    peace
assured under the cloak
                        of M. A. D.).
                                    So
Wiz-dom and **Chloe**
                        agreed to question
Frink,
        who said the two
                        were not only free
to stay,
        but must,
                so long as **Wake** refused
remedial drugs.
                        Who would pay
for their keep
                        was vaguely
glossed.

Only **Sand** and **Chloe**
                              had
the means.
                    And **Sand** had signed
the order
              to admit —
                              Silicon,
having no legal standing,
                              no matter also
being unwilling
              and confused.
                              Seered by
betraying **Wake**,
                      he had not yet
summoned his will
                    to visit her and **Strand**
where he had
              unwittingly
                            consigned them.
Nor could he just send messages by **Chloe**.

All the more poignant then,
                              that both
Wiz-dom's daughters
                            were now together
in this space she'd entered.
                              Windel
she had not seen
                    since **Sophist**'s laws
tore her family
                    when the twins were five.
What happened since
                      made nothing easier.

As she and **Chloe** took their leave of **Frink**,
the new Housekeeper
                        stood in the doorway
to escort them out:
                        the mixed palette
brushing through
                    this woman's eyes —

of yawning blacks and browns
                              and lurid
green —
        shook **Wiz**
                    to the point of vertigo.
Frink started at it;
                        Chloe put
a protecting hand
                  on **Wiz-dom**'s arm.
No flash of recognition
                        as both left
for **Riverstrand**.
                    How much of that
was me,
          not her?
                Wiz stuttered,
                            to ease
her shivering
             with words —
                        while **Chloe**,
who stayed wisely silent,
                          drove.

Frink raised inquiring eyes —
                            but his new
Housekeeper's face shut down.
                            It was one
of her tasks
             to keep accounts
                          and see
that income from inmates,
                          through their carers,
balanced expenses
                  on wages, food and drugs;
and one of **Wilson**'s
                      to press for repairs
of building fabric
                   beyond his own skills,
as well as maintaining
                      all the systems
to keep the Home running.

It did not
take long to see
all this
did not add up —
on the sums
she had to budget from.
This
she now pointed out
to **Dr. Frink**.
Ah!
Yes,
he said.
Remind me tomorrow
I must ring the Bank.
Will double this
meet
all the bills?
Windel nodded,
hiding her
startlement
at such largesse.
As a matter
of fact
continued **Frink**,
I am thinking
of appointing a Chaplain
for this place.
I propose to advertise for one
with skills
in book-keeping,
as well of course
as commitment to
the — er — spiritual
welfare
of our community.
Now which room
would you suggest
we dedicate
as a Chapel —
until we
can build one in the grounds?

                                        Windel,
who so far barely knew
                        the geography
of the main building
                            and had yet
to visit
        half the rooms,
                        was taken aback.
She covered it with charm:
                        Wonderful!
                                    she
said approvingly.
                        Could I let you know later
when I've —
                thought about which room?

Of course said **Frink**
                    in genial mode.
                            Next day,
he wrote the advertisement
                        and rang his bank.

Further up country
                                Witson
pursued his godly studies
                                unaware,
his grandmother had died
                            hours only
after they had left
                    the upheaved ground
they nearly stumbled into.
                                    This
Will and **Viola**
                loved to re-enact:
                                Take me
by my ankle, **Will**
                and pull me out,
                                    Vi
never tired of pleading,
                        nor he of being so

138

obliging
        on those safe, grassy slopes
                       in
the Seminary grounds.

                    Witson soured
at the relaxed Passes rule:
                 black presences
swarmed on buses
              (when he went on visits
to his white parishioners).
                 Violet was
frightened by them;
          Will and **Vi**,
                finding
their energy exciting,
             could not see why.
Witson's superiors
         found
             they could rely
on him
        for duties on the premises.
Violet
       felt more comfortable with this.

Only **Ned**'s letters
          told of **Wit**'s escape.
Nothing revealed
           the whereabouts
of him or **Wiz-dom** —
         from whom **Witson**
had long since
      cut off
         in his compulsive
quest for purity
        of thought and action.
As to the twins,
       he never thought at all.

When,
    two years after

                              they had moved
into this quiet place,
                              he saw
in the Church Monthly
                         a resident vacancy
for an Accountant/Chaplain
                              in a Home
called **Frinkshome** —
                         Witson jumped.
He knew he was only half way
                              through
his training —
                    but times were unusual.
His mentors felt
                         the particular skills
he was developing
                         might well be those
to fit him
              for this quite unique appointment.
It was not after all
                         a medical skill
being sought,
                    but one of bringing order
to a confused,
                    confusing world.
                              Surely
Witson's administrative skills
                              were what
the job description named.
                              So far as
the College were concerned,
                         Witson could
go there on probation,
                         taking full orders
and his finals
                    in a year or so.
                              Violet
visibly brightened
                    at the prospect
                              of another
residential posting —

140

where no out-of-hand
behavior of blacks
need be encountered
by any of her family.

Receiving no other
applications
and delighted by
this man's
supporting commendations,
Frink was
convinced he had his answer.
Witson
was appointed,
without interview,
after
a long exchange by phone.
I may be away
when you arrive
but my Housekeeper
and her family
will be there
to greet you.

Frink spoke truly.
As **Witson** drove up
with his family,
they faced a line of four
across the porch —
white smiles gleaming
from their dark faces.
One face
changed.
Frink had
referred to the new incumbent
as the Chaplain.
Windel had therefore
no more idea
than **Witson**
what she had
agreed

to welcome in.
The children ran
to meet together,
Will more gravely
strolling,
while **Vi**
poured into the arms of
Wick
and **Wind**.
Violet stood dumb
as **Vi**
vanished inside
with **Wind** and **Wick**.

Will, frozen,
realised
for the first time fully,
his father and mother's
feelings
about —
people with black faces.
(He did not know:
the one no longer smiling
was his aunt.)

Witson stood appalled.
Violet,
for whom this black reality
was bad enough,
sensed even worse
in him.
Could **Vi**
possibly be safe in there?
Wilson, always
nonchalant,
led them in,
where,
following
voices,
they found **Vi** and the twins,
playing

on the floor with **Strand** —
                    while a small
black cat,
          white socks and tailtip,
                         sauntered
to coffee-coloured **Wake**
                    to be caressed.

Windel,
          buoyed by **Frink**'s
                         effusive
confidence in her judgment,
                    had made
an uneasy truce
               with **Wake**
                              as
Wilson's firstborn,
                   so found this fresh chaos
quite beyond her.

                   Witson
                         saw the children's
bonding
          made unthinkable
                         attempts
at reversing out of this disaster,
                         and offered
an icebound smile
                   to **Windel,**
                         who covered
her own feelings
               by fetching in a tray for tea.

As they politely
               talked their way
                         through this,
Sap's death
               emerged
                         for **Witson**'s
family.
               Wake became aware

that **Sap** was there amomg them.
                              William
shivered slightly.
                    Witson and **Violet**
were aware of nothing
                        but their loss.
                                      Then
a strange thing happened:
                          as the three-year
olds were playing
                    on the floor with **Strand**,
whose first birthday would be soon,
                                    Will,
nearly six,
              crouched on all fours
to crawl toward **Strand**.
                            She crawled
to meet him.
              They met head on,
brows touching
                and they stayed that way —
for an eternity
                of seconds.
                            Will uttered
a buzzing sound,
                  like a pollinating bee
and **Strand** buzzed silently
                                inside.
Thereafter,
            when they met,
                            Strand
made sure she had her fill
                            of **William**'s
buzzing.
          Thus the new era
in **Frink**'s Mental Home
                            was born.

Will,
      who had learned
                        to read and write

144

correctly,
            joined the class at **Frinkshome**,
where he caught the eye
                        of an unusual
teacher,
            who did not take long to see
behind **Will**'s formal writing
                        a wilful urge
to draw upon his own
                        interior store —
of thoughts and feelings.
                        Thus encouraged,
Will soon
            began to write
                        of his buzzing
times with **Strand**;
                        then
                                    his memory
of the rift
                        between the town
and forest.
            The teacher,
                        who came in
daily from the south,
                        asked where this was,
thinking it likely he had made it up.
                                            Will
named where
                        his great grandmother
had lived.
                        I used to live near there,
she said
            *and who is **Strand**?*
                                            Will
explained.

            When she learned
                        about his sister
and the twins,
            she offered to set up a corner
of the Schoolroom

(the only place **Windel** could suggest
as big enough for the provisional
Chapel —
except the dining room,
already
doubling for use
for therapeutic groups)
as a play area,
which **Strand** too could
come to,
if **Vi** and the twins
took care —
or if
her mother
would like to come in too.
Wake would.
So a quite new way of being
opened up.
Strand,
with **Will** in the same room,
must learn
to choose
the right moments
for her buzzing.

Will and **Vi**
had tried to persuade
Violet
and their father
to go and see the rift again,
but with no **Sap**
they shied away —
even from visiting
their own old home.
Weekends were full.
Laurel, the teacher,
offered to take them all
in her Traveller
one fine weekend,
with **Wake**

as a second grown-up
                    helping out.
                              Violet,
uneasily,
              assented.

                    When **Will** and **Vi**
saw the gorge again,
                              their faces
paled.
          It was so steep,
                    so wide
                              and its length
went out of sight
                    both ways.
                              They could
even hear
              water
                    echoing from the bottom.
Will would not let **Vi** close enough
                              to look.
The others
              stayed far back with **Wake,**
(**Strand** straining against her) —
                              while
Laurel
              peered over the edge with **Will,**
who
              that day decided to become
an Earth Scientist,
                    a geologist.
He and **Strand**
              buzzed almost continuously
as **Laurel** drove them home.

                    When **Will**
was seven
          and Strand two,
                    he said

                                            You
buzz too, Strand.
                        She did.
                                    And he began
to pick up on what she saw.
                                    Sometimes
they buzzed together,
                            sometimes by turns.
Always
                they saw one another's thoughts
and felt their own.
                            When they buzzed
together,
                all their cells
                            came twanging
into life.

                            Wake had realised
from the first day,
                that **Strand**,
                                as reconstructed
Wanda,
                need not fear anything
                            from **Windel**.
She wondered
                if **Sap** had engineered this
for **Strand**'s safety.
                        No
                        came **Sap**'s *voice,*
we do not engineer.
                        But **Will** *has chosen*
a path
                he will not veer from.
                                    Strand,
(Wanda)
                and he
                        are bonded
                                for a life
that will be good
                        for all the planet.

148

About the time
                Witson and his family
                                        made
their move to **Frinkshome**,
                        the government
of **Godwonland**
                        announced
                                that in the spirit
of the times,
            they had decided to hold
                                    National
Elections:
                        nominations were invited
for candidates from every district.
                                    Moreover,
they would,
                    during the campaign,
consider granting amnesty
                                    to some,
as well as freeing
                            certain political
prisoners,
                    held during the past decade.
Exciting news,
                                        unless ...
its ambiguous wording were a trap:
                                    if **Wit**
came out of hiding
                        and was nominated
for a seat,
                what then?
                            And for what
district?
                Riverstrand
                                    was not
their place of origin.

                        They took the risk.
Borrowing **Chloe**'s car,
                        Wit went with **Wiz**

149

back to the shanty town
                              (left recently
by **Wilson** and his family).

                         When **Wiz-dom**
saw
         the squalor —
                         for her first time ever:
(she had spent **Wit**'s years in prison
                              teaching
Biology
         at their own old school,
                              deserted
after the escape) —
                         she began
to understand the look
                    Windel,
                              standing
in **Frink**'s doorway,
                    wore.
                    Much more than
anger
         that her mother was beloved
                              by **Wit**,
it carried
         all of black resentment
                              for what
race
         separation
                    really meant
                              in terms
of who
                    was in —
                         who out.
                              Then they
saw the rift
                    between the forest
                              and the town.
If it grew much bigger,
                         it would swallow up
both the shanty town

and **Sap**'s old home.
Wit knew his constituents were here.

Wiz
went soberly
                    to visit their old School:
they gladly took her back
                    to earn a living.

The upshot of the Elections,
                    when they came,
was that the ruling party
                    were so challenged
by progressive elements,
                    black
                            and white —
minority government by colonists
                    was gone
forever.
        Wit and **Wiz**,
                            returned as
members for their respective districts,
                            would
stand together
                in the new Parliament —
to represent
                shared economic interests
in the land —
                its name now changed
to **Godwilland**.

                Back at **Frinkshome**,
it was soon evident
                    to **Witson**,
that **Frink**'s phone call
                to his Bank Manager
had not brought comfort:
                        to double
the house-keeping allowance
                    (as **Frink** had

offered **Windel**)
                        could throw the enterprise
into such overdraft
                        as neither the Bank
nor the new Accountant
                        could support.

He did not tackle **Frink**
                        directly
                           over this,
but sought to fish
                    for who
                        had been
responsible
               to make ends meet.
                           Frink
muttered
               about the Housekeeper
                        (failing
to divulge
            that **Wake** and **Windel**
                      had not
been at the Mental Home
                    for more
than months).
           Witson went rigid:
                    still not
in touch
           with his own baser nature,
                    he had
no idea
           what motives now impelled him.
Nor did he
           fight **Windel** openly.
                  The new
Administrative officer
             of **Frinkshome**,
as well
         as the keeper of its spiritual purity,
he imposed
         impersonally

upon all aspects
of the running of the Home,
a regimen
the World Bank
would have approved
to deal with an errant
Third World debtor.
In fact,
he handled
what Windel brought
to light —
by slashing services
and salaries.

Now it was **Windel**'s task
to husband food
as she had learned
in the bleak shanty town.
Even easy-going
Wilson
could not shrug off this:
**Have you
seen your father
since we came?**
he asked.
Windel hadn't.
Frinkshome was not
a part of the constituency
Wit stood for;
nor **Wiz-dom**'s —
though its boundary
was closer.
Boundaries did not
mean a thing
to **Windel.**
Understanding
her father was again
a man of influence,
she urged **Wilson**
to help her seek him out
at **Riverstrand**

(where **Wilson** must admit
he knew his way about).

There,
Chloe
told them,
Wit and **Wiz**
had returned
to live in their respective districts.
She
was the member now for **Riverstrand**,
which
included **Frinkshome**.
Could she help?
When she took in their problem,
she
undertook to talk
with **Frink**
and also
Witson —
astonished
he and his family
were in the frame,
confronting **Windel**.
She phoned **Wiz-dom**
who had already picked it up
direct
from **Sap**,
relaying
what other factors
were at work
in **Frinkshome** —
around **Will**
and **Strand**.
(Her heart hurtled
realising all
their young
were now beneath
Frink's roof).
Chloe reassessed:

                                        wiser not
to meddle
                        where deep things
were stirring.

                        Laurel sighed;
shrugged off
                the Chaplain's regimen —
to persevere in her own
                        felt undertaking/s.
Each Monday morning
                                she noticed
in the schoolroom atmosphere
                                a change
she found hard to name.
                                It felt
like one step forward
                        and two back.
The children were quieter,
                        therefore more
amenable,
                        but noticeably less
vital
                than on Friday afternoons.
Who likes work
                after a free weekend?
But **Laurel** felt this
                        in the room itself,
before the children were inside.
                                Long
aware
                the inmates were subdued
through drugging,
                the more urgently she felt
her task
        to arouse their offspring,
                                precious
resource,
        the future
                could not fruit without.

Laurel,
who had left her own children,
Learn and **Leaf**,
of an age with this
new playgroup
at home with **Leo**,
(her musician-poet partner),
when she took
the lot of them
to find the rift —
felt
it was time to talk things through.
Since
they did not
live in
(and thus unlikely
to be ill-affected
by whatever
Witson's dour energy was doing
at least
on Sundays
to her Schoolroom),
Laurel
felt confident
their children's vitality
could counteract,
the grip
this new
Accountant/Chaplain
had.
Learn,
who was learning nothing
at his School,
was keen.
Leaf enjoyed being home
with **Leo**
(who saw **Laurel**'s point);
she agreed
to try things out
in her mother's playgroup.
And 'things'

moved very fast
            from there.

                        Tension rocketed
in **Frinkshome** —
                        as accelerated learning
won the day.
                    Inmates refused their drugs;
Staff left
            as **Witson**'s squeeze
                        on **Windel**
took effect.
            Committed
                        for their labelled
madness,
            now drug-free,
                        people
became creative
                        in often very
disconcerting ways.

                    Will learned so fast
he was ready
            for High School —
                        before
becoming ten.
            By then
                    the whole playgroup
had been in School three years,
                    with **Strand**
ready to join
                    after her fifth birthday.
Leaf had made
            special friends
                        with **Wind**,
and **Learn**
            with **Vi**.
                    Will made sure
Wick was not left out
                    by his deepening
bond with **Strand**.

Less happy change
was visible in the world
(outside this place
of asylum
for the supposed disturbed)
where plans
for building
proper houses
were not materialising
for the black
majority.
Wit had achieved clean water
for the shanty town,
but electricity
and drainage
were as far away
as when
his brother's family
lived there.
Too many
in high places,
resting on their laurels
and high salaries,
declared the country's
interest lay
in keeping sweet
the skilled
white colonists
who still
feared the fierce
uprising
of landless,
penniless
blacks,
too long dubbed feckless.
Wiz-dom,
in her white constituency,
sighed.

Seeker: I'm not surprised:

tell me what difference there is
between **strands of wisdom** —

which this
whole book is —

and the **strands of inquiry**
of this final phase?

Recorder:

A pertinent question,
since we seem so riveted

by the daily details
of this Mental Home —

along with lack of progress
in the much more democratic

world outside.
Strand,

with **Will**,

is the lynch-pin of this 4th
generation,

itself the evolutionary turning
from descent into denseness

to more lively
ascent,

as the next three generations

raise
their sights —

to find the wisdom of experience
added to the light

that **Wisdom** brought.
This phase must see

the birthing of the 5th
generation,

as the inquiry process

gathers speed,
spreading illumination

in its wake.

Seeker: **Wake**

being of course

the mother
of this **Strand** —

and much more luminous
than her surroundings —
            till she and **Laurel**
brighten everything!

Recorder: *Indeed!*
                    And maybe all of us
are strands of wisdom,
                    future foetuses,
                            conceived
of inquiry,
                    broiled in the cauldron
of our parents' stresses,
                    born in the vortex
of the whirling channel
                    we are tossed down
into birth
            on earth.

Seeker: — having forgotten
everything we knew.

Recorder: *So — only learning*
how to ask the questions —

Seeker: (with
                            and of
the people who can answer.)

Recorder: *will fetch*
from our depths
                    what we have lost in transit.
We are richer,
            deeper,
                stronger
                        than we know.

Seeker: So —
            will asking questions
                    really be enough?

Recorder: *Seeking and knocking*

have been also cited.

You are a seeker —

Seeker: and it may be

knocking

is the subtle affect —

Recorder: *of asking*

the right questions

Seeker: at the crucial moment —

Recorder: *so that doors open*

Seeker: on to unimagined heights

Recorder: *from unimagineable*
depths.

Are you now satisfied

that we have raised

as deep a question

as humanity can ask?

Seeker: As to what

it is proper to call mad,

what sane?

Yes.

So long as we do not try too hard

Recorder: *to answer!*

Seeker: Any more than we can fully say

what's bad —

Recorder: *although we talk as though*

we know we can.

Just as the interference wave
                              in **Frinkshome**
reached its height,
                              the government
of **Godwilland** announced
                              its wish
to implement
                   the practice of the North:
no longer locking up
                              the mentally
disturbed;
                   instead,
                              committing them
to the care
                   of the community.
This was begun
                   by shutting down
all Homes,
              whose inmates
                              were instructed
to report each day
                   to Outpatient Clinics
in the towns.

              This would have several strands
of consequence:
                   not least
                   for **Frinkshome.**
Since its inmates were already
                              waking up
from their dulled,
                   everyday existence,
                              it was
hardly likely
                   they would return
for drugs
              when free
                   in the community.
Time would tell
                   how they would come

162

to use
                     this freedom.
                                        Laid off,
or disaffected,
                     staff
                                   would further disrupt
the local culture.

                                   For **Frink** himself,
the change would be disastrous:
                                        to start
his Home,
                     he had been supplied by **Sophist**
with a sum
                     from **Riverstrand** endowments.
This debt,
                  winding things up at **Frinkshome**
would endanger.
                          Frink went
                                   to **Sophist:**
to discover
                     friendship
                                   does not extend
to immolation.
                              One of their institutions
would be made bankrupt
                                   by this new policy,
which **Sophist**
                          had been unable to prevent.
The unauthorised loan
                                   would have to be
returned.

                     Will's advanced studies
in geology,
                     along with careful observations
of what was occurring
                                   in the forest rift,
were, at last,
                                   revealing patterns

in the behavior of plates,
                              pointing to
deeper causes in the mantle
                              (the dynamics
of convection currents,
                              fire being exhaled
in rhythmic bursts),
                              than geologists
had imagined.
                              Will's mind
raced ahead
              in speculation.
                              He could now
use telepathy
                              to reach **Strand**
with his buzzing.
              He found
                              she had already
surmised connection
                              between man-made
disasters
              (local,
                    nation-wide
                              or global)
and subterranean movements,
                              such as he
was learning to interpret.
                              This was a big
step further
              than he'd reached himself.

Then both
          'saw' visually
                              the Atlantic ridge —
extending
              north and south
                              and widening,
as the land
              beneath the ocean
                              cracked
to throw up red-hot

                    lower mantle
                                    which, as
the water cooled it solid,
                                    formed new land.
This was accepted science:
                                    a deep oceanic
scar,
            perhaps from pole to pole.

                                            But,
what if there were another trying to form,
far beneath the continents
                                    and running
east and west,
            making the Equator
                                    not
an imaginary line?
                            Was the whole
earth
            a crusty, leavened lump
of baking dough,
            with an even-armed cross
deeply imprinted in it?
                    That,
                            both knew,
was the zodiac sign
                    for Earth: ⊕
                                    If so,
what implications
                            for our human future
might there be,
                    between hearts and minds,
and subterranean action
                            in the mantle,
some relation
                            not yet understood?
Could these two
                            be mutually causal?
Could their own local turbulence
                                    be linked
to the rate of opening

                         of the forest rift —
now so noticeable,
                         pictures of it
were being shown on National TV?

                                        Will
eased his buzzing,
                         so they could absorb
what they were now proposing.
                                        Their own
local rift
              was so far south,
                         it could only
be, at most,
                         a micro-reflection
of the geo-rift,
                         posed by the phenomenon
of the Atlantic Ridge.
                         Nor was **Will** sure,
whether the tendency
                         of their mini-rift
was to spread
              east/west
                         or north and south.
If north/south,
                         then was its longitude
(what they could see)
                         part of the continuation
south,
       of the geophysically acknowledged
North/South Ridge?
                         Will's mind raced
at the disastrous implications
                         this would
have
       millennia hence
                         for **Godwilland.**

But **Strand**
              was wrestling
                         with the meaning

for future human culture:
                                                seeing
human responsibility
                                    for other forms
of life,
            wondering what kind
                                    of human living
could induce
                        a less inflammatory mode
for the world's engine
                                deep beneath the feet
of all
            who crawl or cry
                                    or run or fly
round the faulted surface
                                of our crowded
globe.
                        The enormity of this —
made them feel suddenly
                            fragile.
                                            Strand
already missed **Will** badly,
                                having so early
learned dependence
                            on his resonance.
Now
                    she longed for his presence
for comfort
                in the face
                            of such big thoughts.
This,
    Will sensed
                        and, knowing his own need,
went as fast as he could
                            to where she was.

One of the outcomes
                        of **Godwilland**'s
new plans,
                    (despite the hardly lessened
deprivation)

had been to set up
a Liberal Arts College
for the enterprising
of whatever colour.
Named Rainbow College,
because its Staff and students
would
embrace
every shade of thought
and racial
origin,
it focussed specially,
on training
therapists
and teachers.
Its Staff included
Laurel.
Wake, who at **Frinkshome**,
had applied herself
in ways not
earlier noted,
would join her
(when qualified),
for a post in teaching
Playgroup Therapy.

Strand had taken
her Leaving Certificates
in Astronomy, Spanish
and Psychology.
She would start as a student
at the College,
when building extensions
were complete.
They were lucky to snap up
the bankrupt property
of **Frinkshome**.

Snake,
returning from her last excursion
found herself invited

                              to set up a department
of Anthropology
                in the new College.
                                        Turned
60, and grandmother
                        of a vigorous teenager,
she must consider
                        tying herself to this.
She could then afford
                                to subsidise
both **Wake** —
                        till she earned herself,
and **Strand**,
                till her mother, likewise,
                                        could.

Will,
        working for his Ph.D.
                                at **Riverstrand**,
chose to specialise
                        in the new science
of rheology,
                        focussed on movements
in the mantle —
                        inferred from their effects
on plate tectonics
                        at the global level;
crystals,
        at the micro-physical,
                                where atoms
deform
                because electrons leap,
responding to seductive pulls
                                we call
strange attractors.
                        He had bursaries
from scientific bodies,
                        he must humour,
if his way-out views
                were not to lose his living.
His father,

having contributed

                to grinding

Frinkshome to a halt,

          had become a more

even-handed accountant

           at the Seminary.

Viola,

      as a teenager,

           had switched

her loyalties

      from **Learn**

        to **Wind**:

          who played

in a different section

           of the same

town orchestra —

         and would eventually

father

      Vivace.

           Learn took **Wick**

under his wing,

       which may have

            singed

his armpit,

      for she did not have

          her mother's

eyes for nothing,

       and fast persuaded him

babies were the very stuff of life.

           Strand,

when **Will** tuned in,

       was for the first time,

living with **Snake**,

        her grandmother,

(her mother, **Wake**,

       being back with **Silicon**,

now that her independent daughter

          needed

no care from her).

       It was therefore here

in **Snake**'s
                        mostly disused quarters,
William found —
                        and went into resonance
with — **Strand**.
                                Perhaps
because of this
                so easily found,
                                affinity
these two had seldom felt
                        the need for sex.
But the vastness
                of their recent
                                geo-thinking
made them feel
                        like microscopic sperm
swimming toward an egg —
                        or that fertile egg
implanting
                in the vast womb
                                it grows in.
With a deep and serious joy
                                Strand
and **William**
                came together now,
                                humming
their resonance
                from crown to root,
                                through all
their centres,
        as they gave loving form
                                to a loop
of energy,
                a cosmic string —
                                drawn
from the plane of light
                        to manifest.
This lovely being
                        they were calling forth,
they felt very sure they had
                                successfully

conceived,
consoled
that in this act
what the world
needed,
nature would bring through.

Almost simultaneously,
Learn,
with less
deliberation,
impregnated Wick.
They would
call this luciferic being
Light-in-the-sun.

Before that time
the rift in **Godwilland**,
which was
somewhat diagonal
to lines
of latitude and longitude
began
a series of eruptions —
for which neither
Will,
nor any of his colleagues
could account
from seismic readings
(unless there were seepage
from the plate
activity
bordering the eastern edge
of **Godwilland)**.
It began,
with a juddering earthquake
that collapsed
most of the houses
in the street (where **Sap**
had brought up **Wiz-dom)**
all abandoned.

People had saved precious things
                                    (like
Sap's woven picture
                        safely reinstalled
at **Windswell**).
                Then the lava
                                trickled
into sight:
                not fast,
                                for the land was flat.
But it was hot, dry weather
                        and a driving wind
blazed through the forest
                        Wit was born in.

He and **Wiz** seemed safe
                                high up
at **Windswell** —
                        so long as the wind
blew toward the forest.
                        They thought
of their plane tree:
                no one had known
for years
        where **Wittle** was —
                        if still alive.

Have you seen this?
                asked **Snake**,
                                handing
Strand
        a single photocopied sheet.
                                Chloe
showed it to me once —
                        *after **Wit** and **Wiz***
came here to hide.
                (She and I
                        used to know
each other well,
                *before she married **Sand**.*
That's one of the reasons

I have been

away so much).

It was written

by **Wit's**

mother,

Wisdom,

before she left

the part of the forest,

which is now

in flames.

You and **Will**

could find it

interesting.*

They did —

especially

the lines:

Who knows what causes faults
or what faults cause?

But, both saw,

geological interpretation

had

moved on

beyond **Wisdom**'s description

of three types of fault.

For **Will,**

the concept of subduction

was the key:

when

the edge of an oceanic plate

is pressured

(by its widening

mid-ocean ridge),

to slip its natural curve

under

the thicker

continental plate

it grinds against —

it dives

---

* see Appendix 4: *Fault-Lines*, or the last pages of **Wisdom Stranded**.

so deep into the mantle,
                              as to trigger
vulcan reaction
                    in an arc,
                              thus causing
what geologists call
                              a 'ring of fire'.
Thus we are now much closer
                              to knowing
what causes faults
                         and what faults cause.
Both are deeply
                    subterranean
                              (and may go
deeper still
                         to convection currents
and exploding heat
                         in the viscous mantle
nearest the Earth's core).
                              For **Strand**,
who would study
                         strands of Psychology
at **Rainbow College**,
                              this held a message.
It could not
               of course
                              provide
an ultimate cause of anything.
                                   But
it suggested to her
                         lines of thought
to be pursued
                    by communities of inquiry,
she imagined
                         as becoming cogent
practice —
                    in the new millennium.

When the baby quickened,
                         Will and **Strand**
began to work out ways

they could ensure
the birth of **String**
without interference
from their families
or gynaecology
(which did not seem to them
the study
of how women
are).
Strand
knew
she wanted Will
as midwife;
he was certain
he could thus support her.
They practised
deep breathing
on the hillside:
he,
holding her from behind
and breathing
with her.
Strand
felt so tuned into Earth,
she understood
its need to breathe forth fire
from between
the grinding plates.
She breathed
with the convection currents,
understanding
this is how the core
reduces heat,
that would otherwise build up
like a nuclear
reactor
that has lost control.
Gaia
has all her systems regulated.
But
have we?

Of all the people
             known to **Strand**,
                              none
came nearer
                    to her high demand
than **Will**.
             Not only did he know her
virtually inside out —
                    with the same
intuitive intensity
             he used
                    to know
deep seismic currents;
             he also
                    thoroughly
read up
       on medical care
                    in pregnancy
and birth,
       consulting friends
                    on after care —
to check against his own impressions
                    gained
from **Strand**,
                    then checked
verbally with her as well.
                    For his flat
(within the sound
             of rumblings
                    from the rift),
Will hired a water pool
             for **Strand**'s labour,
to be filled
       by hose
             from his kitchen taps,
warm enough
                    and not too full,
so he could top it up
                    until the baby's
birth.
             He hired it for two weeks,

on either side

                             of **String**'s expected

birth date,

                    near the spring equinox

in September.

            He got in food,

                      herb teas

and milk.

          Nor did he forget

                  a sharp

and sterile

          pair of scissors,

                   (knowing

to delay

        their cleaving use).

                As the fires

burned out

          across from **Windswell**

Wit and **Wiz-dom**

         had a startling

               visitation:

Wit's mother,

       Wisdom,

           whom they had not

seen

       (like this together)

                    ever

appeared on their inner screen;

           behind her,

Wittle,

      looking not as old

           as he must be.

Wit picked up

        that he had died in the forest

as the smoke began —

          was now recovered

from old age

      and smoke.

         They saw no one

else.

Where was **Wiz-dom**'s mother,
                                        Sap?
You'll see her soon
                            was all this gnomic pair
would tell them.
                        But you may not know her.

Next day
            Will phoned to say
                                a baby girl
was born to **Strand**.
                            He added hesitantly —
never having met
                        either **Wit**
                                    or **Wiz** —
Strand would very much like to see you,
if —
        We'll come
                    said **Wiz,**
                                as insight flashed.
They came:
                it seemed that while **Strand**
was labouring —
                        and momently somnolent
in the pool —
                    a sudden recognition burst.
She knew she had been
                                Wiz's daughter,
Wanda;
                thought she also knew
                                        who
String
            had been before.
                                Looking into
the astonishingly
                        focussed eyes
                                of this bald
baby,
        Wiz was pretty certain
                                she did
too.

Wit nodded,
                    smiling his first memories
of **Sap**.
              Will,
                    who, as a small boy,
had dearly loved
                    his long-haired,
                                    brusque
great grandmother,
                    rejoiced in this new
sense of family riches:
                    as mate,
                                    as midwife,
father, grandson, friend.
                                    Love —
said **Wiz-dom**
                    is indeed
                                    the wielding
of the force
                    behind the worlds.
                                    No
      matter what
                    the cause of faults
                                    or
      what faults cause
                    said **Strand**.

RISKING WISDOM

*I dedicate this final volume
to all those human beings
who share my passion for the planet's possibilities,
and have risked more than I
to bring such possibilities to birth.*

Foreword

I have once again been taken by surprise by the turns and twists of the narrative of the **Wisdom Family** in their last three generations, as incarnations of the 'higher triad' of **Light** and **Love** and **Life.**

In Phase I **Light** painfully discovers himself as firepower, his use of which he comes to control, as he is driven to go North to respond to the inspiration of **Aurora Borealis** (which in past centuries terrified Lapplanders, who sensed its power to burn like lightning, and feared this cosmic 'punishment'). **Light's** consequent insights, as to the possible nature of the Seven Rays, interweave with his grandfather's worrying of the theme of 'cosmic string', the higher key to all that manifests as difference. Since completing this text, it has occurred to me that the **coherent radiance** expressed by the septet in Phase III must be matched at the **cosmic string** level by **coherent sound.**

In Phase II **Love** is seen to be no less strong than **Light,** and even more needed in a world of competing difference such as ours.

But it is only in Phase III that the depths of gender are plumbed as 'the most fundamental of all divisions life on our planet can experience': a bracketed statement thrown up in the brief foreword to the second volume, *Strands of Wisdom.* Consequent to this plumbing, I have myself shifted my understanding of the significance of androgyny in human affairs, as becomes explicit in the final phase, (*Life Spreading).* This is at least partly in response to the theme of a book, with the suggestive title, *God inside out: Siva's game of dice,* which only came my way this year, 2001, though published in 1997 (the year I felt urged to embark upon this trilogy, to bring back the feminine to our understanding of divinity). The subtitle, of course, counterechoes **Einstein's** certainty that 'God does not play dice' (uttered in response to the bewildering implications of quantum theory, as the virtually unpredictable behaviour of subatomic particles).

8

The theme of **God Inside Out** is of the god, **Siva's**, revelling in his (sic) own androgyny (no doubt symbolised by the Sphynx, in a culture farther west), but losing it the moment creation manifests in gender partnership. He thus yields every game of dice to his partner, **Parvati**, quicker in her use of feminine gender, being in effect the wisdom of the partnership, where he is its will. The authors of **God inside Out** make clear that this traditional dice game has nothing to do with chance or statistical probability, as we would interpret such terms. Nor is it deterministic, but rather the unfolding of a tricky, subtle process, with its own inner logic, 'built around the relations between parts and whole, in a dynamic system labelled "play"'.*

This clearly echoes the **Logos Ludens** cited throughout the trilogy, and raises the question whether the task of human evolution is to discover how Will and Wisdom may learn to become peaceful partners to one another over many lifetimes of alternating coexistence as male or female.

How this may work out in practice in relation to each and all of the Seven Ray qualities is a major theme of this third volume, in which the riskiness of being alive at all is unfolded through the supreme qualities of **Light** and **Love** and **Life,** which some of us see as the major cosmic Triad, whose working out in human form may well be the task of the present 'world period' of aeons of logoic activity, through the manifesting of the six pairs of opposites of the astrological zodiac – right now moving from the Ray Six **Piscean Age** of ideology, into the **Aquarian Age,** that is punctuated by the pragmatism of Ray Seven.

Should we ask ourselves why seven, and only seven, Rays are posited, it is worth recalling that nothing (not even the finest piece of paper) can be folded more than seven times at most. This surely represents the maximum degree of complexity a space/time world of three dimensions can accommodate.

---

* see Handelman, D. and Shulman, D., **God Inside Out**, OUP, 1997.

PHASE ONE

THE POWER OF LIGHT

Strand had been enough indulged by her mother,
Wake, and by her lover, **William**, who had known
her from the age of one,
                                    she could look on the world
with confidence, despite her birth in a Mental Home
with no support —
                              except a cat, who licked her dry.

Now she and **Will** had their own water baby,˙ whom
they named for curious reasons **String** — and shared
her caring.
                    Both felt **String** came with cosmic tasks:
she did in fact draw through, for this incarnate life,
honed enthusiasms (encapsuled in her brainstem),
which her great, great grandmother had already made
her own.
                    For **Sap** had, of her own free will, foregone
much sojourning in other realms between her death
and birth,
                    because of a felt urgency for life on earth.

Strand hummed gently from her throat and heart,
while feeding **String** —
                                    to reach **String's** heart,
as through her throat milk poured
                                                  from the breast
between the heart and throat of **Strand**,
                                                  who had,
herself (as **Wanda**˙)
                              been **Sap's** helpless grandchild
in days when black was 'bad'
                                          and being helpless
worse.

˙ see *Strands of Wisdom* - Phase III

But as **Wake's** child, **Strand**,
Wanda had outgrown such helplessness.

It seemed
to **Strand** that **String** held in her tiny body's memory
the full connection
of who she was,
where from and why
here now.
As the sap rose in her baby's springing body,
Strand felt she knew
all of **Sap's** vigorous wisdom
come to peak in **String**.

Yet **Strand** had not known **Sap**
directly, as had **Will** —
though not beyond the age
of three, when he and his littler sister, **Viola**, had come
upon the opening rift*
between the forest and the town,
the day they came to say goodbye to **Sap** and left:
she
to die;
they to follow their father's new-found 'call'.

Neither **Will** nor **Strand** had kept in touch with **Vi**,
who found intimacy with their cousin, **Wind,** through
their shared passion for performing,
each in their
fitting section of the same town orchestra —
whence
the begetting of **Vivace**
in the same month as **String**.

* see **Strands of Wisdom** - Phase II

Though impregnated on the same day as **Strand**,
Wind's twin sister, **Wick**,
                    did not (by some lunar quirk)
give birth to **Light**
                    till the Full Moon of **Taurus**.
Thus **Light-from-the-Sun** seemed strangely born
under a sign of Earth,
                    while **String**, in **Aries**,
was a child of fire,
          autumnal, southern fire.

                    An early
visitor, bearing her home-grown gifts of autumn plants
for **Strand**'s new baby, was **Learn**'s sister, **Leaf** —
straight from **Wick**'s delivery of **Light**,
                    whose eyes
pierced through the darkness of his crinkly newness.

I hardly know what to make of him.

                    He's not like

anyone in your family or mine

                    she said, looking

from **Strand** to **String** and back,

                    as **String** curled

fingers round her passing thumb.

                    But they're both

delighted with him.

                    What kind of birth

     did he have?
                    asked **Strand**, recalling her soothing
pool for birthing **String**.

                    Rather rough, **Wick** *said.*

13

The cord got snarled around his head and arm —
till they realised and freed him.

> *It wasn't an easy birth,*

like **String**'s.

> Remembering what **Wake** had told her

of her own,

> **Strand** empathised

> and phoned up **Learn**.

No one knew as yet how **Vi** had fared.

> **Green**

propagated these.

> **Leaf** pointed, with the hand still

grasped by **String**, toward her proffered plants.

> She

had formed a strange liaison with a gardener, who
had worked at **Rainbow College** since its opening. [*]
Presumed to be one of the thrownout inmates of closed
Frinkshome, he would not leave his chosen plot.

> How

he lived, none knew, but **Leaf**, who had contrived
a flourishing Garden Centre on adjacent land, valued
his growing skills and shared her meals.

> He could

invigorate plants she would have put to compost.

She took to him and called him **Green**, (from which
much of significance for the family would flow).

> **Viola**

[*] see **Strands of Wisdom** - *Phase III*

14

had not fared well:

to her disgust (for she relished
experience that demanded all), the doctors, purely
for their own convenience, sought to induce the birth
and when this failed,

performed a caesarean section.

Vivace thus was never born at all,

but lifted
from her mother's womb, as though a stork
had brought her.

(This missed out rite
would also have its consequence).

String and **Light**
met as their parents' work allowed: **Will**'s thesis
near completion; **Strand**'s assignments flexible,
and one of them a long term study of **String**'s
unfolding with her playmates.

Learn,
who majored at **Riverstrand** in Physics, settled on
Quantum Dynamics for postgraduate work, so left
no obstacle to their children's meeting weekly.

Learn's father, **Leo**, was a dropout poet, who had
threatened as a boy to run away to sea.

He dropped
out of studying Physics, only when his bent
for 'cosmic string' and supersymmetry

brought no
glimmer to his tutor's eye.

He waxed lyrical, when told
his first grandchild, **Light**, had found as playmate
a little girl called **String**.

Taking up his guitar, he began
to strum.
As the strings leapt to his plucking,
he softly sang:

COSMIC STRING

If God does not play dice,
*   what does s/he play?*
It seems s/he plays on us,
*   hir instruments —*
not to make us do,
*   but let us be.*

And what do we?
*   There are it seems*
innumerable ways
*   of making resonance*
on bits of string.

*   We string a bow*
to draw across a cat's gut strung
*   between mellifluous*
points of hollowed wood.

We pluck a flower stem
*   or some kind of string;*
We strike on ivory keys
*   we have connected*
to hidden hammers striking
*   hidden strings.*

We hollow gourds and stretch
*   our skins — or strings*
as tight from rim to rim
*   as tools or nimble*
fingers can contrive.

Contemplating cosmic string
and basking in autumnal sun,
I wonder who is plucking strings
and how the hidden work is done.

Are we puppet marionettes,
dangled by invisible strings?

And not the plucky mariners
we fancied climbing sheets
and staves to lookouts
high in rigs, we'd strain
to view from to behold
the possible —
                              but out of reach?

Unwitting of the cosmic space, **Leo**'s guitar plucked
out for her, **String** was resonating to the tunes
Light's restless nature played on all surrounding him.

Before they were two, both knew that focussed sun
could smoke a hole through paper.
                              Light had often
watched his father use a magnifying glass.
                              Clambering
on a chair, he reached and seized it from **Learn**'s
desktop,
          handed it to **String**
                              and scrambled down.
On bare, unsteady feet both made a beeline
for a patch of dead winter grass on **Learn**'s neat lawn.

Sprawled on their tummies in the sun, they held
the glass steady on a dried up blade, elbows planted,
all four fists
                    straining to focus the hot sun's rays
at the very centre of the burning glass.
                              When a spark
took and smouldered at the leaf's dry edge —
                                        both
cackled like a pair of tiny witches, and rolled over
in the warm spring grass.

                                Life with **Light**
was so absorbing, **String** hardly noticed her mother,
swelling again, would soon fetch forth her baby
brother, **Still**.

                  Light's first real lesson in the power of fire
came when he was four,
                         Still two, and a competing
pleasure for his sister's time.

                        On his own and feeling it,
Light casually unwrapped a sticky sweet
                            and dropped
its covering.
                 A micro angel with a fairly fiery sword
stood in his path:
                     Pick it up.
                         The voice was cool
and mellifluous as a flute, the sword pointing directly
at the discarded paper.
                    Startled, **Light** stooped
and reached.
             Flame flared from the wrapper,
                          scorching
his nose and watering his eyes.
                 The paper was cinder
before his fingers touched it.
                   Light looked up:
the little angel was no longer there.
                 But **Light**'s brain
etched its form.
             Thereafter, when he saw dirty paper
not in bins,

Light could direct his eyes to incinerate
any litter that was dry.

By seven, his first glance
would vaporise damp litter,
his next
burn it to a crisp.

Then **Light** began to understand he must control
his glances
if he would burn up paper,
not his friends.

Indeed mysterious blisters had come up below the eyes
of children at his school, which no one thought
of tracking to their source
in **Light**.

By the age of nine,
Light was avoiding looking people in the eye — unsure
if what his eyes could do was just haphazard —
or due
to grudges he did not even know he had.
He knew
his urge to burn up litter came from distaste for mess:
a surge drove through him,
a tornado,
twisting
to extinguish ugliness.

String felt, but did not fear,
Light's power, knowing he would not harm her.

But was **Still** as safe from searing **Light**?
String was
less sure
and so was **Light**, who knew he did not like

their closeness.

Still was deep and quiet,
String his shield from what might invade his peace.
This could make them prey to Light's dark side.

Wick,
only half aware of powers inherited through
her mother's eyes, was more so of her son's.
Sometimes she had known shocks, when soothing
his baby crying, and seen red spots across her chest,
laying him down after fraught feedings.

But Wick
knew nothing of Light's feats with litter, none of which
gathered in her home with Learn.

*H*ave you seen this?
Learn's mother asked her partner, Leo, as they sat
over breakfast with the Sunday papers.

*The Brits
are saying on TV that all their institutions are race
tainted:*

Police, Home Office — everything.

*Why don't
they open Colleges like ours?*

*Or intermarry
as our children have?*

Laurel, said Leo,

plucking
his guitar,

are you so sure there's none in this new
College ?

From what I've heard,

racism in Britain
is not a conscious thing.

'Unwitting', they call it,
which maybe covers nearly all we do.
Though
we are both white, we come from quite different
cultures —
apart from our goings on as man
and woman
(and much of that's reversed by me
being home, while you go gallivanting ...)
No, I don't
Laurel's indignant eyes shot at him.
Leo grinned.
Listen to this:

FIRE

The ancients knew four elements:
earth, water, air and fire —
to which the Chinese added wood,
the cellulose fire likes to eat.

Yet fire is not an element at all.
And water's two;
while air is seldom found
as purest oxygen.

As for earth, what's soil?
Wet enough mineral mixed with veg
to grow things in, when worms
have passed all through
and cast the product.
So
(like the chicken and the egg)
all three
must come together
for the soil to flourish.

Once it does
it can extinguish fire
like water.

Water so bonds its fiery gases,
                        they shrink into it
to quench the flaring thirst
                        that's given rise to —
when living carbon drains away
                                its moisture,
sweating to outstrip
                        its many selves.

So,
            what
                        IS
                                fire?

Explosive product of a misjudged bond
                        it feeds on cellulose
and leaps in air —
                to yield an energy so high,

its light is hot enough
                        to shrivel flesh off bones
it only blackens
                and then leaves for dead —
releasing spirit, the electric fire —
                        that had informed
their carbon structure.

                        Though **Laurel** felt no
need to rise to **Leo**'s windup,

                        this was the outcome
Light most feared,
            as into puberty
                    his firepower soared.

Light spoke to no one of his fire or fear; but told
his father when he reached fourteen, he wanted
to go abroad
            to find the North
                    as soon as he'd finished

School
    and knew his worth.
                                        Learn, aware
Light's adolescence was giving him a rougher ride
than he and **Leaf** had had to feel through, acquiesced.

So did **Wick**, who, anguishing for her own litter, but
not again conceiving,
                    acquired cats —
                                        to ease
her ancient impulse.*

                                String,
who found **Light**'s restless nature stimulating, was
dismayed when he shared with her his future plans
and said his parents would be backing him, once
he had won his spurs.
                    He planned to include
political geography, as well as physical, among
his advanced options.
                    Poring over maps, he left **String**
hanging.

            None of the family had relatives in the north.
Yes, we have
            said **Strand**,
                                *my aunt **Carol**,
my father's sister,** is a **Camford** Professor — I think.
She has no family.*
                    *I'll sound out dad about her—
if **Light** would like a base in **Britain**.*
                                *Does he know
where he wants to go and why?*

---

* see **Strands of Wisdom** - *Phase III*
** see **Strands of Wisdom** - *Phase II*

He's very vague
for someone so incisive,
String admitted.
He's just
a restless devil
put in **Still**, preferring art and music
and with no voyaging aspirations, that were clearly
driving **Light**.
Aren't we all different ?
offered **Loam**
(born surprisingly to **Leaf**, and evidently **Green**, soon
after **Still**, when **String** and **Light** were two).
Of course
we are,
said **Strand**,
a full-time Counsellor at the College
most of them would go to.
She ran an informal group,
all in the Upper School were free to come to, and chat
over the ritual cup of tea that followed.
(**Light** usually
seemed too busy to attend).

Strand saw her parents
seldom:
Silicon worked on the technical side
at **Rainbow College**, where he was indispensable
to all in jams with processing —
and thus to everyone.
He didn't really know where **Carol** was.
Their mother,
Chloe, would:
retired with **Sand** (and now **Snake** too),
they still lived in **Sand**'s Ecohouse, where **Carol**
sometimes visited from **England** —
soon might again,
if **Light** would like to talk.

> **Strand**'s idea
of a family gathering lay somewhere between now
outdated Encounter
> and new Community of Inquiry,
where all participants, whether previously known
to one another, would by various strategies be mixed —
over issues they had views on — and could disagree
to heads and hearts content.

> **Strand** foresaw
such mingling in the coming festivities for **Wit** and **Wiz**,
whose 'diamond' celebration (marked by the day
Wiz-dom met **Wit**'s glowing mother in the forest˙)
could embrace four generations of ensuing dynasty —
if all would come.

> **Wiz**, (who knew **Strand** was already
her reincarnate daughter,
> and that daughter's daughter
her own mother, **Sap**˙˙) hoped she, at eighty, would
not become confused by who was who.
> **Wit** was
exhilarated, when he heard the news:
> a fitting
send-off to the North for **Light**, who had just passed all
exams with flying colours — even as he had, so many
years before.˙˙˙

Seeker: My goodness, we're whirling along a bit!

Recorder: *On a tide of light, yes —*

> *approaching top speed.*

˙ see **Wisdom Stranded** - *Phase I*
˙˙ see **Strands of Wisdom** - *Phase I*
˙˙˙ see **Wisdom Stranded** - *Phase II*

Seeker: After which **Light** will vanish, I presume, since —

Recorder: *nothing can move faster!*
Quite —
because it turns
into pure energy thereafter.
Invisible, but —

Seeker: all the stronger.
Where are we now in time?
Has the Millennium come and gone with never
a mention?

Recorder: *Yes, there's much less emphasis*
on tracking dates in **Godwilland**, *than there would*
have been in musty **Godwonland**.

Strand's
plans for a climactic family experience fell flat:
Carole
wrote from **England**, regretting she could not come
to **Godwilland** that year, but welcoming **Light**, whom
she could meet at London Airport, if he came by plane.

Light felt thrown:
he had visualised trekking northward
up the continent until —
he reached the sea.
Then —
who knew?
This offer was too new to feel through ...

Learn firmly bought his ticket.

As **Light** and **String**
took leave of one another in a cloudy drizzle
at **Godwilland**'s main airport, they sensed
                                        a break
that might not be repaired:
                              was that worse than what
Light risked by staying?
                        Still he had not spoken.
                                                String
could only guess
                    deep reasons for his wretchedness,
feel herself wrenched, despite her joy in **Still**.

                                        As **Light**
entered the belly of the vast beast — to carry hundreds
far above the world he knew,
                              to one he did not —
such was the weight he felt, he could not imagine how
this weight could leave the earth.
                                        Space rockets
he had seen on television, in perpendicular propulsion,
wreathed in flame.
                        But this crouched animal, bigger
than very many elephants,
                              had to ascend from belly flat.

It bellied slowly forward, stalking predator,
then in a rush it gathered speed
to a frenzied roaring over rough terrain,
no beast would utter.
                        As its nose tilted sharply up,
the frenzy fell away and only wind through wings was
hearable, while the metal monster climbed and circled,
through thin and ever thinning air.

Light, entranced,
looked down through his porthole,
for the land he left:
saw only seas on seas of bright cloud lit by sun,
not
the dim world he left behind with **String**.

Light,
dozing in ecstasy —
was roused by the first of far
too many meals ...
Light-headed, he looked again
for Earth,
and this time saw, down through the layers
of dissolving cloud,
a coastline slowly whipped by seas
so far below
they broke in slow motion,
to be lost in swathes that hid earth's beauty from this
cleansing sun,
source of the fire he used to burn up litter.

Light knew his mind had never soared like this;
saw blindingly,
he was pulled by a magnet
to the planet's North, to find
answers to questions he had yet to frame.

Not **Britain**, but somewhere to the north and east,
to **Scandinavia** —
from which to scan
what?

28

Carole in **Camford** was a staging post:

from there

he would take ship across the seas —

to where?

Seeker: Surely
to the magnetic North?

Recorder: Maybe.
*Inspired as he is by
leaving Earth, he's doubtless tuning in to the research
of a Danish scientist a hundred years ago, who wrote
a book:* **Under the Rays of the Northern Lights** *—
far ahead of auroral scientists of his time.*
                                                                         Light
*is in line to understand their true significance, once
he is hooked by the very sight of them.*

Seeker: Are you saying
Aurora Borealis is the source of the Seven Rays?

Recorder: *Not the source exactly, no,
                                                        but it is the least
invisible way of seeing,
                                          and therefore understanding,
the force of rays upon our planet, and how it seems
they reach us.*

Seeker: Seems?

Recorder: *The Northern Lights occur
(and thus make visible the rainbow rays)
                                                        when air
molecules collide with charged particles from the Sun,
trapped in the Earth's magnetic field.*

Seeker: So, what
                 about the South Magnetic Pole?
                                          Are there no
                 Southern Lights as well?

Recorder: They are much less visible.
                 There really is no land to see them from,
                 so they are hardly held in human consciousness.

Seeker: What about **Antarctica**?

Recorder: That continent surrounds
                 the Pole itself.
                                          For best displays,
                 you need to watch from further north
                                          (or south)
                 than 60° of latitude,
                                          but nowhere near the 90
                 of the actual poles, where magnetism is invisible,
                 though intense.

Seeker: Like radiation!

Recorder: Yes.

Back in **Godwilland**, **String** found she turned, not
to her brother, **Still**,
                          but to **Light**'s grandfather, **Leo**,
who knew, it seemed, more than she did herself,
of what she missed in **Light**.
                          What, said **Leo**,
makes a fire fly ?
                 Listen.
                          Leo's voice
and plucking spoke together:

30

WHAT MAKES A FIRE FLY?

What makes a fire?

                              What makes a fly?

What makes a fire

                              fly?

Air through it sparks up flame from smoke —
till smouldering Earth becomes a raging fire.

But what of more delicate phosphorescent
things?

                              Filaments of phosphorus

on wings

                              prosper in glowing dark.

Small enough amounts of anything
combine to form the tension that a string,
played on by every element (selected
for endurance in spacetime), weaves
in and out of living, like a shuttle
flying back and forth from there to here.

There's your flying.

                              Where's your fire?

It is hidden safely

                              in polarity —

whether between people or in things
that manifest because of hidden strings,
whose tension tells us what their nature is.

So —

                  when we ask what makes a fire fly,
we ask what tension it experiences,

                                        what

its earth,

            its wavelength,

                              must endure,

to bring them back together close enough
to bring forth more, so keep the Earth
caretaken by the life she spawns —

                              yet is

polluted by,

                                    for too much richness
        weighs down wings —
                                    till even fireflies
        cannot fly.
                                    And golden Midas,
        fighting to draw breath,
                                            crystallises
        in his metal death.

                        Do you mean, said **String**
that light and fire are really the same thing?
                                In a way —
but so are all of us.
                        Everything is made of starry
fire (wrought out of tiny strings).
                                What we have
too much of
                        needs to be brought back
for balancing.
                                Light has so much light
his fires are in danger of becoming incandescent,
setting fire to what his seeing touches.

                                            Yes,
said **String**.
                        he seems the opposite of **Still**.

Yet he doesn't burn up me —
                                No, because you
are his true polarity.
                        You have known wisdom.
                                            He
is safe with you
                        and will come back.

                                Carol,
who had spent most of the previous day wrestling
with corporations as to who should pay for oilspills,

32

when the offending ship was hired, found **Light**'s
enthusiasm brightening.

He had watched dawn
from the stratosphere hours before sunrise was visible
from the earth below.

Nor did he yet show signs
of jetlag, as **Carol** drove them back to **Camford**.

**How
far is Camford from the sea ?**

he asked.

*Quite
a distance; it's an inland market town in the middle
of* **East Anglia** —

**which is a billowing bulge,
quite unlike anything else in the British Isles,
where all the western coast is scored with deep
inlets like a dragon's teeth.**

**Why would you think
that is ?**

*Well, as you know, prevailing winds
are westerly, which must rip up the sea's eroding
coastline —*

just leaving rock skeleton —

**whereas
East Anglia is muddy flats, often awash — though
not yet washed away.**

*The day for that may come,
though — if the Poles are melting*

and they surely are.

Both sat in the silence of a shared reality, peaceful
in spite of distant implications ...

till **Carol** braked —
outside her flat near the ancient heart of **Camford**.

An unfreckled replica of her mother, **Chloe, Carol**
had outgrown her childhood preference for whites.
Camford was full of intellectual blacks, where **Light**'s
dark face would not stand out — except (as **Leaf** had
noted from day one)

his piercing eyes.

As they supped
in the gentle light of a late English summer, this visitor
from the South brought up to date his hostess on what
he knew of the family she'd left

to find her place
at one of the oldest 'bastions of light'

in a new, but now
prestigious, discipline.

Had ecology done more

or less
to change world thinking on how humanity needed
to conduct itself, in the face of changing world
conditions, than had her brother **Silicon**'s lure,
P/C technology?

Fascinated by all such debatables,
Light almost wavered at the plan his flight had brought
to light.

With **Leo**'s conviction
that **Light** would return, **String** sought contentment, as
she ploughed her own uncertain furrow in the world's
now plastic,

now unyielding

substance, aware
of her parents' sudden anxious watching of what was
happening to **Still**.

Vivace, whose preteen childhood

did not sit lightly to her non-birth status (ripped untimely
from her mother's womb), had persuaded that mother,
Viola, at eleven, she badly needed to consult a plastic
surgeon —
                          Vivace being certain she had such
unshapely ears
                    she was scarcely human.
                                              The surgeon
thought otherwise, as did her mother,
                                        but nothing
would persuade **Vivace** she was a lovely, normal
human being.
                    Her father, **Wind**'s, thwarted ambition
to become the first black cosmonaut in **Godwilland**,
pushed him to flit from job to job to subsidise a passion
for paragliding —
                    and to buy his flute,
                                        while **Viola**
kept one foot firmly grounded (no doubt the one **Will**
had so often pulled her out by, in their far off games
in childhood: *"Beat the Rift"*)*
                                to hold down a steady job
in the local bank.
                    For both **Viv**'s parents,
music was their true sharing, and both knew
                                        Vivace
did not have a perfect ear:
                                her voice was pure,
her nature more than lively, her attention flitting
like a humming bird from flower to flower
like **Wind** with work
                          but underneath
(like him) she was dissatisfied — and blamed her body
for her imperfections.

* see **Strands of Wisdom** - Phase II and III

Still, whose quiet, compassionate heart had tuned unconsciously to the need **Viv** hid, was magnetised by her vividness from first meeting — at **Strand**'s informal group — and thus unwittingly revealed himself to those who knew him best.

Though **Will** remembered fondly **Laurel**'s playgroup, back at old **Frinkshome** (before **Rainbow College**) where all of them had first met **Strand** (**Wake**'s baby),˙ neither he nor **Strand** felt comfortable, as **Still** began to bond with **Vivace**.

String knew there was nothing they could do, or would, to put a stop to this, but shared their deep unease, and understood it —

even

while she yearned to bring back **Light**.

The day before **Carol** undertook to transport **Light** (to where he would embark for **Scandinavia**),

she was moved to ask her close friend, **Belle**, to tea and dinner.

Belle had in late middle age resigned her post as senior mathematician at one of **Camford**'s best known Colleges, and now devoted all her time to psycho-spiritual therapy, more blandly known as transpersonal psychology.

Behind **Light**'s bright (though dark) exterior, **Belle** saw a dowsing fear, not reached

˙ see **Strands of Wisdom** - *Phase III*

36

by **Carol**, who was cooking her favorite vegetarian meal, and leaving both of them together.

Light
felt **Belle**'s concern — and something he found deeply reassuring.

Belle had spent years in esoteric training, knew the dangers, and the strengths,

of handling force.
She had reached a certain level of containment, that felt, and could offer, routes to being safe.

Light,
for the first time since his early boyhood discoveries of power,

dared to unburden.

Belle asked him
what he understood of fire.

Mainly that I can make it happen,

Light confessed.

But can you control it?
Light's frantic eyes told all.

*Maybe you need
a working model — to help you fit your powers —
and your beliefs,*

*into some organic system you can use,
because you recognise its truth.*

Light
was near to sobbing his relief.

Tell me, he said,
trusting his eyes to bring no harm to her.

*What do you
hope to find in* **Scandinavia** *?*

*Are you looking for
the source of fire?*

**I really do not know.
I had a vision a few days ago, watching the dawn
as the plane flew here.**

                              I thought that maybe
in the Arctic
          I would see something about the world
I need to know, yet do not understand.
                              What else
must have driven me up here ?
                                        That, only you
can answer.
                    Will you come back this way?
                                        as **Carol**
called them to their feast.
                              He knows he's welcome to.

A noticeably lightened **Light** regaled them as they ate:
told tales of his mother, **Wick**, who found new life
in dancing with her cats.
                    Though **Learn**, his father,
raised his eyebrows at his wife's self-therapies,
he delighted in their outcome and even photographed
her cats' astonishing
                              mid-air

                                        dynamics.

Light's ship ploughed north and east.
                                             This
was too unlike his angel flight from South:
untouched by airsickness in the stratosphere,
here
          Light was plunged

                              in nauseous
peaks
          and troughs;
                              a chilling wind
flung in faces,
                    bellies,
                              stung eyes

with spraying salt,
                        dug into pockets,
knuckles sought for shields.
                                        Feet
wallowed in water,
                    as legs,
                        struggling against
the drag of waves
                        to find their level,
were thrown
                off balance
                        to the biting rail.

As **Light**, half-drowned,
                        pondered this dark
assault —
                                the ship
juddered beneath them
                        and began to break.

Alarms barely sounded
                    before **Light**,
                                cast
in icy blackness,
                    drowned in dark,
                            was gone.

He woke alone and bruised on a bleaker beach
than any imagined in the South he knew.
                                        No bones
felt broken,
                    but his stomach's pit
                                    snarled
for attention he must give to it.

Some residual
fire called out in him:
through the half-light
of whatever dawn his washed up body resonated to,
Light thought he saw a lit up window, could not judge
its distance, could not even tell if it belonged —
to the world he had come so far north to find ...

Body
forgotten,
Light lay still
and looked:
the light was playing,
like a ray from a moving source —
a headlight?
As he gazed, it spread,
took on greenness,
doubled back and folded on itself,
a curtain fringe
of restive green that grew to fill the sky —
not framing
a window,
but the window's pulsing self:
a panorama
swelling the night sky.
Nothing to do with sunrise
or the dawn.
And yet it was a dawn.
Why did it
make him think of curtains billowing?
What drama
was this gold green curtain rising on?
Never
in **Godwilland** had **Light** seen anything resembling
this.

Nothing in his Geography programs touched on it —
though dark in the south he knew came early to display
such plays of rays:
                    sunset and sunrise could outshine
each other's reds and turquoise not seen now.
                                        Then,
as he watched the greengold folds,
                                    a red began
suffusing them,
                spread from their focussed source:
                                        a fan,
a flower,
        a dancing arc,
                    held the sky captive for an age,

before it very slowly faded,
                            through every shade
of mauve and indigo,
                    back to the green white he had
seen first,
        and **Light** fell slowly, slowly into further sleep.

When he woke again, **Light** was lying warm and fed
in a neat ward and a not uncomfortable bed.
                                        Parts
of him he did not seem to feel ...
                                    Was he
sole survivor of the capsized ship?
                            They said a man
called **Hans** had spotted him from his helicopter,
long before the dawn, as he searched for wreck
remnants —
            maybe people clinging.
                                    Light
was far further north than he'd supposed, well within

the Arctic Circle —

                               and during those icy hours,
some of his fingers and his toes
                         frosted.
                                  They might/
might not
               return to life —
                              as he had.

Yes, it seemed (so far} he was the sole survivor:
the man whose name was **Hans** was speaking on TV
of having seen a glow, and marked it ...
to find **Light** lying on an iced up beach
no guiding torch, no flare ...

                               Light wrestled
with the significance of this, and wrestling,
recalled his vision of the night before:
coloured curtains hanging in the sky,
an ever shifting play of radiating rainbow spectrum,
focussed on yellow green.
                        Had he dreamt all —
hanging between ebbing life
                        and frozen death,
to which everyone wrecked with him seemed
consigned?
                      Light could not know.

Hans came to see him, still astounded

                              by the light
revealing him —
                the more so when he learned the name
of this sole survivor,
                    rescued solely by his own

internal glow.
His face lit up, when **Light**
asked him about the radiant lights he thought he saw.

Hans told him everything he knew of the **Aurora,**
that miracle of ever-changing lights
that keep up spirits in the arctic dark —
less often during milder nights of spring or autumn;
never when the sun forgets to set.
Light dawned
on **Light:**
Of course not, he said,
**when sun is there,
such lights would be invisible.
That does not mean
what causes them is not still present:
the force,
the rays —
must be coming from the earth itself,
the planet.**

And yet, said **Hans,
I think the sun is also part of it.
From observations
when sunspot activity is at its height,
Aurora
increases till they say it can be seen even
at the Equator —
as though the sun embraced
the Earth
to set off shivers of delight
throughout the planet.**

A pause enveloped them,
a small exchange of inner sun,
and this began to melt
Light's frozen limbs.
He cried out with pain,
but **Hans** only nodded sympathy:

it was good news, although excruciating.
Painkillers could relieve the worst,
but nurses must know his senses were returning,
so physios could work on him, lest **Light**
lose bits he would prefer to keep.

His mobile lost,
Light asked if **Hans** or the hospital could somehow get
a message to his family in **Godwilland**, who would
not even know his ship had sunk.

Carol however did,
and it took long enough to find out that the sole
survivor of the cargo ship, that she had watched weigh
anchor,
was her recent guest from the Antipodes.
She sent a fast fax to brother **Silicon** — to spread
the disturbing, yet rewarding word

that **Light**
was recovering, in a hospital in arctic **Spitzbergen**,
from frostbite
and the total loss

both of the ship
he sailed in
and of every other soul on board.

Wick woke to see one of her dancing cats

pirouetting
on a forefoot
off the back
of the only other
in the room that night.

Bad news from the North
not yet arrived, **Wick** felt sure that some good thing

had come to **Light**.

Learn listened to her, but
he heard a lot more clearly, when word from **Silicon**
arrived within the hour.

Where was the ship
bound for ?

Leo asked,

when a shaken **Learn**
came in to share his news.

Stavanger in Norway,
Carol's message said.

She saw him off on it,
**but he's landed up a great deal farther north —
in Spitzbergen, it seems.**

And he's the only one
picked up, they say.

Almost unbelievable.
**Wick is convinced that something wonderful has
happened to him, but as he's lost everything,
it's hard to imagine what!**

His life, perhaps?
suggested **Leo** mildly.

Imagine the waters
he's been plucked from, Learn.

Only sealions
**and some bacteria strains survive for long enough
in Arctic seas.**

Light is used to this climate.
I'd say Wick's right.

Have you told String ?

Wick's
on her way to tell her now, said **Learn**.

Good!
Do you like this ?

continued **Leo**,

I'm just
composing it:

When light has gone
                am I a thing of death?
What am I now?
                    An organism —
organon/instrument
                   like this I play:
strung wood, sprung tree,
                  stringed instrument —
organic thing
                 defined by the tension
of the string I'm strung by —
                      hung
from heaven till my feet touch earth.

                      Planted,
I grow in a bubble
                and come forth in time;
then give birth in turn
                to further organs,
instruments of string,
                invisibly strung
from earth to heaven
                to be sounded;
thence straining into colour
                to subsist:
to root as plant, as petals —
                visible life,
organic complement
                of hidden strife —
like matches struck
                to spark a flaring life —
as quickly stifled
                by the staring dark
wrapped round
                the striving string
of life.
                When light has gone,
am I a thing of death —
                who will not, cannot
draw another breath?

                    Listening

to his father's deeper thoughts,

                             Learn let a little shiver
of relief for **Light**'s survival issue forth.

                                While **Leo**

sang, **String** came in with **Wick**,
                           then **Vivace**
and **Still**, (relieved at **String**'s release from tension, for
he knew her sleepless in the hours of **Light**'s enduring).

To this rejoicing, **Laurel,** returning from her day
at **Rainbow**, quietly brought in tea.

Seeker: What exactly are you trying
         to do here?

Recorder: *Actually to marry our two major themes:*
         of rays, which are light (whether visible or not
         to human seeing),
                     and cosmic string,
         the always invisible, less than microscopic, base
         of all existence in the world of senses.

Seeker: Which pairing
         Light and **String** will consummate?

Recorder: *I think so, yes,*
         though it is not yet obvious what will be the outcome.

Seeker: Not less than wisdom, I would stake my oath.

Recorder: *Indeed*
         not less —
               nor is the intensity of their passion lessened
         by the upheaval of **Light**'s *northern venture.*
                                It will

take a deal of wisdom to withstand the strain of all
this fresh experience **Light** *is now heir to.*

Seeker: Perhaps

he will talk with **Belle** again —

to help him assimilate
what he and **Hans** are understanding.

Light

spurred on by his auroral vision and by **Hans**,
recovered swiftly from the exposing Arctic, as both
arrived at a new view of what is causal in our Solar
System — as well as on our planet, **Earth**.

When
the hospital pronounced him fit enough, he went up
with **Hans**

to see if the play of light and dark
looked any different from the sky.

The helicopter
could not climb like the transworld jet he had flown
North in, but high enough to show the curve of **Earth** —
Sun blazing up

to dispatch **Aurora** to a darker space
where it could play its soundless tunes,

display its hues.
(Can sound be causal, even if you cannot hear?
Light wondered).

Hans urged that timed
observations from **Alaska** and the **Canadian Arctic**,
as well as **Greenland**, supported the satellite view
that true **Aurora** was an oval,

not the arc
all earth perceptions had conveyed.

More like a hand

of cards,
                    said **Light** recalling his own arc vision.
**But what you are saying would be like a halo
on a giant saint !**
                              Light had seen pictures
of Italian saints in books, and thought them silly.
But now he saw these haloes with new eyes:
what if there were a Being of the planet,
a Guiding Spirit, whose forceful energy emanated
from the magnetic north as from a head?
                                        If so,
was the South Pole this Being's feet?
                         Or was this Entity
more like kings and queens in packs of cards,
                                   reversing
halfway to become their own image upside down?
Two heads, no tails
                    like tossing fraudulent coins.
Hans laughed at **Light**'s irreverent flight of fancy:
  Surely that's checkable.
                         **Encyclopaedias speak
  of Southern Lights — Aurora Australis.**

                              **I'll have
to go back and check that out then.**
                         **I'd love
to believe we have Southern Lights as grand.**

But Antarctic research is done by Europeans.
                         **You
never hear of southern scientists at the Pole.**

  Why don't you go then ?
                    **You must have been
  preserved from death for something!**

                         Light
had never considered either of these two propositions,
but he was beginning to feel the pull of **String**.

                                                    Nothing
was yet arrived at as to how the Baltic ship
had proved so fragile in a freakish storm —
till weathermen reported a small shower of meteorites
over the North Sea that night, one of which could well
have been of a size
                              to spill the sea's contents —
like a plate of milk put out to feed a cat,
then catapulted by a naughty boy.

                                              Was that
Light's picture of a playful god?
                                              Could
Logos Ludens act so spitefuly, condemning all but him
to icy death in the cod-strewn bottom of deep northern
seas?
              Or were the dealings of a spacetime world
only obliquely due to that world's maker?
                                              Once
Logos Ludens has let go the reins, bestowing freedom
on created things, all consequence is simply what it is.

If traceable at all in all their knotted nets,
effects will be outcomes of chains of earlier effects,
also becoming causes.
                         An accident that causes havoc
is still that —
              however we may seek to lay the blame
on whomever we deem responsible for our welfare.

Nor was body death to be dismissed as snuffed out
consciousness:
                         this side or that of bleak,
black happenings was still a place for gaining more
experience.
                                        Or was it?

And where did that leave **Hans'** conviction
that **Light** was destined for a major role
this side the curtain of the Northern Lights?

                                    Belle
and **Carol** listened to his thinking, saw deep changes
and a brighter eye than even his ecstasy, as he flew
North, had given.
                       Belle noted his new confidence
with some misgiving:
                       behind the seeming modesty
of this last question,
                       she felt a bursting of the bonds,
from that self deprecation he had let her see, before
his adventure in the icy waste.
                       Now he was not
a fearful flame-thrower,
               but a Light-bringer,
                       Lucifer —
with all the painful potency of **Icarus**.
                       Carol thrilled
to his visions of **Aurora**, his expanded sense of solar
causes, and the **Sun**'s dynamic role in magnifying
Earth's own energies.
                       You know, said **Light,**
as he bathed in her appreciative warmth,
                       I think
maybe each colour (in Aurora or a rainbow)
is expressing a different sort of force, an energy
with its own particular effect on us —
                       and in us:
green and blue,
             yellow and red
                   all feel different.
Don't they for you ?

                              Belle and **Carol**
looked at each other, nodding.
                              I wonder,
Light added in a final flurry,
                              if we are really made
of coloured rays,
                              each one of us with different
dominants,
                              chords in music, all of us instruments
in harmonious interaction
                              like players in a cosmic
orchestra.

                    If so, then who or what conducts
this symphony?
                    pealed **Belle** and **Carol** on one note —

and **Light** stopped short, seeing a real question
in their eyes,
                    as they stood together, champions
of Nature.
          Ah! said **Light**,
                    all of whose thinking
had been hatched with **Hans,**
                              I haven't yet
thought that one through.

                              Maybe **String**
will help, when you get back to her,
                              they said.
                                        Yes,
said **Light** thoughtfully, as they all prepared for bed.
Then who indeed conducts this symphony?

And does it feel the same at both the Poles?

PHASE TWO

THE STRENGTH OF LOVE

Before **Light** flew back to **Godwilland**, buoyed
with what he had come north to find, **Belle** shared
with him a prayer that shook the core he now thought
shake-proof.

> **From the point of Light
> within the Mind of God**˙
>
> he read,
> **Let light stream forth into our human minds,
> Let Light descend on earth.**

Try as he might, **Light** could not but feel himself
the subject of this stanza.
What was **Belle** doing
to him?
The second stanza in like fashion invoked
the point of Love within the Godhead,
as though
available to human beings everywhere,
while the third
implied a centre where God's Will is known,
and done by those who know.
As **Light** gasped
at the implications of such claims, **Belle** showed him
two variants and invited him to look for differences.

Mostly the changes echoed the gender tussle, implied
the night he had come back from **Scandinavia**,
enchanted to feel humanity might, quite unknowingly,
be playing out a vast symphony on **Earth**.
But who
directed it?
The Goddess Nature?

˙ see Appendix 1: **The Great Invocation**

54

Or a Logos
known as 'He'?
Or might Nature's wisdom be
simply overlighted by a naturally loving will, beyond all
gender —
who brought into being, maybe through
the power of loving sound?
As **Light**
attuned himself to this ecstatic possible,
his point of light
was drawn to **String**
and overwhelmed
by love.

Could this drama of the human race be due to play out
in the South, in **Godwilland**,
when he and **String**
enfolded to bring forth **Love**'s plan?
This passionate
possible enveloped **Light**, as he took tender leave
of **Belle** and **Carol**.

But as he flew again
through the stratosphere (those rare upper layers,
where clouds do not shroud judgement, nor seduce)
Light was sure
the last line of the fourth stanza
of **Belle**'s prayer, which handled the human bent
for separateness,
was wrong to speak of sealing evil off:
to grow fearsome in the dark, because excluded,
instead of uncovering our unmet need —
which is what
makes us monsters.

High above the biosphere,
where marauding insects do not fly,

                                          Light thought
of **Leaf**'s Garden Centre, where aphids were slain,
because they breed on plants, ladybirds welcomed
for preying on those tiny bodies, nectar full,
which ants delight to keep as captured wine —
to savour their cellared flavour.
                                         How could we,
thought **Light**, drunk with altitude, dare to seal off
as evil, whatever of Nature we find inconvenient?

Light did not know that as he flew (as swallows fly
for winter betterment),
                                 thousands of feet beneath
the plane,
                thousands of dispossessed from **Godwilland**
trudged North (as he himself had planned to), through
heat and dust and drought
                         to break their spent waves
upon barbed beaches,
                   barred by rich Europe
                                   to keep
out 'the scum'.

                        Among these would be some,
dislodged by **Frinkshome**'s closure years before, less
blessed than his gnomic uncle **Green**, his cousin,
Loam.
               Light in his soaring had soared out of touch.

As his plane circled for its landing signal, **Light**
fingered in his pocket the huge opal ring he had
acquired for **String**, by opportune offerings of himself
in **England**, to Agencies who found his survival story
promoted their products on TV.
                     (What little he had when
he flew North, **Light** had nothing, when returning
from the dead).

This shimmering oval set in silver,
symbolised, not what he had seen, but what **Hans** said
was seeable from man-made satellites —

so, not
from **Earth**, but maybe from the **Sun** (her lover?).

String,
urged by **Leo**, went alone to meet him.

Seeing
Light's countenance, she knew him changed, even
before she met him in the Customs Hall, exuding quiet
power — not the restlessness she knew.

Under the eye
of the nearest officer, **Light** fetched out his opal, took
her hand

and slipped it over the knuckle history hallows
for such corralling.

String shied a micro-second
before relaxing into **Light**'s intent.

The Customs man
saw **Light** had nothing to declare but this his loving,
so waved him and his travelling bag back into the light
of **Godwilland**

from Autumn Britain to October spring.

Thus they conceived their love-child **Light** would like
to have named **Aurora**,

but **String**, to reflect
its father's pulsing, suggested **Lyric** would fit either
gender.

Neither name would yield a nest
for nurturing.

Will, now salaried with tenure
and a roving commission to investigate all instances
of pyroclastic flows, wondered what niche **Light**

might be minded to make his.

Antarctic exploration,

When **Light** murmured

Will asked what skills
he had to offer.

Light came down to earth,
as **Strand** pointed out routes, both in the Sciences
and in Humanities, which could help him toward
acceptance in a polar team —

but not for some years.
Only his A in geography, and untoward experience,
could count toward a career so dearly sought —
in the bright world of tomorrow, where grants were
scarce, and working one's passage more or less
assumed.

Light shrugged this off:

I can do anything.
String, arching one eyebrow, held up her ring finger:
Perhaps he can.

Light's exploits as noted here
as in the North, he could fund a living for them both
trading commercials as 'the man who did not die',
while he studied at **Rainbow** or at **Riverstrand**
(from which even **Sophist**'s influence had now
faded).˙

Which of these must turn on whether
he would take a general first degree

or choose now
between 'sub' or 'objective' disciplines — for both
of which he had some aptitude.

It's up to you,
said **Laurel** briskly, when he and **String** presented
proposals to her.

˙ see **Strands of Wisdom** - especially *Phase II*

Her own earlier training had given her
some grasp of curriculum choice at almost any age,
though there were many more specialist options now,
in various therapies, as well as in new techno-science.

Have you thought of Anthropology?
It counts as science,
but involves humanities too.
(We've done it here since
Rainbow *opened).*
So, of course, does ***Archaeology***
we intend including in our new millennial courses.
But,
she smiled,
I suppose there isn't much to excavate
at the Pole — unless maybe ***Scott****'s last expedition.*

I don't want to be at the Pole itself; they say you
can't really see Aurora from so close.
Mainly
I want to check whether the same magnetic
effects are present in the South, as I saw myself
when stranded in the North.
I don't believe
the world has a right and wrong way up.
We float
in space —

We charge our way through it!
interrupted **Leo**,
but on a pretty regular orbit
that's predictable —
by astrologers as well
as astroscientists
put in **String**.
Light had shared
with her all his illuminations in the Arctic fall, as well as
the part **Hans** played, both in his rescue from the ice,

and his interpretations of what caused **Aurora**.
                                                        Born
himself at **Wesak**, annual festival in **Tibet**, held
at the Full Moon of **Taurus** (**Belle** had said),
                                                    Light
was essentially a Light-bringer, being of illumination,
while **String** had deep umbilical connections, both
to her own forebears
                        and to the future she now held
in trust.

                        Strand could feel **Light** did not have
the soothing quality that smoothed her life with **Will**
and brought tranquillity to rearing **String**.
                                                        She
wondered how aware **String** was
                                            of carrying
Sap's nature in her veins, as well as this new being
in her womb.

                        When the baby quickened
String experienced a double revelation:
realised with some shock that she herself
was **Sap**, who had made woven pictures
for a living and had mothered **Wiz**; knew
also she had been very close to **Wit**'s mother,
Wisdom, who vanished from the forest when
the gold men came (**Wit** imprisoned in
oppressive **Godwonland**).

                        But now, as
she felt this beloved seed of hers and **Light**'s
spring into life,
                        String knew
the being she and **Light** agreed on calling
Lyric,

                        was **Sap**'s beloved **Wisdom**
come again.
                   This was so startling **String/Sap**
could not keep still, but paced the room till
dawn, twisting her opal, while **Light** stayed
fast asleep.
                        When it was daylight,
String called **Wit** and **Wiz**, now in their eighties.
Two decades earlier they had been called by **Will**˙,
on the day that followed **String**'s own birthing —
and the shared conviction she was **Sap** reborn.
                                  Aaaah!
said **Wiz-dom** with a satisfying sigh,
                         then we can go.

  What will you call her?

                      She is **Love-Wisdom**.

  Did you not know?
                       String found she said.

Light was awake when **String** came back and told
him their baby was a girl called **Love**.
                      Love-Lyric, then,
said **Light**, reminding her his choice had been **Aurora**
— dawn, the theme of many northern lyrics.

                          Light had
plumped for a general first degree: was now studying
World Poetry in the English Tongue, along with the Art
and Science of Colour, and Linguistics.
                        This allowed
some focus on Antarctic Studies, a new course **Laurel**
worked up in response to **Light**'s perception that
Southerners were being overlooked for projects
to explore **Antarctica** — carved up for years, between
the European powers and **USA**.

All that would change,
thought **Light**, once he was there ...

Let him dwell,
meanwhile, on the lyrics love poets the world over
wrote — exploring feelings such as he and **String**
wrapped round the seedling they were fostering,
twining their thinking and their strung up hearts —
to sense a tension that lay so far beyond the seeable,
Light could find no images to shape it.

Who was
this **Wisdom String** was telling him she knew?
As
Light pondered this, half aware she had conceived
the family of all **String**'s forebears, the post brought
word from **Belle**

enclosing a manifesto from **UN**,
proclaiming 2000 the International Year for Cultural
Peace, inviting them to join 100 million signatories
worldwide, pledged to respect all life and share
with others.
That was last year, so they had missed
the moment, but signatures were pouring in, said
Belle,
to focus this crucial theme,
so bring together
Wisdom and Love.
Was the link, **Light** wondered,
hidden in the mystery of the world
as sound and light —
to be brought to expression by the birth of babes,
whose seeing and sounding surely are the heart
of mystery?

Had not **String**
tried to tell him she believed she was herself the friend
of **Wisdom, Sap,** reborn
which gave her a unique
relation to the fruit she carried in her basket belly,
they were choosing to rename **Love-Lyric.**

String,
meanwhile, who had taken Astrology Studies among
her 'A's, balanced them by absorbing every month
the gist of **Global Linkings**
so she could devote
herself (as **Sap** carrying **Wisdom** into the new age)
to activities that would feed her baby's braincells
for forming networks helpful when she birthed.

Carol had focussed on this vital monthly, owned
by a collective trust in **England**, linking elsewhere
in the North, and needing stronger expression
in the South.
Members took turns to edit it,
choosing ahead a theme to be explored, and digging
deeper than the corporate world would wish.

The current
issue invited 'sapient salesfolk' from the South to use
their skill to spread this journal's wisdom to a wider
public, thus make better known the use of power
to make the world's rich
sound like the benefactors
of its poor.
The scheme was offering a pack to each
prospective agent, at various levels of commitment.

---

see **Wisdom Stranded** - *Phase I*
see *Appendix 2*

A truly **Sap** activity, thought **String**, to feed her foetus
in these months between; the sooner the better,
as her belly swelled to slow her more each month,
and it would take two more to receive her pack by sea.

Gazing at last year's issues, **String**'s eye lit on a huge
pair of interlocking hands, imprinted by the continents
as they clasped the globe — in rich contrasting blues
and greens and purples, encircled by warm flesh —
cover design for the practice of Fair Trade:

                                            vivid image
of love's strength **String** knew she must carry with her
for the bringing forth
                        of the world's wisdom

                                            through
the form of love.

                            With exquisite care,
she fashioned a template of this fragile imaged world —
to preserve it from the clashing, scarlet lettering,
though reason said
                        nature and commerce

                                    must learn
to live together.

                            Just as **Light** had 'sold'
his **Aurora** experience to buy her opal, so would she
work to increase subscriptions to this journal, by selling
pictures to her friends and family of what the world
might look like from the air.

                        As **String** thumbed through,
her eye was caught
                        by the photoed pages of an open
book:

Seen from Above —˙

                            superb aerial pictures
by a French photographer, offered at discount to all
paid up **GL** readers.

˙ see *Appendix 2*

This too **String** would delight
to sell, once she became an agent for the collective
trust whose energy rayed forth **Global Linkings**
to a world that is dying for the love it does not give.

Three full months later, **String**'s starter pack arrived,
her body then so heavy she could barely lug the box
up to their apartment, then knife her way through too
tough cardboard..
　　　　　　　She flopped sweatily on the bed
and fell asleep surrounded by the contents.
　　　　　　　　　　　　　　　　**If you
don't stand for something, you'll fall for anything**

was the succinct greeting she surfaced to, with a fresh
surge of energy to take her beyond the appearance
in the world of **Love-Lyric/Wisdom**, who would make
available the tools
　　　　　　　for helping all to help themselves.

String wondered if even modern **Godwilland** was
free enough to make proper use of what it wrested
long ago from **Godwonland**'s oblivious founders.
　　　　　　　　　　　　　　　　　　She
thought of **Vivace** and her father, **Wind**, whose
mother, **Windel**, none of them had seen since
Frinkshome closed.
　　　　　　　　　　How easy to overlook
bits of the family seen as marginal …
　　　　　　　　　　　　　　Yet **Windel**
had been a violent central force.‎˙
　　　　　　　　　What had become
of her?

˙ see **Strands of Wisdom** - *Phase III*

And what was troubling **Vivace**,
her granddaughter, who had won the heart of **String**'s
beloved **Still**?

                 Vivace, wriggling to evade
the doom that dogged her, shunned her pure voice —
to hold the stage as lead singer in a band of boys,
where, mike in hand, she projected a raucous shout
most of her generation ached to hear.
                           Still didn't,
but he felt her need so keenly he attended every
concert, hoping his poignant meditation would turn
her heart and free her for his love.
                          On stage
Vivace looked spectacular — (or was a spectacle?).
She wore a mix of jade and crimson so arresting,
eyes were riveted as she sang (or yelled) lyrics
the boy band backed.
                 Hair dyed in beetroot juice,
eyeshadow silverjade, her mouth and platform shoes
and uncut fingernails crimson to almost black; tunic
and trousers striped in jade and shades of red, mostly
the colour of venous blood, **Viv**, with the elegance
of a zebra coming into heat, projected outrage
from each cell of her misused body.
                   (She had swung
between bulimia and fasting most of her tweenage
years of puberty).
               The pain of her mother, **Viola**,
made her wish their childhood gully˙ had swallowed
her and her brother, **William**, before such poison
to her pride could reach them.

˙ see **Strands of Wisdom** - Phase II

                                 Viola knew
that he and **Strand** deplored **Still**'s adoration; felt
seared by this stigma with her colleagues —

                                       though

she longed to reach
                   her out of reach,

                                not even

borne down, daughter.
                         Viv's father, **Wind**,
seemed to take this lightly, went paragliding when
the papers blazoned a photo of the boy band icon.
Viv still worked from home, and if they protested,
she would move in with the boys — and be lost
to drugs as well.

                    Strand and **String** watched **Still**
lose weight, as he struggled with **Viv**'s near total
ignoring of his love.
                       Clearly she thought
so little of herself, she felt him a fool to waste his quiet
energy on her.
                    Anguish seeped everywhere.

Will, far off in the ring of fire to the east
of **Godwilland**, where he was waiting
for a mountaintop to blow, received
an agonised letter from his sister, **Vi** —
and felt she probably overstated the antics
of his niece.
                      It would all come out
in the wash he assured her in a fax more
facile than was maybe fitting.
                        Nature
was Nature and would do whatever all
her elements found congenial.

What drove
Vivace would
until her spent energy laid bare
another facet of her tortured being.

Strand
half took this view, but felt more might be
done to close in on **Viv** and listen to her.
But,
might it be like offering cups of tea
to a charging rhinoceros (whose troubles
we know lie just beneath her thick skin folds)?

The night the mountain blew,
String went
into labour seven days early.
Light adroitly
got her into hospital where by dawn,
the cherished **Love-Lyric** of their dreams
was born.
Light melted into a glistening bead,
as spent **String** sank into dreamless sleep,
and he held his baby daughter in arms
that had held her mother as she came.
'Came'
thought **Light**, what a weight of work
that word's assigned!
Faces contort in ecstasy
as well as pain.
Is it to do with work not yet complete
that agony registers before release?
The tiny face
before him crinkled, lips pursed for the teat the nurse
was poised to offer, as she tested the bottle's heat
against her arm.

In a few hours **String** would offer her
a meal more natural.
Light went home satisfied.

When **String** gazed at her baby in the morning light,
(all soreness banished by her healing sleep), she felt
her 'Sapness', as she searched for features from those
far off days
of finding **Wisdom** as a friend long lost.˙
Love-Lyric had those same dark pools of eyes,
whose fathomless wisdom, linked with a new kind
of love,
looked back at her
with readiness to read
what lay behind her own.
O, my little love,
String breathed,
are the strains of being born
and birthing, the only way we know of meeting need?

The night the mountain blew it rained boiled ash,
for miles and hours through and around and down
people and places it could sulphur-skewer.
Will was
almost caught in a flow he could barely see for acid
mist,
one of his men incinerated instantly, by its speed
he could neither sidestep nor outrun.
Will watched,
helpless — and barely able to draw breath.

˙ see **Wisdom Stranded** - *Phase I*

And that
same night, as she finished her day's work,
                                        Vivace
sighed and turned to **Still** for love.
                              Still, who had
longed so long for this, he had become content to long,
could not express his turmoil of delight,
                                    so bring content
to **Viv**.
          Her very appearance, when she closed on him,
drew forth revulsion, which his body spoke, although
his mind denied.
                      So, an uneasy equilibrium
only **String** could fathom.
                          Viola held her breath.
Strand, observing that **Still** and **Vivace** now did
everything together, could only wonder what
the 'doing' was.

                  When a shaken **William** returned
from his vulcan task,
                          less one of his most trusted
helpers —
                      but to the glad addition of their first
grandchild —
                      he was disposed to look more kindly
on **Still**'s love.
                                        Vivace
had toned down a little her eccentric dress, so offered
a less disturbing presence.
                          Strand, whose closeness
to **Will** had never depended on erotic union, thought
Still might be similar —
                      but not **Vivace**;
                                    doubted,
in fact, if true intimacy were the bond —

or some
more complicated codependency.
                                                        Viola could only
nod agreement.
                              Wind expressed no opinion in words.

They met to celebrate **Love-Lyric**'s birth, and mark
the passing of the family elders,
                              Wit and **Wiz-dom**,
who 'left' benignly within days of one another (as **Wiz**
had virtually promised **String**).

                              At such a gathering,
surely, betrothal between **Still** and **Viv** would be
declared.
                                             Silicon,
who had since **Light**'s ordeal, used his special skills
to link the whole family on the Internet, wherever they
might live, had rigged a camcorder in his parents'
home, with an interactive video link to **Carol**'s
English website, so all could participate as they might
wish, in this triple family celebration, centred on
the home of **Strand** and **Will** (as roomier than **Light**
and **String**'s apartment).
                              This did not have quite
the timbre **Strand** had envisaged before **Light**'s
English venture: a touch more muted and inclined
to overlay deep differences as to what the point
of life (or love) might be.
                              Yet it would surprise.

Love-Lyric slept throughout: fresh family angel, lulled
by **Leo**'s pixie plucking,
                              Wind's flute,
                                             the bow of **Viola**,
sometimes all three in spirited improvisings, managed
more cunningly as the day unfolded.

Only
when **Wick**, who never went anywhere without a cat
or two,
        began dancing with her Balinese,
L-L's eyes opened (at the rush of wind
across her cheek)
            to gaze,
                  rapt,
at the sight of pirouetting **Wick**
                trailing
her shawl like a matador ...
             then lifting
it high,
          while one cat leapt higher
and the other crouched.
           Then they reversed:
the orange leapt,
         the Balinese stayed still.
Did you see that ?
                 Light
gasped in sudden recognition.
             Yes, said **Belle**
clearly from her English site 10,000 miles away.
                They
are grounding and expressing energy in a shared
polarity.
      Wick *has the measure and they work as one.*
I had not expected cats to put so much effort into being
alive.
      Belle, I told you about my mother's cats
before I left for Scandinavia!
            But this is so public.
Cats are private people.
        Love-Lyric purred gently
at the beauty of the world she had come back to.

Laurel was rejoicing quietly in her first great grand child, when **Wake** came up to sit with her:

She's yours too, of course!

they both saw suddenly and laughed. Though their paths crossed often at the College, they much less frequently paused — to talk as family.

But now:

*Do you believe in reincarnation, **Laurel**?*

I'm not against it, but I have no reason to accept it — why?

Wake issued a luxurious sigh, and shared with **Laurel Strand**'s past identity as **Windel**'s twin

and **String**'s, as **Wiz**' mother, **Sap**.

'You're joking, of course', **Laurel**'s raised eyebrows said.

But **Wake** went on.

Not only that:

*since **Wick** and her cats got dancing, I've had the strangest feeling this great grandchild here of yours and mine*

*is **Sap**'s friend, **Wisdom**, come again as **Love**.*

*I saw her first at **Sap**'s funeral at **Riverstrand**, when **Wit** was on the run.*

*That's really how I came to be in **Frinkshome**.*

Laurel nodded, not yet taking in what **Wake** was telling her.

*But where is **Wilson** —*

*and what became of **Windel**?*

***Wilson**, my father, is watching at home with **Silicon** and **Chloe**.*

*As for **Windel**, who knows?*

(**Laurel** felt abashed to have forgotten her long absence).

Wake sighed and shrugged:

No one has seen her since
she left when **Frinkshome** *closed, and only Dad*
was asked to stay.
She took it badly,
he shrugged it off.
She could well have gone back to the shanty town ...

which is probably rife with AIDS by now.
O God,
Wake, *what a mess lies just beyond our noticing!*

Laurel's own children, **Leaf** and **Learn**, were having
a rare get together here.
(She still could not absorb what
Wake had told her: what could it mean to say **Light**
and **String**'s baby, **Love**,
was really **Wisdom** come
again?)

Though **Leaf** had not persuaded **Green**
to come, their son, **Loam**, had willingly put on a shirt
and slinky pants, then gravitated to a corner, whence
he watched.
Now, as **Wick**'s dancing
climaxed and subsided,
Loam leapt
from his corner and stripped off his shirt.
Looking deep into the eyes of **Wick**'s orange
Javanese, stretched in total relaxation
on the floor, he whispered
Wax.

Engaged
fully as its name was sounded,
                                        the cat gazed
back.
                Loam began circling very slowly
round.
                The cat's body had to swivel
to keep in contact with Loam's eyes, its tail
piloting its body movements.
                                        Gradually,
Loam stepped up his speed,
                                        till the cat
was spinning on the carpet like a top —
                                                        then
elongated as it found its legs.
                                        Loam slowed
to a standstill
                and then flopped,
                                        till he lay
as relaxed as Wax had been.

                                Wax now
upright, tail thrust out, front paws touching
high above its head,
                        began weaving circles
around Loam, who held eye contact, just as
the cat had done with him ...
                                The whole
performance was repeated, cat in charge,
Loam swivelling in response to Wax.
                                        When
Loam reached spinning point, he hummed.

Vivace, watching quietly from the side
with Still,
                got up as suddenly as Loam had.

*(I thought at first **Loam** was misusing magic,*
Belle whispered across the Internet to **Light**.

**Me too, how did he manage to reverse
the power like that ?**
By leaving space,
I think; why don't you ask him?
**I don't want
to break the flow.**
Viv seems willing to risk
that).
When **Light** turned back, he saw two
pairs at work
in what had now become
a performance arena:
Loam and **Vivace**;
Wax and **Win**, (the austere white Balinese,
dark marks round face and feet).
Both cats
stood upright opposite each other, tails
stretched to balance them, front paws raised
to form a circle high above each head (like
Wax before).
Loam and **Vivace**
copied them — as for the starting of a circle
dance.
Wick rose at the same moment
as her twin brother, **Wind**.
All six danced
a pretty stately minuet —
till by silent consent
the pace stepped up to reach a crescendo
of Saturnalian revelry, quite the highest
energy expressed that day.

When it wound down,
Love-Lyric closed her eyes again, and the gathering
dispersed:
      Wick returned home with **Learn** and her two
cats; **Wind** and **Viola** packed their instruments and left
— **Leo** and **Laurel** linked arms and took their leave.
                        But
Loam did not return to **Green** with **Leaf**.
                And nothing
had been said of **Still**'s betrothal.

               The energy in the home
of **Strand** and **Will** had changed.
            Everyone there
or looking in could feel it.
          Loam and **Vivace**
had become 'an item'.
       And that feels much more fitting,
Strand observed.
        Out of this celebration,
Vision was conceived.

Seeker: Did you make up
      all that cat stuff,
             just to create an atmosphere?

Recorder: *Indeed I did not!*
       Cat dancing is an astonishing fact,
    quite recently uncovered.
       *Only **Loam** and the spinning*
    goes beyond what we know from photographs
    and books.

Seeker: Even cats taking initiatives themselves?

Recorder: (nodding)   Many cat owners (and their children) will tell you they feel fed by their cats' energy.
I doubt we know the half of how intelligent animals really are.
          But **Loam**'s natural instinct for earth magic can take almost anything that bit further than is so far known.

Seeker: Will you have more to say on this?

Recorder: Well, this trilogy is about human evolution, but our relation to animals has a vital place in what we humans will become,
                    as **Life** takes over.
                                        Cat dancing, as **Belle** observed, involves the balancing of etheric energy,
                    the core of all relating,
                                        as indeed of relativity: $E=MC^2$ — yang and yin aspects of the Seven Rays[*];
                              again the two lines of force (from creative will to incarnate manifesting).
                                        This invisible energy is at work throughout all Nature, in plants and minerals, as well as animals and humans, who all have animal forms they vitalise by eating plants,
                    while they are structured by their mineral skeletons — held together by the planet's magnetism, being explored by **Light** ...

Seeker: guided by the Sun —

[*]see **Strands of Wisdom** - Seeker/Recorder Interlude after *Phase I*

Recorder: *Yes, cosmic ray influence reaches us through signs of the* **Zodiac**, *by way of the Sun's planets.*

Seeker: And thus
our individual difference manifests.

                                                    Still
did not deceive himself: he felt more relief than pain
at **Viv**'s abrupt removal.

                              What **Leaf** experienced,
when **Loam** brought **Vivace** back to her and **Green**,
may have been more suppressed.
                              Leaf had to learn
that **Wisdom** incarnate in the **Word** arrives as both
gift and burden.˙
                              The nine months leading to the birth
of **Vision** would surely have been both.

                              Leaf could not,
as she watched **Viv**'s belly grow, have been unaware
of what took place, while she and **Learn** savoured
re-meeting at the Celebration.
                              Nor could she know how
significant a part this new child would play in the life
of **Love-Lyric**, whose birth the family had gathered
there to honour.

                              Leaf did intuit that **Loam**
was a more likely carrier than **Still** of vibrant sperm
for impregnating **Viv**.
                    String agreed

˙ see **Prelude** - *2ⁿᵈ scenario*

(without sharing
her misgivings as to whether **Still** might not be sterile —
from those early years before **Light** understood
his frightening powers).

Enough to acknowledge
Still was not designed for fathering, at the grounding
level we call birth on earth.

Loam was.

But what
of **Vivace** in the role of mother?

Not having borne
herself
    down the canal
            and through the reluctant opening,
how would she fare at bringing **Vision**

to a world
that did not know it cried for him?

Light became
an expert nappy changer.

Having almost no sense
of smell, he could aesthetically enjoy the golden
mustard, extruded from **Love-Lyric**'s tail in rhythmic
cycles, through all the hours and days of sleeping,
feeding, being bathed or held.

String supplied ample
provender, both for assimilation and for 'waste'
(essential ingredient of a natural cycle).

Light recited
poems or sang songs, often his grandfather's (so
tapping into another kind of cycle), and he cooked
for both of them as often as did **String**, who was
making a quiet, professional task of selling **GL**.

Though
slowed by the baby's birth, she had gained several
new subscriptions, through sharing with friends and
family the lively cassette from her Starter pack, backed
by vigorous 'first nation' drumming.

Leaf and **Vi**,
and one of **Vi**'s banking colleagues, had all responded
warmly to the tone of **GL**'s outreach, but **String** chafed
that **Earth from Above**, the entrancing book of aerial
photographs, had not arrived from **England**.

Light
continued working for his place in a polar team, while
funding his family through TV adverts.

Though
the impetus of his prowess in the North had waned,
his comely face and bearing were by now so known,
he could count on a steady income.

But he and **String**
had nearly come to blows, when the Agency suggested
the babe would be an added incentive to consumer
spending.

But, why not ?, said **Light**.

**All I'd have
to do is hold her in my arms,**

**and you know how
much I like doing that.**

**It's not like a politician
kissing babies only to attract their mothers' votes.**

String gulped.

She could see it was in ways an issue
similar to her distaste for garish **GL** fliers.

Yet surely
there was something more: both had watched English
adverts, in which photo'd two-year olds had generated
really funny copy, simply through face expressions,

while an adult voiceover made innuendoes the small
participants would have no clue to.

                                       But
what when these children grew old enough to see
how their budding personalities had been exploited?
Even **Christopher Robin Milne** last century had said
his life was blighted by being the unwitting dynamo
of **Pooh Book** stories.

                         Was that because his name
was used, making him foolish with his peers at school?

Yet, why should a small boy, relishing his cherished
toys, be cause for adult shame, confused identity?

Which kind of betrayal really was the worse for male
maturing?
                    This stark denial of our tender feelings,
distorting our true nature
                         to make us ...
                                 String
had a sudden flashback to her life as **Sap**,

                               saw
Sophist who had fathered **Wiz-dom** with her —
perhaps the most cynical operator of his age, and that
less openly cynical by far than this ...
                        Where draw
the line, between commerce and our precious privacy,
without becoming either smug or vulgar?
                              Light
and **String** chewed on it night after night, while **L-L**
slept her innocent sleep.
                    Viola (whom they met more
often now that **Viv** had left, expectant)
                        saw the logic
of **Light**'s argument, but felt **String**'s driving anguish —
for they needed such extra money for their own goals'
furthering.

Perhaps, said the bank clerk thoughtfully,
*it is a case of feeling how the flow of living really does
depend on meeting people's wants,*

in ways that tickle
their palates,

without being either crude or vicious ...

or downright lethal, put in **String**, fresh from the latest
issue of **GL**, which had bought space in **Godwilland**'s
most radical press, **The Participant Observer**,
using those two huge human hands to cradle the earth
with its 5 continents.

Six, said **Light**.
Look at that!
Isn't Love-Lyric to be a sponsor of *Fair Trade* **?**

But are your Agencies such sponsors?
Probably not —
but I could make that a condition of bringing in
L-L.
And so **Light** won on points
and the babe became
ambiguous party to procuring money for her family —
by being the presence that earned her father most.

At **String**'s suggestion, they had sent an E-mail off
to **Belle**, when the impasse threatened souring
of their bond.
Some of her answer was dismaying:
Lucis (the Trust distributing **The Great Invocation**
and sponsoring **World goodwill** activities, as well as
the **Alice Bailey** Esoteric School)
charged nothing
for their work,

˙ see *Appendix 1*

subsisting wholly
                          on student donations,
legacies, and other goodwill offerings.
                                          The Trust
had its commercial arm, **The Lucis Press**, for selling
the books channelled by **Alice** through 'The Tibetan',
and for **Beacon**, their esoteric quarterly.
                                          But its day
to day work depended wholly on the giving of those
committed to its tenets.
                          Divine circulatory flow,
Belle called it, quoting this same Tibetan adept, who
expounded the theory of the **Seven Rays**.˙
                                          Markedly
he linked this flow also with the body's health:
                                          when,
like blood circulation, it was blocked or too much
stimulated,
                  sickness followed,
                                  whether in the body
politic, or individual human.
                          Healing would then depend
on finding the hidden cause, most likely in the nearest
organ to the disrupted centre, focussing ray energy
and so releasing flow, at a rate most equitable
to that body's need.
                          'Of course', **Belle**'s E-mail added,
'the human genome makes mistakes in copying, which
puts another twist on things.'
                                  So where does that
leave us?
                  sighed a bewildered **String**.

˙ see *Appendix 3*

Using
our intuition,
Light replied too glibly.
Yours or mine?
said String tartly, L-L having just shot excess milk
across her chest.
We have to learn it all through trial
and error, as well as our sense of what is right.
Light
tried to get a word in, but String swept on:
If I'd been
attending, I'd have known she needed to bring up
wind before she could take more milk —

and I think
she needs her nappy changing too.
The expert took her
from String's arms and went on reasoning (while
String mopped up her front).
So Belle sees a clear
analogy between what happens at our individual
level/micro
and the whole planetary picture/macro.
But I feel it's rather more than that:
our bodies
and the body politic
are all inside
the body
of the Planetary Being.
This must mean
some psychic penetration of each one of us
by big disturbing world events.
Especially when
so disturbing we have unconsciously excluded them,
String interjected —
which means we wouldn't have
a clue what's bothering us, but the larger cause
will be the body politic, so national ...

more likely
global, now that electronic markets sweep the board.

Light had brought **Love-Lyric** back, clean and pure
and listening to their interchange:
**that we are all
interlinked at every level, only a useless ostrich
would deny.**
Don't project our folly on to animals,
laughed **String**, as she proffered her second nipple.
That's been exploded long ago; I read it in **GL**.
**How
reliable is their research ?**
The best there is, I'd say —
and they always cite its origin in footnotes.
**So do all
Scientific Papers, but it's still only 'best opinion',
Light** countered,
**even when they claim their source
is primary, which I don't think GL often does.**
But
all its articles are based on what its reporters see
and hear!
GL *is primary source material.*
They found
the fruits of a further primary source on their doorstep:
the precious book from **England, Seen from Above,**
weighed more than **L-L** (who had put on tidy weight
her full three months).
Here was evidence more telling
than a raft of footnotes.
This French photographer
had the eye of a tender eagle as he caught images
of little, striving bands of earthly beings:
a dromedary
caravan lost in the shadows of scorched dunes, stark
at sunset;

tiny, unpeopled islet in the Pacific deep;
a helicopter looking no less lost as it wound across
a gully, dark as **Milton's Satan** flew from; vast vats
of bright coloured dyes in **Fez; Everest** mounting
guard between **Nepal** and **China** — and that was only
the first few pages.

String was exalted by this global
feast.

Light, does **Belle** *ever talk about the moon?
I've just had a thought about its cycles, as it wanes
and waxes: how tides and planting times and women's
eggs and stuff — affect our lives.*

**She says full moons
are most significant, but because they reflect
the Sun, not in themselves.**

Why?

Light shuffled.
I think I'm still trying to find that out.

**She and Carol,
as you know, are both keen feminists, and insist
on the newer wording of The Great Invocation,
but when it comes to keeping the Full Moon
Festivals, it's always the larger picture of the Solar
System, and beyond.**

**And of course my Aurora
understanding is about the Sun's effect on Earth's
magnetism,**

**so the moon seems overshadowed:
like local government by central.**

*But each
has its proper place,*

objected **String**.

*The sun may be
creative, but it is the moon that shapes*

*to yield the form
we come in, on the stage of life, and make us familiar
to one another.*

It may not be our permanence,
but it is what brings our daily bread.
It is your form
(plus **L-L**'s) that makes you successful on TV.
**Surely
it's what L-L stands for, as small and vulnerable,
not her shape —**
String snorted.
She stands for
a whole lot more than that —
but it's not what I mean.
I think I'm saying that **Sun** and **Moon** and **Earth**
form a triumvirate that brings to birth
and it is the **Moon**
that licks things into shape — to stand against the wind.

**It certainly is solar wind that presses on the Earth.
And there must be some pretty pressing reason
for celebrating Moon's main phases — as Belle
says Lucis does.
Maybe I'll see it all more clearly,
when Aurora Australis appears in the Antarctic.**

Perhaps **Belle**'s **Tibetan** is only saying form is not
everything.
But it is what we work with at the sharp end,
surely.

Vivace soon discovered this.
She had enough in her of her mother, **Viola**, to bear
stoically the long nine months of hefting, to the day
and hour, when **Vision** evidently knew he must bestir:
switches clicked off,
provisions failed;
he felt pinched,
and propelled toward deeper, narrower darkness
than the half-lit belly he had grown in.

                                  No going back,
he fought for moving forward.
                        This shattered **Viv**,
who had no latent memory of her own to match it with.
It felt a butting rugger scrum inside her.

                                  Leaf and **Vi**,
seeking to offer comfort, were puzzled —
                                  till **Viola**
remembered:
                  she too had been deprived of the painful
value of the birth experience.
                                  Leaf had not,
and had found **Loam** vigorous enough, to blot out
most of the memory of labouring.
                                  But something
told her **Viv** was not cooperating.
                                  Nor could **Loam**
be there supporting **Viv**, for **Leaf** had to leave him
in charge of the Centre, when they heard **Viv**'s cries,
Green being too vague with money, for balancing
growth with parting from its products.
                                  (If **Green** liked
a buyer he would give his plants away; if not,
he'd name a price too high to pay.)
                                  Vision had
no such quirks:
                  he wanted out
                        and pressing for release,
he tore his mother's cervix as he came.
                                  This was far
more serious than snicked labia.
                                  Vivace screamed
and spurted blood and fainted.

Vision came
before the doctor, who pronounced him fine, but
wanted to take both in, for care and monitoring.
                                                    This
revealed both mother and baby HIV.
                                            Loam's check
proved negative,
                              but the day his repaired family
were returned to him,
                              Vivace fled.

Seeker: That's put the cat
            among the pigeons, hasn't it?
                                              But where is all this
            risking leading?

Recorder: *Perhaps it is time*
            to remind ourselves that we are moving out
            of the **Piscean Age** *and into the* **Aquarian**.

Seeker: Remind
            me again what that will mean in terms of Rays.

Recorder: *It will*
            mean that the 2000 year dominion of Ray Six,
            which began as the birth of Ideal Love (begetting
            Christianity)
                        has now crystallised —
                                              to become
            our modern conflict between the dried out ideals
            of religion
                        and **Marx**'s *dialectical materialism*.

Seeker: Both of which would seem to have lost sight of love
            in action.

So, what is coming in to replace the spent
Piscean energy of Ray Six?

Recorder: ***Aquarian** Ray Seven.*
Purely pragmatic:
                            if it works,
                                        go for it.

Seeker: So that's what is rasping everyone these days !
Pressure to ignore, or override, all principles — with
corresponding outrage when it happens.
                                              While
the public hasn't an idea what's hit them.

Recorder: *No,*
and nor have governments.
                            But we must wrestle
for the core of truth in every decision made
                                        and lived.
***Light** and **String** have struggled for solutions.*
*What they (and **Leaf** and **Loam**) have landed now*
will really smudge the boundary between present
rules for living
                            and alive compassion.

Still shook his head in answer to **String**'s unspoken
questions, when news of these disasters broke.
                                              No,
he knew nothing of **Vivace**'s whereabouts — and no,
his medical condition would not require a test.
                                              Still
sighed, but seemed unsurprised by what **String** said.

Efforts at tracing **Viv** drew only blanks.
                                        Viola knew

the more frantic she became, the less likely the currents
to return her child.

So **Leaf** and **Loam** and **Green**
were left to bring up **Vision** as they best could:
with earthy care, they fed and watered him, and gave
him supplements, watching his unfolding in the sun.

As **String** worked from home, **Leaf** often transplanted
him to play with **Love-Lyric**.
                    Because of his viral status,
rigid routines in handling his body fluids were as vital
as unsplit rubber gloves.

                    But how to be sure **L-L**
was safe?

                    String did not forget
Belle's words on keeping the divine flow unblocked.

Wick, for **Love-Lyric**'s second birthday, brought her
an orange kitten:
                    what if it scratched them both —
and bleeding mingled?
                    String held her breath,
as **Love-Lyric** beamed at the kitten
                    and began to dance
on pudgy unstable legs,
                    Vision likewise.
                                        The kitten
sat on its haunches,
                    front legs in the air
                                        and watched.

String was again pregnant, and by the time she went
into labour, **Orange** was fully grown and danced
adeptly — with two ardent partners oftener than one.

Skill was thus born into an arena in which clumsiness
was not rewarded.

He took the hint.

He and **Vision**
developed a game of using sticks as fencing swords,
lunging and parrying, like French musketeers.

Though
nearly three years younger, **Skill** was tall.

His reach,
at four, could match **Vision**'s (coming up for seven).
Vision was scrupulous not to trick his younger cousin.

Love-Lyric trained **Orange** and her various broods
to give wide berthing to this sparring pair.

One day
that would not leave anything as it had come to be,
Wick appeared, with her long gone mother, **Windel**,
who had news, and not good news, of **Vivace**.
Windel had worked for years among AIDS sufferers
and had by chance discovered **Viv**, alone, near death,
uncared for.

Having got her into hospital,
where she died days later,

Windel saw something
familiar in this woman's dried up face, and wondered.
She sought out **Wick**, unseen for many years.

Wick
identified her niece hours only before they buried her.
(There was no dallying with such infectious corpses).

Thus **Windel** learned this dying neglected sufferer,
she had nursed, had been her own grand daughter.
Wick called up **Wind** and **Viola** too late for them
to see their daughter's body.

                                        Loam
went into a powerful ritual dance with **Vision**:
                                          cats
stood in a circle round them, paws uplifted, as though
acknowledging grief expressed.
                                   Love-Lyric
looked thoughtful:
                        was this more separating than
her father's going, two years back?
                                    String shook
her head:
            Not necessarily, darling, no.
                                        That now
depends on **Viv** *herself,*
                        on where she may choose to let
her presence spread.

                              As **String** spoke,
the faces of **Wit** and **Wiz**, as she recalled them,
                                          hung
in the air.
          Love-Lyric saw them too.
                                They did not speak.

But the room held a presence
                              Windel felt.

PHASE THREE

LIFE SPREADING

Beyond the reach of **Windel**'s anger (once
expressed with such violent silence it had winded her˙),
if **Wiz-dom** registered her daughter's presence now,
it would be to enfold her in a new compassion,
wrought by a place where black and white had no
more meaning than they ever had
                                                    for **Wit** and **Wiz**
from their first meeting by the plane tree in the forest,
where **Wit**'s dropped arrow pierced his own foot —
to draw toward both all the events that shaped
their future stress:
                                marking the end of **Godwonland**,
the start of the multiracial state of **Godwilland** —
whose compromises **Windel** turned her back on,
for the now AIDS-ridden shanty town, where she
had born her twins,
                                (forsaken when she and **Wilson**
brought them to enjoy new life at **Frinkshome**).

                                                            A tear
oozed shyly out of **Windel**'s ageing eye, as the faces
of her parents swam into her sight.
                                            Now **Vision**
saw them too
                        and so did **String**
                                                    (who had been
Wiz' mother in her life as **Sap**).
                                            Love-Lyric was
the first to hear **Wiz** speak:
                                    Vivace is safe and well,
but needing care.
                                She cannot come yet to share
with you like this —

˙ see **Strands of Wisdom** - *Phase III*

but when she can,

she may want

to tell you of her **Life-Review**.

Did you hear that, Mum,

L-L breathed.

What did she mean?

And who

is telling us?

Loam too looked to **String**
for explanation.

She, recalling flashes
of her half-forgotten Life Review as **Sap**, was hesitant.

This broke the connection, and the presence faded —
but not the impression it had made on each:

Loam

as anxious as when **Vivace** disappeared;

Love-Lyric

deeply thoughtful;

Windel silent, wondering.

String,

as though emerging from a trance, shook herself;
while **Skill** and **Vision**, glancing at each other, went
for their fencing sticks — to work it out.

Wick turned,

to begin dancing with the cats,

who, for the first time,

spoke:

not in English,

nor in cats' tongue.

They sounded an unearthly melody that drew through,
for all who reflected soberly on **Wiz-dom**'s words
concerning **Life-Review,**

more than a hint

of conscious existence when the body's gone.

                                        Cats

were special very long ago,

                    when **Egypt** built pyramids

to focus energy, so direct that world's attention —

to the permanence behind decay and change.

                                        Now,

trained by **L-L** from strains that **Wick** had bred,

these cats shared readily their ancient feline wisdom —

to feed the questioning they felt

                              deep in the people

gathered in this space.

                        They stood in their circle

and they uttered sounds:

                          some deeply gutteral,

like Buddhist monks,

                        some with the tonal purity

of a brass bowl struck

                          by the surest gong.

These tones were heard

                  as telling the secrets

                                of the inner

person.

        Each listener learned that per-

                        sonal-ity

                                means

that which is formed essentially through sound:

                                        first

the creative sounding of the Will that sets in motion

atoms for building protein molecules —

                                and so make

genes from double strings of chemicals;

                                      thence,

from resounding impact of whatever reaches us —

                                        we

minded to receive.

                                   For like attracts like, we say,
forgetting that what we do not like seeps also — as
discordant sound
                             into the deeper reaches of our being,
to form traits unexpressed
                                   that work like poisoned
splinters irking our psyche.

                                   All this the dancing cats
now wove into movements they expressed
                                              in leaps
and crouches
                             each listener 'heard' in hir own
distinctive way
                       with blocks
                                        or openness,
according to hir nature, hir readiness to face ...
the meaning of a **Life-Review**.
                                   And each could only
wonder
         how **Viv** would be experiencing hers
                                        and where.

Windel, who did not dance (with cats or humans),
but had begun to learn to listen and was glad to have
made peace with both her parents,
                                   felt in herself
discordance,
                 as the cats displayed it.
                                   And she gloried
in it:
                 not till the last white, western face had gone
back to the North it emanated from,
                                   and every AIDS
sufferer was dead

would **Windel** seek to tame
her nature to fit the requirements of a **Life-Review**.

Her daughter, **Wick**, as surprised as any by her cats'
new skill, and ever ready to temper with more prudent
ways the effect she caused, if it would ease her future
passage (still far enough away to feel remote),

saw
that her niece, **Vivace**, could be facing

extremely
painful recognitions:

battered by demons maybe
in her new abode.

Vision saw **Viv** suddenly
assailed by harpies

(of her own imagining, ugly fruits
of misfelt self-beliefs),

biting, pecking at her eyes
and ears.

He cried out,

as **Love-Lyric** trained
her light to banish them,

and **String** saw through them
to their aching hearts within.

Skill looked scared,
and **Loam** distressed.

This lay as far outside his sphere
of understanding, as his athletic acumen with cats
beyond most of the Garden Centre customers.

Death
as the end of things,

even the out of order perishing
from AIDS of his own partner and mother of his son,
he felt he could accept.

But that she should be

suffering now
                    revolted him.
                                        He had seen and heard
nothing,
                    and he felt confused
                                        by what the 7 year olds
had seemed to do.
                                String picked up his silent pain,
as the cats gathered round him to commiserate
                                                    (silent
this time, but soothing with their fur).
                                        String sought
for words she hoped would reassure:
                                        Loam, *I think*

  we are made of many parts
                                        and some of them

  get out of hand
                    or hide.
                                        All of us run

from what we do not like ...
                                        But what we hide

returns again to haunt us,
                                        as though not us at all,

but enemies.
                    That's what I saw
                                        cried **Vision**.
They attacked her.
                            But who ?
                                        asked **Loam**.
**They looked like female furies from the dark, who
don't like light.**
                    They don't,
                            said **String**,
                                        but until

Vivace *understands them for herself,*
                                        and ... makes

her peace with them ...

How can she do that ?
Loam reasonably asked.

Windel, who had stood
stock still through all of this,
erupted.
Why should she
make peace with everything that's wrong!
No one,
not even the cats, could answer this.

Out of the silence
came again the voice of **Wiz-dom**,
again heard easily
by **Love-Lyric**:
Windel, it is not so long
since your father and I experienced this process.
We left soon after **Love-Lyric** *came, because we knew*
Wisdom *was born again into the world (where we*
were tired and old).
Would you like **Wit**
to tell you what we went through then?
Yes, **Windel**
hardly breathed.
Wit's loved voice:
Windel, my heart,
I very quickly knew how far from helpful, as
your dad, I'd been.
The essence of the Life-
Review
is that you experience all,
as though
you were the person you had influenced.
I really
thought I had loved you purely,
but found I had
spoiled you —
by coming closer than was wise.

We made a bond that left your mother out —
$\qquad\qquad\qquad\qquad\qquad\qquad\qquad\qquad$ **as**
also your brother and sister.
$\qquad\qquad\qquad\qquad\qquad$ **Wanda put this right**
by coming back as Strand.
$\qquad\qquad\qquad\qquad\qquad\qquad$ **(Windel** gasped,
but saw **String** nod).
$\qquad\qquad\qquad\qquad\qquad\qquad$ **But Witson ...**
$\qquad\qquad\qquad\qquad\qquad\qquad\qquad$ **Wit** paused.
Witson could never accept that you and I are
black.
$\qquad\qquad$ **Nor you perhaps that he is white.**
$\qquad\qquad\qquad\qquad\qquad\qquad\qquad\qquad\qquad$ **All**
this you will be wise to work through,
$\qquad\qquad\qquad\qquad\qquad\qquad$ **before you**
reach the space we live in now.

$\qquad\qquad\qquad\qquad\qquad\qquad$ **Windel** heaved
in her cauldron
$\qquad\qquad\qquad\qquad$ and could not draw breath.
$\qquad\qquad\qquad\qquad\qquad\qquad\qquad\qquad$ Two
of the cats withdrew from **Loam** to help her.
$\qquad\qquad\qquad\qquad\qquad\qquad\qquad$ **String**
felt **L-L**'s attention pricked again.
$\qquad\qquad\qquad\qquad\qquad\qquad$ **Wiz-dom,**
who had taught biology most of her working life,
and not lost interest in genetics since,
$\qquad\qquad\qquad\qquad\qquad\qquad$ had more
to say:
$\qquad\qquad\qquad$ *not everyone knows that through no fault*
of hers or her mother's,
$\qquad\qquad\qquad\qquad$ *Vivace had no normal birthing.*
This was deep loss to both of them.
$\qquad\qquad\qquad\qquad\qquad\qquad$ *Viv is angry*
with herself that, through her restless folly, she picked
*up the virus and has passed it on to **Vision**, although*
***Loam** is free.*
$\qquad\qquad\qquad$ *She cannot yet forgive herself for this —*

so her feelings are projected —

exactly as **Vision** saw.

What she and all of you now need to know (and a few
Earth researchers have begun to see this)

is that AIDS
need not be the killer it became once the H.I. virus was
identified.

Nor need drastic drugs be manufactured
by rich countries, still less tested on laboratory animals
(often apes captured from our forests, our very closest
gene relations, whom we poison for our imagined
well-being).

All this is literally dead end research,
though it may be many years before afflicted peoples
feel they can live without this chemical ritual.

Vision
may well be the first to make this true.

If he has children,
(and I think he will)

they may or may not carry the virus,
but it need not harm them.

Skill, who at four, had
never really thought of the virus as doing more than
add some zip to life,

laughed aloud.

Vision
stole a glance at **L-L**, who held his hand.

Wiz
continued:

a virus is the very simplest root of life,
not the real enemy mankind has been taught to fight.
This is now coming to the brink of consciousness
and it will deeply change all healing practice — as
human beings come themselves to see

what makes

them susceptible to what disease.

                    The cancers too
are under closer scrutiny, revealing gene mechanisms
never known before

                    to kill off cells when lethal mutations
damage DNA.

              Remember that genes also can mutate —
to protect from viruses evolving blindly (not realising
that to kill their hosts is fatal for them too,

                                        not

the 'live and let live' Law of Life).

                              Wick,
aware her mother's turbulence was increasing, as
she listened, said:

              Mum, why don't you and **Loam**
    use the children's fencing sticks —

                        to have a workout
    (like I do with cats)?

                    Vision got up at once
to take his own to **Windel** and bring **Skill**'s across
to give his father.

                    The cats stood back,
but they remained attentive.

                        Doubtfully,
for they did not know each other, and felt no
quarrel to resolve — even across the generations —
(indeed **Loam** had reason to be grateful for the care
this ravaged woman had brought to **Viv**'s last days),
Loam and **Windel** faced each other with their well-
used sticks.

Seeker: What's all this!

                        And how has **Wiz-dom**
        covered so much ground in seven years?

Recorder: **Wiz**

  began looking deep into her own life,
                                  mostly her part
  in the family tragedy,
                          while **Wit** was away in prison
  (**Windel** too for several years).*
                                  So she had already
  faced in herself
                      what **Vivace** is painfully rejecting still.
  Both **Wiz** and **Wit** you will recall
                                  had a new lease
  of life, when he (shall we say)
                                  came out —
  to find themselves caught up in dynamic change,
  which brought about the state of **Godwilland**.

Seeker: Yes,

  I can see all that would give them a flying start.
  But what about this astonishing understanding
  of the virus —
                      not to mention cancers?

Recorder: **Wiz-dom**

  always had a special feel for how genes work,
  and even in old age she kept up with the genome
  project
                      (although that is not recorded here).
  She half intuited all she told us there
                                  and found it
  confirmed
                  from the higher perspective open to her now.

Seeker: She doesn't miss a trick, does she!

* see **Wisdom Stranded** – Phase III

But what about
this bright idea of **Wick**'s?

Recorder: She has sharp enough
perceptions too!
                              With easy-going **Wilson**
for her father, **Wick** never let her troubles distort
her outlook,
                    as her mother has.
                                    She saw enough
of therapy at **Frinkshome**
                                    to grasp the value
of a workout.
                    (**Frink** only drugged those who resisted
such group treatment).
                              And you have learned enough
of how ray energies work
                              to see what earth **Loam**
could gain from **Windel**'s fire.

Seeker: And she
from his solid common sense,
                              if they can amicably pit
their blocked energies —

Recorder: against one another.
                                          Quite !

Loam held his stick like a quarter staff instinctively —
to parry blows he felt would come from **Windel**.
                                          But
her next move disarmed him.
                              Though her eyes
were rheumy with the pain of bitter ageing,
                              they had
not lost a power **Loam** had no means to parry.

Some
age-old instinct rose in him:
he must either fight
this woman
or be lost.
He moved his stick
to readiness to thrust.
Windel, surprised,
did likewise.
Though **Loam** was as white
as both his parents, she found she felt no animosity.

But she did feel opposed by something she had not met
before:
stolid resistance to her inborn charm.

Into this paralysed standoff came the agonised voice
of **Vivace**,
caught in her own bewildered non-event,
but glimpsing the two she felt she had reason to be
grateful to.
No!
she moaned as she sensed
their squaring up.
Loam turned instantly,
but could not see.
Vision, who had virtually never
seen his mother, could.
He knew her sound, her smell
and felt her now.
Daddie, he cried,
as the cats came
circling in,
surrounding him and **Loam**
and **Windel**
and the voice.

108

Slowly the tension eased,
as **Windel** sobbed and clung to **Loam** and **Vision**,
while **String** drew both her children to her,
                                        and the cats
moved to rearrange themselves,
                                        enfolding also
                                                Wick.

As **Light** in his icy region of the South, watched
the play of Aurora in the cold, dark sky,
                                        he knew
he was witnessing some secret of the cosmos.
                                        Behind
the familiar greens and golds,
                                        he felt all seven
colours of the spectrum lay,
                                as rays of different energies
relayed to earth, not only from the sun,
                                but way beyond
from the twelve constellations of the Zodiac, shedding
their age-old influence upon whatever came within
their visual focal distance, whether to be seen
or seeing him.
                        From here in the most southern
continent, he could see
                                not the Northern Pole Star,
but the Southern Cross.
                        In awe, **Light** felt he knew
something of the sacrifice a **Logos** makes
                                        in making
manifest long dreamt creation.
                                        Was this what
he had to come so far South to find?
                                        To grasp

the perhaps unending process, following an ultra burst
(an **Outbreath**)
                                    of unfolding growth in sunlight
from the colliding electric particles round atoms,
whose nuclear elements translate to different chemicals,
thus a controlled release of their colossal energy :
first in simple virus rods,
                                            which still dart
among the building blocks of natural life,
                                            one-celled
bacterial conquerors of land and sea, whose progeny
have survived whatever circumstances nature posed —
of annihilating heat or cold or pressure.
                                            Not all
bacteria, or we could hardly boil away the most
invidious in cooking, or keep foods safe by freezing ...

And what of those strangest microbes of them all, who,
finding oxygen a poison,
                                    take refuge in our gut,
where they have made themselves as indispensable
to us,
        as we find breathing the air that killed them.
                                            Yet,
when they first needed respite,
                                    there was no US
to hide in.
                        By what amazing concilorium
did microscopic beasties,
                                warmed by sun falling on
stagnant pools,
                        agree to form alliances round nuclei,
to build up shapely bodies, multiplicities of specialising
cells, able to preserve their own integrity,
                                    by excelling
in some one essential skill each learned to offer

for
the greater good of all:
                          that individual
                                    we have each
become?

                    All this at least a billion years ago!
What, thought **Light**, have we individuals done since
to equal this?
                                    And how
did this ancient microcosmic triumph link
                                    to the even
tinier cosmic strings
                          his grandfather, **Leo**, claimed
were the basic entities enshrining difference?

                                    Then
he saw:
          the manifesting **Logos** uttered sounds —
                                    to hold,
in exquisite tension,
                          these not quite pinpoint particles,
these vibrating strings, which,
                          touched,
                                    float into colour
in the cosmos,
                    submicroscopic bubbles of a billion hues,
visible as bands of light —
                          until, in their own naturally
selected time, those that survive the bracing solar wind
form viral life:
                          hence at last the complex biology
we know today, forms best adapted to conditions
found.
                    (**Light** stirred in his thermal sleeping bag
to scratch an itch.)

Perhaps some forms took passage
on great comets, sent from their sky HQ as messengers
or maybe as wilful travellers on their own, to spill
their seed,
                    as the comet's orbit sought like a moth
the sun,
          thus melting ice droplets
                              (Icarus wings)
to leave a trail
          carrying not death, but life
                              in its long tail.

And what a tale such comets have to tell ...
                              The bleep
of **Light**'s mobile broke his reverie.
                              E-mails
from his far off family had bounced from a satellite
to find him here:
                    String's vivid account
of the return of **Windel**/news of **Vivace**'s death
and her exacting further life/the new interventions
of the cats —
          welded by **Wiz-dom**'s solemn input
as to how AIDS might be disarmed.
                    This helped to melt
the ice **Light** lived with —
                    most of all a note
from seven year old **Love-Lyric** (unaware
of her father's childhood powers), to tell him how
she kept the garden free of snaring brambles,
by simply asking them to remove themselves,
having no business to be there —
                    which they did
she said by shrinking back into the ground, not
shrivelling.
          Light conveyed gravely to his only daughter

his reassurance that his absence from the household
had not left his family resourceless —

                        with messages
to her mother that he hoped to be back within the year
having learned all that he had come to find.

                                 He was/
he had:
                         String found him gentler
and more noticing, as though something inside him
had connected up, which had before been loosely
dangling.

                            What
they did not anticipate were the kinds of influence **L-L**
and **Vision** would respond to as they grew.
                        The new
century was bringing changes faster than almost any
could adjust to.
                  When the two children, hardly
teenagers, yet well into puberty, took off without
a word,
         it seemed frighteningly like **Vivace**.
                          But at least
they could assume (consulting **Leaf** and **Loam**),
                          both
would be together.
                  A fax from **Belle**,
though enlightening, was no comfort.
                        She said
her esoteric sources had some time ago predicted
that as the new millennium began, the energy
of the First Ray of **Will** would pour directly on to, and
so through,
        humanity,

not mediated by the force
of **Love-Wisdom** at the heart of planetary life,
as in the past was so.

Vision and **L-L**
would likely be specially sensitive to such a force,
but also ready to make positive response —
though
hardly to reveal their whereabouts.

This
sounded a strong chord for **Light**, whose enchantment
in the presence of **Aurora Australis** had faded
in the too anxious present.
In a flurry of faxes
between him and **Belle**, **Light**, for the first time,
discovered **The Treatise on the Seven Rays**,˙
whose five volumes formed the inner core
of **Belle**'s esoteric understanding.
From her account
of each such Ray (the first book even linked the seven
to the colours of our spectral waveband),
Light
saw at once his dominating ray was Three, with not
a little of the force of One (of which **String** too was
clearly not devoid).
Love-Lyric, he felt,
would be predominantly Two, and maybe mostly
on that second line of force,
even numbers, 2/4/6,
the indispensable relating rays.˙˙
The First Ray line,

˙ see – *Appendix 3*
˙˙ see **Strands of Wisdom** - *Interlude*

of driving force (uneven numbers, 1 through 7) were
usually seen as masculine.
                              But how to deduce
Vision's ray make-up, so sense whose motivation lay
behind this?

                         Vision had shown no signs
of awkward adolescence, but he was increasingly
responsive to **Love-Lyric**'s loving nature,

                                                    she
to the world's need.
                         Indeed it seemed he saw not only
other worlds, but more of this.
                              And what he saw
he shared with **L-L**
                         (more than he sought to balance
skills with **Skill**, who in his turn turned inward —
to imbibe the skills of learning schools provide).

L-L in her blossoming cried to know firsthand
people and places **Vision** said he saw.

                                        String,
who now ran a full-time office for **GL** from home,
(the first established in the southern world)
                                        was torn
between mother agony
                    and pride
                         Love-Lyric should
so very early feel
                    ready to fulfil her global task.

                                             Though
she guessed **Skill** would know something of the plans
they'd laid
                    (he had taken on caring for the cats, as
though he always had, so must have been instructed

by **L-L**),
                    she did not press him for what he likely felt
he could not share.
                              Light, more confident
in **L-L**'s survival skills, was a shade more sanguine.

A picture postcard from some remote and forested
mountain town, far to the west of **Godwilland**,
rewarded weeks of waiting —
                              but even that
made clear the two had left some days before
the card was postmarked.

                              For as much
as **Vision** could see pictures at a distance,
                              Love-Lyric
could see inside the people they would meet:
                                        she
seemed to know, especially, what might trigger
the unstable to explode.
                              She thus trod gently
round their wounded places,
                              while not avoiding
tender issues crying to be salved.
                              Since
many trained psychiatrists ignored this skill
                              (or had
they never understood it?),
                              it drew **Vision** and **L-L**
closer and yet more close to border places, territorial
boundaries, where the disaffected gathered —
and 'border cases' multiplied.
                              This coinciding
of geography and psyche

                              plunged them
into a strange milieu
                    of opportunity and danger:
sought after for their felt wisdom, they continuously
lived,
          where distrust and doubt
                                        weighed
like corrosive kerosene containers.

                                        Only
their own unsevered bonding, almost from the time
of **Vision**'s birth (within a year of **Love-Lyric**'s),
could hope to keep them safe —
                    now welded
on a blacksmith's anvil by the hammering the world
rained down.

                              Slowly it dawned,
as the months grew to a year
                    and thence to two,
that explosiveness they met in people seeking healing,
was not so much due to border conflicts over territory,
or even to race difference, to skin colour, or speech
patterns.
                    It was a deeper and more inner thing
to do with gender,
                    yet not so obvious as wives
and husbands fighting to dominate their households,
                                        nor
children bursting for freedom from their parents
(though both were often reasons people came).
                                        It was
more, they felt, to do with inner conflict of both sexes in
the same person
                    crying out
                              not to be suppressed.

Women, they came to realise

                                            (though not
from their own childhoods),

                                had been so long
repressed,

               their breaking bonds today

                            had upset
a balance men had come to take as theirs by right.

So why doesn't this happen between you and me?
Love-Lyric queried, as they rested together
in the hills under a tree, whose branches shaded them
when sun rose fierce.

                          **I suppose because
you've never felt I bullied you, so you don't have
to escape from who I am.**

                        But that seems to mean,
said **L-L** wondering,

                      that you must have as much
feminine in you as masculine.

                    **Yes, and you as much
male as female.**

                 **We seem to have between us
a natural balance —**

                which I suppose is why

                      **people
seek us out to heal them,**

                Vision finished vigorously.

L-L, after a dreamy pause:

                  Vision, *what sort of child*
do you think we would produce?

                      Life,
said **Vision** instantly.

                  **Our child would be so like life
it would be androgynous — with all the attributes**

of either gender.
                                        It might even not
be possible to tell which sex it was.
                                        It would be us
in one:
              able to have babies and to impregnate ...

But you're not old enough
                                   he added soberly,
and fidgetted as he felt delicious writhings.
                                        We're both
still under age.
                                   I wouldn't be
by the time the child was born,
                              said **L-L** demurely,
responding to **Vision**'s instant imaging, and excited
by the thought their task in life, now they had learned
so much just being in the world,
                              might be to birth
a new kind of human able to dissolve the barriers
they had come to see
                         as obstacles to human beings
everywhere.

Seeker: Aren't they straining out a gnat
                 and swallowing a camel (as the good book says)?

Recorder: *How so?*

Seeker: Well, I thought the point of all this 20th
                 century healing of the psyche was for weaning
                 people from dependence on their mothers — to get
                 on their own two feet as separate individuals
                 with their own true identity.
                                        Surely that's bound
                 to be uncomfortable, not soothing.

Recorder: *That's half*
the truth, I'm sure, but maybe not all.
                                                  And it's not
only mothers who have to be outgrown.
                                                  People
these two come across are in that space already,
or they wouldn't be congregating at these conflict-
ridden borders, where **L-L** *and* **Vision** *find them.*

How is **Love** *ever going to manifest on this planet*
(as our intuition and **Belle***'s esoteric sources, as well*
as religion for the past two thousand years, tell us
is now grossly overdue) —
                                        unless discerning people,
like **Vision** *and* **Love-Lyric***,*
                                                  respond to them
with healing love?

Seeker: (deflated)   Yes, I suppose that must
         be right.
                              Perhaps that's what I've been seeking
         all this time …

Recorder: (drily)   *Perhaps it is.*

Seeker: The children of course
         have done their own uncomfortable bit by leaving
         home and fending for themselves.

Recorder: *Exactly!*
         At least they've made a start —
                                        though I doubt
         it'll all be plain sailing for them from now on …

Seeker: Yet
         they still seem very far ahead.

Recorder: *They're meant to be.*
                 They are the harbingers of the New Aquarian Age.
                 Life *will be growing up well into this twenty first*
                 century we've just begun.

Seeker: But what about
                 this business of androgyny?
                                                     Has anyone
                 suggested Aquarians will be androgynous?

Recorder: No,
                 I don't think anyone has
                                    so far.
                                                     But it's a fact
                 that babies are increasingly being found to be
                 of indeterminate sex —
                                    which parents consider such
                 a stigma, they are only too glad for gynaecologists
                 to designate them male or female —

Seeker: even if it means
                 surgical manipulation —

Recorder: *which may not fit the child's*
                 own self-perception, as s/he grows.
                                          Vision *and* **L-L**
                 will never allow that to happen to their progeny,
                 I promise you.

                      What neither **Love-Lyric**
in her zest,
                 nor her beloved **Vision,**
                                     had allowed for
was the stigma that would attach to her becoming

'casually' pregnant as a nomadic teenager.
                                        Like many,
she suffered nausea during her early months, as
the rampant, sperm-driven blastocyst
                                                    dug
into her sheltering womb wall.
                                        Moreover,
the more of her body's attention the foetus claimed,
the less **Love-Lyric**'s gift of drawing in supplies:
a kind of comfort they relied on.

                                        Vision found
he must resort to begging;
                        often he was turned away.
He remembered films of cheetahs he had watched:
lean creatures, who four times out of five, after intense
bursts of speed,
                                would lose their prey —
relief for a TV viewer
                        as a baby impala
                                        leapt away,
but not for a would be father with an expectant wife
and precious embryo to feed.
                                Vision thinned,
while **Love-Lyric**'s belly swelled.
                                As the third month
slid into the fourth,
                        their sore feet brought them
to a backpackers hostel, where **Vision** found a guitar
abandoned with a broken string he mended swiftly.

For the next few months, they paid their way
                                        by singing:

in markets
                or at border posts,
                                wherever folk formed
bottle-necks —
                waiting for the next train out, the bus
back home, or just for their cars to pass through
check points.
                While **Vision** strummed, **Love-Lyric**
mischievously sang her favorite song,
                                when her belly
swelling became visible.

WHAT IS NATURAL?

What is not nature — if our nature made it?
When we say:
                        'It's against nature'
we can only mean:
                        against our conception
of what nature is.
                        And what could be more
natural than conception?
                                Nature's way
of making more
                        of what already is!

Nature is
                what is
                                when seed
is carried to its fruiting,
                                nurtured
in inner contact
                        with what
                                sprouted it —
and then let go,
                        if mammal,
                                to come back
for outer nourishment.
                                Do plants
take greater risks

                    or less —
                                        by trusting
        wind or water
                              to disperse their seed
        to favoured habitats?

                                        Mammals
        push their fruitings
                                  out of darkness
        into glaring light —
                                  often before eyes
        are ready
                          for the gift
                                        of sight.

        Birds and reptiles
                                  fashion shell
        to house their unborn young,
                                            then
        build a rampart
                                  out of earth
        or twigs:
                          a nest for nurturing —
        a little fortress to prevent marauding:

        Nature protecting nature from herself!

        So nature already knows a part of her
        attacks,
                    a part defends.
                                        Nature
        is nature.
                          Nature is the given,
        but by whom?
                          Nature is data.

Then **L-L** would rest on the ground, while **Vision**'s cap
would fill with coins or bills dropped in —
                                        as much
for her pluck and new found radiance, as for any
understanding of her song.

124

And **Vision**

would take up the theme:

STARDUST

Is Nature only data?

          Or is it also cause?

Is not the will to live and reproduce

          as natural

as growth and nourishing of seed?

          What

immediately caused us then?

          Are we stardust?

A star is a vast particle

          of dust:

some so vast

          they burn too fast

          and bust.

We live on a piece of named debris.

          Dust

left over when our Sun was formed:

          a star

of moderate size

          and cool decorum,

which did not suck in and swallow up

          all

dust available

          as it grew itself.

          So

we,

          our brother/sister planets,

          formed:

of the same spewed out dust —

          but smaller,

cooler,

          not nuclear factories;

          finding

rock and grass and trees

          more satisfactory,

and grateful for the distant heat

that let's

lungs breathe

and makes hearts beat,

that photosynthesises

wheat

and all the other plants

we eat.

We are all manufactured

stardust.

By the end of the seventh month, **Love-Lyric**'s weight
in front was causing a shifting in her balance
her joints and muscles found it hard to bear.
Her mind kept turning to her lissom cats

and all

the kittens **Skill** must by now have taken care of,
or found homes for — (she was sure he would not
drown them).

Her sixteenth birthday having come

and gone, time felt propitious for returning home.
It was three years nearly to the day, since the two
had launched themselves to meet the world head on,
without the sheltering love of parents.

(And **Vision**

anyway had hardly known his mother).

Both felt

confident of welcome, despite the worry they hoped
their picture postcards had allayed.

These

had not revealed **Love-Lyric**'s pregnancy.

Mother,

I knew you would understand I came into the world
with work to do.

A part of it is giving birth
to the next generation and it had to be prepared for.
You know you would never have agreed if we had
told you.
                    I know, I know **String** sobbed,
as she hugged her pregnant prodigal to her.

                                                    Light

enlightened by **Aurora Australis**
                                        refrained

from rebuking **Vision**, who,
                            before he left to make
his peace with **Loam** (and **Leaf**, his grandmother),
wanted to share his thoughts about the baby's
likely nature, problems it could face in School —
playground and changing room especially.
                                        Let's

wait and see,
                    said **Light**, brusquely,
                                        as he recalled
his own childhood hardships.
                            We have still to find
out how sure Wiz' prophecies concerning AIDS
turn out to be —
                    though you look fit enough.

I think he could do with feeding up, said **String**,
                                                    but

you've certainly taken care of **Love-Lyric**.
                                        Stay here

and eat with us.
                    Leaf *and your father both*
are coming here to join us when they close.

As

Windel had let herself feel soothed by her family
and their cats, she had drifted into sleep where were
no barriers between 'here' (where we live),
and 'there', the life hereafter, where her father
and mother and **Viv**, her grandchild, dwelt.
That did not mean there was no difference in the felt
conditions: it did mean you could not escape
from feelings into doing (as we try to 'here').

                                                    Only
changing feelings could release from pain.

                                             But how?

Vivace felt the urgency of **Windel**'s thought,
was penetrated by it to a new perception
of who she was
                        and where
                                    and why she had
felt assailed by female demons, but no longer ......

Peering into the dark,
                        Viv half felt,
                                         half saw
a bewildered wraith float by,
                                    another —
like purposelessly drifting jellyfish ....

They don't know they are dead.
                        Help them.
                                    How?

Windel felt her energy blend with **Viv**'s, saw too
the floating wraiths.

Who are they?

her mind asked,
as more and more came drifting into the field of vision
she and **Viv** were sharing.

Unwitting victims
came the unknown voice both she and **Vivace** heard:
They will go on drifting till they understand.
They trusted blindly and they paid the price.

You

trusted no one and have also paid.

Time now

for balancing accounts.

Am I dead too, then?

Windel asked the voice.

No, said **Vivace**

I can see
your cord and it is still attached —

You are asleep

and dreaming

said the voice
that seemed to know and wished to share its knowing.
You are also strong enough to help Vivace
help these ghosts to know they need to reconnect
their consciousness with who they were and are —
and so begin to live again.

The shock of sudden

death is always that:

a shock.

But how

did they die then?

Windel and **Vivace** asked.

They went to their doctor, trusting him to take
away their pain.

He did.

But how?

By translating them from your world into this.

They trusted blindly —

                           and therefore do not know

they died.

                Were they very lonely then?

                                Viv asked.

Ask them.

            Some of them were old

                         and some well off.

Ask them how they felt.

                        But ask them gently

or they will refuse what they now need to know.

You and Windel can together do this.

                                It will

release your pain somewhat and bring you both

to better understanding —

                       of yourselves and them.

I will be there —

                although you cannot see me

                                  yet.

And so it came about over the next months and years
(while **Love-Lyric** and **Viv**'s infected son travelled
this world),

        that **Windel** 'here',

                              Vivace 'there',

joined forces:

                  for **Viv**'s purifying, through her Life
Review,

            the other side of death,

                        and for **Windel**'s
redemption from her unforgivingness — before
time came to leave her body in old age
(as had her parents).

                                Nor
was it only the old who drifted toward them, lost —
and sometimes terrified:

                              a little, shivering, scabrous,
bleeding girl — her scarred wraith still tied to her earth
memory —
            swam into **Windel**'s ken
                              and broke her heart.

This **Windel** had resisted through all her labouring
for AIDS sufferers — including her caring for the waif
Vivace had become.
                        But her parents' presence,
combined with the cats' concern, had lowered
the ramparts that had made her heart a fort.
Vivace felt the difference as they worked:
                              first to free
this litle battered human from her body's clinging,
then to warm her frightened wraith in space.
Here several cats **Wick** or **L-L** had kept on earth
(their essence long since passed into feeling realms),
brought to her all the imagined tender warmth
her soul had starved for in the northern place
her parents sent her to for 'betterment'
                              from southern 'less-
developed' **Godwilland**.

Seeker: How is all this linked up healing
            possible?

Recorder: *By tapping into the one energy source.*

Seeker: The source behind the Seven Rays, you mean?

Recorder: (nodding)   Yes,
            the energy of the vacuum, which is tapped, when
            our meditation goes beyond our mental focussing
            to reach the space where everything is one.
                                          This

happened first to **Wit**, *you will remember, when
at his wits' end after 15 years in prison, he first saw*˙
Wanda *and his mother,* **Wisdom** *(who is now
back in the world, as* **Love-Lyric,** *and about to give
birth*
            to **Life**
                        with **Vision**'*s sperm).*

                                        Love-Lyric
was by now so vast and weary with her baby's weight,
it was not hard to persuade her into **String**'s car,
for a checkup in hospital she had not had anywhere
since conceiving.
                        The scanner revealed a medley
of tiny hearts with no clear indication of their gender.

But —
        how many?
                        L-L asked,
                                        excited but nonetheless
aghast.
                **We can't be sure, but certainly not less
than four.**
                                        There could be more.
The puzzled expert looked at her:
                                        **Aren't you
concerned**
                        **we don't know whether they are girls
or boys ?**

                        No, because I hope they're both.

I mean we cannot tell the sex of any of them.

˙ see **Strands of Wisdom** – Phase I

That's what I thought you meant, said **L-L** calmly.

It was the specialist's turn to feel aghast.

                                A few weeks
later,
       L-L's waters broke —
                     and she cascaded,
(rather than laboured)
                       to bring forth.
So many were the babes,
                  and therefore all
so small,
           they almost tumbled out of **L-L**'s
womb.
        More like a litter
                said her brother,
Skill, as a further surge convulsed his sister
and he wrapped the fifth of **L-L**'s fruitings
in a dry, warm blanket by the fourth, while
String and **Vision** did so
                 with the sixth
and seventh.
          That at last was it.
                  Seven babies
came into the world through the loving penetration
of the minds and hearts and bodies of **Vision**
and **Love-Lyric** in their teens, knowing they sought
to bring together once for all
               the qualities of male
and female gender in one form.

              All seemed healthy
as they yelled for the body warmth that had expelled
them one by one,

weighing barely a kilo each.

In hospital each of these babies would have been
placed in an incubator till they doubled in size
and weight.
Much would be later said
as to their indeterminate gender being due
to lack
of peri- and post-natal care.
No one
had ever reared seven babies born from a single egg
and nurtured in one womb simultaneously.
The scandal
was compounded by their mother's having no history
of IVF.
Nevertheless, since they had been registered
and diagnosed before their birth, the authorities had
no recourse but to allot them housing
and one helper.
That was enough, with **Skill**;
for several of the cats,
(who had gathered round to witness this event,
so much more like their own than human birthing)
were fully ready to assist with grooming, and one
or two with suckling —
their own kittens overdue
for weaning, and the need of these mewing newborns
obvious.

In nearly as many colours as the cats,
from velvet black to pink albino, with red and brown
and yellow to fill in, the whole clutch of babies (plus
grass to play on, blue sky beyond the sun and deep
mauve ocean rearing to break the shoreline) made
up the rainbow spectrum human beings live with.

And one was pied (human genetics not always quite
preventing).
                    First to emerge was duly labelled **Life**.
The next two, of distinctive mammal gender:
                                        a girl,
then boy,
            they called **Vera** (for veracity)
                                    and **Lucy**
(for **Lucifer**, Bearer of the Light to Earth), thus dowsing
the emphasis on gender difference.

                                    The fourth
was **Laughter**, and s/he surely had to be:
                                        caught
in the middle of this sevenfold tribe, s/he must seek
to relate to trios fore and aft.

                                The final three,
as their grandfather, **Light**, was quick to see and say,
had to reflect the coming down to earth
                                    of the Fifth
and Sixth
            and Seventh Rays,
                            and also the paternity
of **Vision**.
            So they named the albino fifth child, **Verve**,
because of the mind energy required, for bringing
through diversity in Nature (with overtones of the nerve
it takes to do so).
                    The sixth, after some deliberation,
they named with an adjective and not a noun, thus
emphasising with what sensitivity
                                s/he would link
the fact of being
                    with the actual form —
                                    so called hir

Vital,
    and matched it by naming the seventh, **Vigour** —
to carry the full weight of being physical.

                    L-L adored
them all, but with so many needed helpers, it was hard
to tell who was who —
             and bond with each.
                        Only
for an hour or so each day could she try to hold
and feed each one,
               since she, as well as they,
must have rest and sleep.
            Had **Skill** and **Vision**
not been so attentive
          (as also **String** and **Light**,
whose home they would litter till the new house
was ready), **L-L** could only have felt like the woman
who lived in a shoe in the nursery rhyme (and why
was she old ... unless their grandmother?)
                   L-L
drifted into blissful sleep, with one of her babies
perched on either arm:
          black velvet **Vigour**
and albino **Verve**.

       Vital was as beautifully pied
as reindeer, in shades of fawn and white and brown.
The yellow baby, **Laughter**, had the wrinkled visage
of a Chinese sage, carved in ancient ivory, with turned
up corners to hir mouth, and eyebrows raised.
            Lucy
was the copper red of fired earth, with the eagle nose
of an Amerindian chief;
         Vera, a fresh-faced svelte
brunette, born with hair down the back of her neck.
             Life

was born hairless, but would soon become a blonde
with sprouting duckling down all over.

How long,
Love-Lyric wondered, before s/he would become
a swan?

String had virtually abandoned
her P/C (and thus her **GL** work) for the task of keeping
everyone supplied with food — the multiple mother,
specially, in milk enough to feed as many as she could
for as long as they felt inclined.

The seven
babies did not share the same metabolism, but rather
tended to mature in different areas of experience
or expertise, according to the dominance of their rays.

Vigour, being most attuned to physical earth, was
faster than the rest to crawl and walk; while **Lucy**
would talk soonest, and show traits in common
with his mother's father, **Light**.

Though **Life**
had come first to meet the Earth (or did those who
named hir call hir **Life** because the first to come?),
s/he seemed in no hurry to become a swan, but kept
hir duckling down so long, s/he was outstripped
by the later babies, who preferred more solid food
and orange juice, months before **Vera** and **Lucy** —
and this 'slothful' **Life**.

Laughter seemed easy
either way.

It was a full six months
before the family of nine with their helper, **Hermia**,
could be transferred to the four-bed bungalow, (leased

by the local council) only two of which must house all
seven babies, if parents and helper were to have
some solo space.
But for the time being it was luxury,
compared with the flat they came from, where every
chair and corner was a creche, a niche to bloom in,
if you could.
But the cats missed them
and they missed the cats.

Though **Hermia** had
gone in daily, to help with the never ending baby care,
she had not had nights to deal with.
Indeed
the cats had been the main source of succour
in those hours when adult humans like to sleep,
and cats to (hunt or) play.
Hermia soon realised this
and would take a couple of wakeful babies back
to bed with her, to relieve the cacophony (that reigned
in the absence of the feline energy), while **Vision**
brewed up tea and **Love-Lyric** suckled whosever turn
it seemed to be for milk.

Cats or no cats, **Hermia**
found herself responding to the energy that came
from the seven siblings, growing now from swarming
babyhood
to a radiating centre of coherence.

Despite (or perhaps because) of their small space,
the seven siblings tended to keep themselves in check:
so different in their temperaments, they noticed faults
in one another and could be generous in allowing
for them.

If someone spilled or broke whatever
they were using, another would help to clear the mess;
and maybe, in a crisis, all would come rushing, so
no one was to blame —
                    not three but seven
                                musketeers.

Thus, by the time they were due for Nursery School,
at three, all had taught themselves or one another,
to read and write and use their number skills.
                                    (**Verve**,
here, was especially helpful to the last two siblings,
Vital and seventh ray **Vigour**, who never dropped
or broke or spilled a thing.)
                        Thinking in sevens, they
'used up' their five right fingers by the age of two,
but adding in **Hermia** and both their parents, they
brought a triumphal use of both their hands by three.

These skills meant they would outgrow the Playgroup
almost before they reached it.
                        They were therefore soon
passed on to 'proper' School,
                        where they arrived
on a small fleet of motor scooters, which they parked
neatly at the cycle shed.
                        This would probably
have drawn from older boys the cry:
                                "Here come
the Seven Dwarves!" —
                        but for that radiant energy,
which came from each, no matter whether all were
present.
                        So no one bullied them, because
as soon as one seemed cornered, the rest sprang
into visibility around them.

Before long
this was true if anyone at all was bullied: there were
the siblings
                              like the Seven Samurai.

Seeker: Well,
            they're certainly ahead of things this time!
                                              But what's
            all this about coherent energy?

Recorder: *You know coherent*
            LASER light, which surgeons use instead of knives
            for certain crucial operations?
                                    Well, this is that same
            energy of photons, no longer distributed at random
            (as has been considered normal throughout nature),
            but gathered to a focus by the mental energy latent
            in all living things, though only in humans coming
            into consciousness, and never to be used unless
            evoked by need expressed.
                                          It is still awaiting
            mastery at group level (where we see it here) —
                                                    while
            at this time, of course, it is wholly beyond the use
            of nations —
                        still less the international community.

Seeker: Ah … yes !
                                    I wonder if this would be
            an underlying factor in that remarkable synchronicity
            we witnessed,
                        back in the days when **Wit** was still
            to be delivered from his prison, and all the lights
            in the Great Stadium went out, just as his singing
            reached its powerful climax.

Recorder: *Yes, indeed:*
that would be a pure example of cosmic coherency
of energies,
                    available at a most propitious moment,
to yield a transhumanly desired effect,
                                    which most
call 'miracle'.
                    (Actually, though none would know this,
Hermia *is the great grand daughter of* **Wit***'s helper,*
Herm*, whose expertise took* **Wit** *beyond his peak*
and so to freedom, as you said, at the televised
concert in the City Stadium.˙)
                    The difference here is
simply that these seven children have this coherence
in their normal span.
                    Together embodying
the Seven Rays,
                    and nurtured nine months
in the one womb space, they have come forth here
with one another's special qualities as well.

Seeker: *So,*
what each may not have, another seems very
willing to supply.

Recorder: *Yes, these children are the height*
of evolutionary endeavour, while still in human
form — which after all derives from mammal life.

This may be entirely different on the other planets,
none of which shows signs of being at present able
to sustain condensed (and therefore viable) bio-life,
as we understand it.

˙ see **Strands of Wisdom** *– Phase I*

Seeker: Do you mean there could be Intelligences on the other planets — angelic life?

Recorder: *There could be,*

but then, many are aware of devic life on Earth, especially in growing plants and soil. Some see it as the substance of our being, a parallel evolution to our own, intrinsic to it, but not in dense matter.

They manifest just beyond the electromagnetic spectrum, where ultrasound precipitates in drops of light.

And devas, of course, have no freewill. Joy, for them, lies in surrendering to whatever seems required of them.

Seeker: No!

And you say they are the substance of ourselves?

Surely that would account for our positively wilful waywardness, as to whether we want our own or one another's way.

This must make them our **yin**, traditionally known as 'female', where our freewill, human side — is **yang**.

Recorder: *Yes, in effect, that's right.*

There are devas of all four ancient elements: earth and water, air and fire — each pair of which is allotted also gender in astrology.

Seeker: Yes,

Fire and Air being masculine, while Earth and Water are dubbed female, which makes them doubly so !

I wonder what will happen to that conception, if androgyny is to become a norm.

Recorder: *I wonder too, especially as the opposites in astrology*
retain their gender signature,
while altering the element
they work through: **Leo***, for example, is a fire sign,*
but **Aquarius***, its opposite, is a sign in air,*
both male.

Elsewhere, the kind of norm androgyny might become
was working out in more than one dimension.
Heedless
of the world's dispute, as to whether the age of puberty
in girls, especially, was hastening,
the radiant septet
was forging faster through its adolescence into so-
called adulthood, than anything the world had yet
perceived.
And simultaneously physical gender
imprinted itself upon the final three:
Verve
and **Vigour** becoming noticeably male; dappled
Vital a full-blown woman.
But there were subtle
differences:
though albino **Verve** retained the mental
adroitness of Ray Five, this came now with all
the psychic vulnerabilities we associate with female
gender, and indeed with menstruation (though **Verve**
lacked the internal apparatus to induce this).
He was,
of course, protected from incoherence by his siblings'
radiant strength, no less available at this crux.
Reindeer
Vital was now his firmest ally.
So phenomenal
was her development, she virtually became a female
warrior, displaying all the grace of the hidden dragon

and the Chinese tiger, as she learned to box, not only
with her hands, with **Vigour**, nothing detracting from
her femaleness.

Since **Vigour** also practised
Kendo swordsmanship (encouraged by his father,
Vision and his uncle, **Skill**), these last three formed
a formidable trio before they reached their teens.

Verve
also often linked with his brother, **Lucy**, in seeking
the sense behind the cosmos.

Learn, who at 42,
rejoiced his father's heart by becoming involved
with cosmic supersymmetry and thence with various
theories of strings (after his Ph.D. received acclaim),
had been approached concerning this by two
of his great grand children, **Verve** and **Lucy**, who
were not yet twelve.

Feeling unable to reduce
this complex theme to terms they could encompass,
he passed them on to **Leo**, who, coming up to 70,
was already being hugely entertained by **Laughter**,
asking him such questions as what is the difference
between playing an instrument

and using one?

Is it what you do with it?

Or does it have to be
a different thing?

A P/C,

suggested **Laughter**,
is surely an instrument you use.

Does that mean,
Leo, you are only playing,
although you have made
your living out of your guitar ?

I haven't really,

Leo laughed.

I swapped with Laurel

and she earned

our bread, while I brought up the kids.

OOOoooh!

hooted **Laughter,**

we brought up ourselves —

didn't we ? —

as **Verve** and **Lucy** joined them.

What

*do **Vision** and **Love-Lyric** do, now that you're all*

grown up?

Laurel swivelled round from her P/C

to ask.

Ah, yes! said **Laughter,**

I think you've raised a question there, as to what

is happening now people live much longer,

(though it is a wholly open question as to whether

this truly is a sign of humanity's development)

as well as what parents do, when we no longer

need them.

Actually Vision sees clearly

into the next dimension, so he and our mother

do much to clear the fog, gathered between

our human physical bodies

and our feeling-

thoughts she has always known the way to heal.

(Among us, Vera does this best).

Verve and **Lucy**

were closing in on **Leo**, to ask him what 'M' Theory

really was:

Ah, said **Leo**,

for whom this overarching

and mysterious thesis had not yet been posited —

in his young 'string' days,

maybe we need

a family gathering with **Learn** and **Light**, as well
as your parents,

                              to explore this fully in a way
that might 'throw light' for all of us.

                                                 Where are
the rest of you?

                                            Verve said he thought
Vital was helping **Vigour** with the animals they kept.
We don't eat them, you know, but we make
a living out of selling them to those who do.

                                                             We
just eat the eggs and drink the milk and knit up
wool.

                    When we were little, our parents needed
lamb and bacon for the household.

                                                 The animals
like us,

              so we keep them,

                              for they have no fear.
Lucy explained:

                              We kill them reverently
and they know it is not the end for them,

                                                             but
release —

              so they are very willing

                                            to let us use
their bodies for a living.

                                            They probably
wouldn't mind it, if we ate them,

                                            but our bodies
do not seem to have the need.

                                                     Yours
could do with some red blood, said **Laurel**, *looking*
up and down at albino **Verve**.

                                            So, when
are we going to have this Conference?

Recorder: *That*

              points up some of the directions this new androgyny
              seems about to take.

146

Seeker: Yes, it does,

but it raises other
issues I also feel the need to question.

Recorder: *Such as?*

Seeker: Well, **Laughter** just there threw out the notion
that living longer is a highly questionable virtue.
Yet medical scientists are proud to tell us it is now
a fact of life we should all of us aspire to — so even
centenarians will be commonplace.

And many
octogenarians take the view their wisdom is required
to keep the balance because the young grow up so
fast.

Recorder: *Yes, there may even be two opposing trends
at work here.*

*There often are, as Ray Six moves out
and Ray Seven presses in, with what works best.*

*Most
esotericists (**Belle** among them) are convinced
that civilisations rise and crystallise*

(so die)

*much
faster than they did.*

*Growth certainly is speeding up:
technical as well as physical.*

*It would be surprising if
our individual micro-patterns did not reflect the macro
culture —*

*though the world's poorest
have hardly yet reached anything like the three score
years and ten the Bible boasts.*

Seeker: And only the rich west has shown the trend to live to its eighties — and beyond.

Recorder: *Death we must learn to understand, as not our enemy but our friend,*

for not our end,
yet also not to be deliberately sought, just to evade our tasks.

Seeker: Which brings me to my other question: **Lucy** and **Verve** seemed very keen to assure **Laurel** that he and his family do not eat the beasts they rear, but make a living out of them instead.

That really seems to me the last word in hypocrisy!

Recorder: (laughing): *Yes, it does rather, doesn't it!*

But there are several levels you can look at vegetarianism from.

Lucy *is not taking a moral stance, because he knows, as all the seven do, that there is in the end no death — whether we incarnate again*

or remain where ***Vivace*** *is about to find herself.*

What may be much more relevant is the effect on all of us of using animals as though they did not matter —

squandering them (whether painfully or not) for medical experiments that solve very little in the sickness stakes.

Seeker: How so, when lethal genes get passed on so dramatically, and we need to isolate precisely what is happening?

Recorder: *Being precise is hardly what most research can hope for.*

Most often we find different interpretations given rise to from the same findings, which are then fought out, as on a battlefield.

Genes are not so easily isolated.

Like causes, they come in consequential chains that interlink.

There is really no such thing as a lethal gene — merely unfortunate effects tied up with gene efforts to rebalance something else — exactly as we find in social living.

What **Wiz** *had to say about viruses is much more germane than animal research.*

Viruses are life — and we are full of them;

probably at root they make us up.

They and we must learn to live together.

'Getting rid'

of anything is fatal —

Seeker: as back we come again to learn the lesson in a different form!

Recorder: *Form is the only thing that ever dies.*

And as energy dynamises form, conscience arises from complexity, as consciousness unfolds itself.

Viv,
accordingly, was startled to begin to find herself
in sunny uplands.
What could have given rise to such
a change in her surroundings?
You willed it,
came the unseen voice she now knew well.
***You worked
so hard with Windel in Bewilderment,
you let in
light, and now it is your lot to bask in it.***
Look !
Toward her were coming a rejuvenated **Wit** and **Wiz**,
whom **Viv** had not met, but who seemed to know her
well enough.
Etched in their black and white past forms,
they matched the munching Friesians (slain too recently
for daring not to produce their expected yield of milk.
The swishing grasses were glad to be cropped to make
them healthier than had cattle cake and bonemeal).
*Did
you know, **Viv**, you now have seven grandchildren?*
Vivace blinked at **Wiz-dom** in astonishment.
*They are
growing up so fast the earth family have called
a conference to try to answer all their questions
on the universe.*
I think, said **Wit, the answers —
some, at least —
will come from the seven,
rather than their grand, or great grand, parents!
Life and Vera are already quizzing Light, who had
great insights from the North and South Auroras.**

*And we think **Leo** and **Learn** are on their way,*
Wiz
added,

150

along with their parents and also **String**
and **Laurel**.

They'll need to hire a hall to house all those!
This was **Viv**'s first joke for longer than anybody could
remember.
Unless the weather there's as nice as this.

The weather was,
(thanks maybe to the seven siblings,
to whose coherent radiance, it seemed, the elements
were as responsive, as they had proved antagonistic
to global twisting for greedy human ends).
So
they met in open air,
Light having left a message on
Belle's website, inviting her to phone from **England**
or maybe join them telepathically.
Strand,
away with **William** on his latest vulcan project, found
herself able to attune, through **String**, to thoughts
of **Light** that also may have helped precipitate
this focussed gathering.
For **Light**'s experience,
gazing at the **Southern Cross**, he had not perceived
as deprivation —
rather as a state of timeless ecstasy,
in which all we know of   .
comes into being and is held,
by the **Logos'** conjugation with the **Spirit of the Earth**
and devic helpers, for all recorded time.
Thus can we
say:
"in whom we live and move and have our being."

Light found in **Lucifer**, his first grandson, an austere
brightness that carried all the poise of being alive

in nature, his own childhood experience had lacked,
(his fieriness not then truly grounded — until he met with
Belle).

                  Lucy and **Veracity** together
reminded **Light** of lightning playing through
an earthern vessel of almost unearthly composition:
rare earths fired in molten metal, such as only **Vigour**
could have forged,
               while **Verve** held his mind steady,
and the pitched hum of **Vital** helped in fashioning
life's instruments.
                Strand's heart and mind
imbibed and held this, as the family gathering focussed
on the earth reflection of that sunny upland, where **Viv**
had met with **Wit** and **Wiz**, and, with them, looked in
now.
                 Grounded between
the forest and the town, (where no evidence of the rift˙
remained), this fertile land began to draw together
more than the members of this human family.

                     As
Laughter also tuned hirself to **Light**'s intuited vision,
and the sun came up over the world's lip,
                Life began
to gather for a fuller focus than hir long slumbering
had seemed to prophesy.
          At last, thought **Love-Lyric**,
as she too was drawn by this magnetic rising,
                  Life
is like a swan about to launch.

             Freedom, said **Life**
in a voice no one had heard before,

˙ see *Strands of Wisdom* – Phase I

is the most
precious gift humanity has received —
                                        also
the most difficult to live with.
                        We need more space
than our teeming billions here seem able, or
willing, to negotiate.
                        I see two obvious
solutions:
                        either we cease to procreate and turn
to widening channels between this biosphere
and where we came from (and return to) —
                                        or
we spread our wings, the seven of us, and lead
a search for other places in the universe, where
life is as sustainable as here.
                        A startled silence.
  You realise,
                said **Lucifer** at last,
                        that only volcanic
planets can sustain the kind of bio-life we have
lived here.
                Conditions of risk and danger
seem essential to the human undertaking.

                                        Fire
is of the essence at all levels,
                        Life agreed,
                                        but
it need not necessarily
                        be fire-by-friction.
Faultlines, thus engendered,
                        have their own beauty,
as the past history of our life here shows.
                                        But
the lesson of difference has been almost too well
learned.
                                        Now

· see **Wisdom Stranded** – Phase III

at the dawn of this New Age, is perhaps the time
for discovering something of the vast extent
of the great cosmic symphony we all partake in —
greater by far than any earth musician
has dreamed of giving birth to,

                                  wherein each
individual
                is both instrument
                        and player,
though none has known this while in incarnation,
and none can perfect hir playing
                      or hir instrument,
except through this earthly bio-living.
                      This is both
human tragedy
            and joy triumphant.
                      Only by living
in the present moment, with no eye to past
or future glories,
                can human loving reach
its lovely peak.
                      Life paused
to glance at hir first sister, **Vera**, whose shining eyes
mirrored her sibling's words.
                     Life shifted tone:
Some of you write from left to right, some right
to left; others by scrolling down the page; while
some write upward from the page's foot.

                      Some
of you do not write at all, but share your thoughts
even without the spoken word.
                  Other mammals
do this all the time
              in tones and pitch so various
it may not be known that any more is uttered
than a cry of pain —
           or joy.

              Heard or unheard,
a song is being sung.

**It vibrates through all of us
and causes change.**

While **Life** was speaking,
a silent happening was taking place.
Strand
could just 'see' it from her distant viewpoint:
first
the cows, no longer munching, joined the gathering,
forming a circle round the family.
Then pigs and sheep
began to find their way,
and all the family's cats,
as one by one,
animals came from the forest:
deer and monkeys, wolves and jackals, wild boar
and bears,
turtles and lizards and the smaller snakes.
At last tropical animals emerged:
spotted, striped
or blotched, the big cats came, forming an outer circle,
with gorillas, a maned lion,
and a giraffe surveying all,
which included crocodile, hippopotamus, as well as
a huge python and a rearing cobra —
every animal
that could live on land.
Finally, an elephant
matriarch, with her rubbery new born, lower than
her knee,
trod into the centre of those circles
in the open air.

Laughter gave voice
to what seemed hanging there:
**What Life has said
seems to have changed the form**

of what you
thought we had come here to do.
I want to speak
the meaning of androgyny, here in the presence
of these gendered forms.
This little elephant,
and all the rest of us, came into the world
through loving mothers sired by loving mates.
That is the way the Logos seems to choose,
although our genetic makeup surely could
have replicated otherwise (and did for billions
of years of sturdy bacteria,
who still do).
Nature
it seems, now plays with us:
more and more
producing what the world calls 'freaks',
although
an androgynous state of being clearly is a norm
of higher consciousness,
that holds together
qualities of both ray lines of force.

The other day
I saw a lovely picture by a European painter,
several centuries gone:
a delighted baby, cradled
in its mother's arms, fingers winding joyously
the dangling tendrils of her beard.
Laughter
paused.
Might it be that,
just as the crocodile's eggs assume their gender,
due to the air temperature, below which she has
buried them in earth,
so are we altered
in our electro-chemical forms
by purposes
playing on us through the notes and tones
that thrill the air round us and pass through ?

Life intervened:
                    I have come to realise, Laughter,
although I am as androgynous as you, that not yet
(if indeed the time will come on earth at all)
will procreation be brought about through
physical androgyny.
                              The beautiful story
you have told us of the painter
                              is unmistakably
about secondary sexual characteristics, and not
primary.
                    The baby had a mother with a beard.
The mother who carried the baby in her womb,
and fed and fondled her when she was born,
was still fertilised by the baby's father's sperm.

If change is coming in the way of our conceiving,
it will be because rapport between women
and their men
                    has reached such ecstatic heights
of mental penetration
                              that conception itself will be
a mental act.
                              Already, we know,
sperm counts in men and boys are falling fast.
This need not mean that human beings cease
to procreate.
                    Nor yet that animals will cease
to carry young within the womb
                              (both now
and as they individually evolve through human
forms, as apes are very close indeed to doing).

It does mean that parents will share absolutely all
responsibility for nurturing —
                              both for the babies'
sakes,
            but also
                    so that mothers may develop,
as Vital has,
                    all the qualities of driving thought

and strength we have till now attributed to males.
And men will be as beautiful as women.

Laugh

looked at his oldest sibling —
and assented:

This

is the place where truth and beauty meet.

A murmur of approving joy went rippling through
the gathered circles, as the baby elephant lifted
its tiny trunk in its first salute to life.

Vera knew
it was time for her to speak her truth as 'Wisdom, who
knows the possibilities'.*

(Vision

caught her eye — and did not blink,

as **Love-Lyric**

nodded with him over **Life**'s correction of their first
thinking on androgyny):

VERA'S TRUTH

What Life has said is how it indeed will be:
Beauty and Truth are met together here.
Truth is sounded by the God
of unconditional Love,
which 'moves the Sun and all the other stars,'
moves them to be
but also to become.

Only the form knows death and Death shall be
seen as Life's playful bedfellow.
For out of the death of each perfected form
shall rise another form more beautiful —
conceived, as Life said,
through loving penetration.

˙ see *Possible Scenarios*

Only the interpenetration of two minds
can sound the note that carries
every form:
the rainbow light of joyous difference —

whether of living beings like ourselves,
or myriads of manufactured things,
like books or dynamos or dams
or recipes for food —

or Nature's mountains, forests, rivers,
flowers or birds.
For plants and animals have given
of themselves:
their coloured chemistry is patterned
by their atoms,
which, played upon by sound, induce
the shapes
we see solidified in warp and weft
of Nature's weaving —
as ray meets ray
in intricacy so deft
we sense it as we name
Life's tapestry.

This is the truth we know shall make us free,
this the beauty that we need to know.

So play your instruments
and learn to be
the instruments you thus
shall learn to play,
as you discover and sound out
the chord
of your own unique
and individual ray.

Thus shall sound the Cosmic Symphony:
             thus shall the aeons come and go,
with human freedom choosing
                        all the airs to sing,
and Nature's wisdom
                   all the winds that blow.

             That is all on Earth we need to know.

As all imbibed in silence **Vera's Truth**,
                                    the septet,
as seven swans,
                  took to the air and circled seven times,
each time with a different sibling in the lead:
                                        Vera
and **Lucy** spiralling higher even than had **Life**,
                                        Laugh
evening out,
                  while **Verve** and **Vital** spiralled down,
and **Vigour** led the septet back to earth, so human
form.

       Belle, after due reflection, faxed through to **Light**
her thought:
                  she had seen the swans and had devined
the next project the septet would undertake would be
the very problem, to avoid which, **Life** had offered
his 'too obvious' solutions:
                              Earth's teeming
billions — and how her resources might be better used,
by humans truly expressing right relations, through
the seven siblings' own example, as they never wasted
time or energy in quarrelling, because they valued
their own,
                  and one anothers', offerings:
                              not alone
toward one another,

but toward every animal and plant
and mineral the planet harbours.

For the first time
Belle revealed the esoteric teaching that a band
of enlightened individuals stands at the planetary heart,
between the **Logos** and Humanity, watching invisibly
over the needs of every form of Life (but not ever
encroaching on essential freedom).

The Teacher
of these illumined ones (known also as **The Dragons
of the Wisdom**) she called **The Coming One**.

Clearly
Belle saw this Septet from the Southern Hemisphere, as
the long awaited reappearance of **The Coming One**,
embodying **The Seven Spirits before the Throne**,
our earthly **Logos**,

who looks, for inspiration,
to what is hidden by the Sun —

Recorder: *as in turn the* **Solar Logos** *looks
to the* **Great bear, Sirius** *and the* **Pleiades**,
*whose synchronised energies inspire hir work,
by means of the* **Seven Rays**

*and the twelve, safely
stepped down, forces of the* **Zodiac**.

Always it is:
'As above,
so below'.

*There is also an unknown band
of human helpers (of whom* **Belle** *is one), existing in
and out of human incarnation, who link between
the enlightened adepts and the bulk of human kind —
to form a vast meditating throng, who work,
especially at the Full Moons and the New, to bring
into being the kind of world we want.*

The human
project is to ask the deeper questions; it all too easily
assumes it has the answers.

Seeker: Is humanity
perhaps a great community of inquiring minds?
I find what you and **Belle** have said reminds me
of the story of the two green caterpillars nibbling
on a leaf, while a gorgeous butterfly
was lifting off from one nearby.
                                              As it nudged the other,
one caterpillar shook its head:
                                              "You'd never get me
to go up in one of those!", it said.

Recorder (smiling tenderly):   Apperception has
to be the key:
                        we see what we see.
                                              Not often will
that be
                        enough to hold all things together.

Seeker: Until,
like the sibling septet,
                                              we have accessed all
the perspectives of the Seven Rays,
                                              so can control
the ways we use them.

Recorder: Very true, but since
the true route to such control is by way of a total
letting go, at risk of losing all control whatever,
I think the time to make this known has come.
                                                                Not
for nothing have we called this final volume:
Risking Wisdom.

          Wisdom *is subject always*
to the focussed **Will**, *for that is* **Life**.

                  Let us then dare
to see
       the dragonfly we are to be —

                        when
we have learned to hear and learned to sound
our individual chord upon our own particular set
of instruments, our bodies resonating to our rays,
with every other differential form, thus causing even
Sun and stars to move.

Seeker: *If it is sound that moves,*
    what moves the sound?

Recorder: *Ask* **Life***!*

He meant this to be rhetorical,
                but, true to the bias
of human freedom down the ages, the dogged **Seeker**
did:
                Love,
               said **Life,** responding,
is the implementing of the Will of Life through
Sound.
       When Sound is moved, it moves to manifest
in all the realms of colour difference: we speak
of quarks with qualities of charm, of ups and
downs, and turnings left or right.
                    All these
are moves, which may attract, repel — or hold
together what already is.
               The spell, when cast,
is constant for an aeon of loving, interpenetrating
cosmic song.
             The moves of chess, or sex,
are equally expressive of this cosmic, choral
symphony —

as are rainbows, bolts of lightening,
refracting, hexagonal snow crystals, waxed cells
of honey combs,

      or the great six-pointed Star
of human destiny —

     when the Logos of the Seven
Solar Systems

      whirls into action to create through
Sound,

    thus setting in motion every cosmic string.

But, said the **Seeker** doggedly,

         which are
these Seven ?

       Of that, said **Life**,
nothing may yet be said —

      except that ours is one.

The **Seeker** dared to cock his brow again.

          Life
obliged:

    Earth's place in this,

       when Humanity
shall at last be ready —

       is to become
a Sacred Beacon to the Cosmos.

POSTLUDE

Seeker: Did you know that sperm carry all the possibilities of change, while female eggs prefer to stabilise inheritance?

Recorder: *I confess I haven't given much thought to what that might imply.*

Seeker: Well, the current trend to have babies rather late in life is very bad news for DNA and so for faulty genes (as Nature plays with us), because sperm vibrancy wears off with time (just as rocks weather and hills reduce in size).

Recorder: *Then it is just as well that many of the **Wisdom** children brought forth as teenagers, especially **Vision** and **L-L** — so helpful mutations could occur.*

*What you say bears out my contention all along about the creative driving force of the **1-3-5-7** line as male, with **2-4-6** providing the relating and therefore stabilising female influence.*

Seeker: It surely also highlights the need for rays of both,

in one person —

to make a truly balanced individual.

It would also seem to me to justify the fact of sex as the means that humans use for reproducing

Recorder: *until the mind, not genes, can carry the two opposing,*

highly creative,

trends.

166

Seeker: Isn't this saying something vital about the relation between consciousness and energy,

maybe the place of reconciling in the dance of life.

For life is a dance, as well as a deeply orchestrated symphony.

Recorder: *Yes, it is a playful dance, and therefore open-ended — as the risk through mutations always has to be.*

*The **Logos** and **Nature** must be taking unbelievable risks to bring into being all the elements of Life.*

Seeker: That men see women as the unpredictable, and so unstable element would seem to me the paradox!

Recorder: *Yet always has the female been the constant, by way of the trillions of cells that make our bodies up — conserving the energy sperm need, to carry through exciting new mutations —*

when we treat our bodies properly, that is.

Seeker: I wonder if what we feed them with,

and how,

could make the difference?

Recorder: *Feeding our bodies rightly is indeed a part of what I meant.*

Seeker: I'm coming to see that food may not just be something to fill our bellies with for energy.

Recorder: *No, the relation's much more subtle.*

It is indeed our task to bring on our cells' evolution
by feeding them food that will be spiritually
nourishing — for them as much as us.

Seeker: That makes us
almost our bodies' priests
                                                                            as in the Eucharist!

Recorder: *That's right: all four kinds of elementals are at work*
each hour — bringing forth ingredients for our use.
Some say that earthworms have the task of passing
the soil of the whole planet through their systems,
to raise it a notch in the scheme of evolution.
                                                                            We
complex human beings have this task for all our cells.
By the same token, no doubt, we may, through
our absorbed experience, become the fodder
for whatever higher beings feed on us!

Seeker: So the great Chain of Being is really how things are!
And the food chain must constitute its base (as **Marx**
contended all along)

Recorder: *even if he went too far*
in toppling the top to let the bottom up.
                                                                            There really is
no inherent contradiction once you grasp
that the opposites must all be reconciled
by a third factor,
                                                                            our perpetually evolving
consciousness —
                                                                            achieving polar union at last ...

Seeker: as we know the joy of loving and forgiving: these
are the possibilities **Wisdom** always knew.

APPENDICES

1

THE GREAT INVOCATION

As first given out through the **Lucis trust** in 1945:

From the point of Light within the Mind of God
  Let light stream forth into the minds of men.
    Let Light descend on Earth.

From the point of Love within the Heart of God
  Let love stream forth into the hearts of men.
    May Christ return to Earth.

From the centre where the Will of God is known
  Let purpose guide the little wills of men –
    The purpose which the Masters know and serve.

From the centre which we call the race of men
  Let the Plan of Love and Light work out
    And may it seal the door where evil dwells.

Let Light and Love and Power restore the Plan on Earth.

        OM   OM   OM

The alternative rendering offered by the **Lucis Trust** in 2000

From the point of Light within the Mind of God
  Let light stream forth into human minds.
    Let Light descend on Earth.

From the point of Love within the Heart of God
  Let love stream forth into human hearts.
    May the Coming One return to Earth.

From the centre where the Will of God is known
  Let purpose guide all little human wills –
    The purpose which the Masters know and serve.

From the centre which we call the human race
  Let the Plan of Love and Light work out
    And may it seal the door where evil dwells.

Let Light and Love and Power restore the Plan on Earth.

    OM   OM   OM

Light's Invocation (used early in the 21st century)

From the point of Light within the mind of God
  let light stream forth into our human minds.
    Let Light descend on earth.

From the point of Love within the Heart of God,
  let love stream forth into our human hearts.
    May Christ be felt in Earth.

From the centre where the Will of God is known,
  let purpose guide our human wills,
    the purpose every adept knows and serves.

From the centre which we call the human race,
  let the plan of love and light work out,
    and heal the space malicious discord fills.

Let Light and Love and Life restore the planet Earth.

    OM   OM   OM

The **Lucis Trust** is concerned to safeguard the original wording of **The Great Invocation** (as arrived at between AAB and the Tibetan in 1945), because the English rendering has been scrupulously selected, not only to convey deep esoteric meanings, but also to carry the numerology values of the chosen words, in order to make the deepest possible mantric impact on the inner subjectivity of users, hearers and indeed the very substance of the planet's etheric nature.

Nevertheless, for the sake of reaching a wider human constituency, **Lucis** decided at the turn of the Millennium, to reword certain contentious phrases, such as "minds of men" et al (which feminists had always found alienating), as well as substituting the phrase, "the Coming One" in place of "the Christ" (which had tended to restrict to Christians the religious appeal of this powerful prayer). Albeit reluctantly, these changes were agreed..

Lucis feel that any adaptation of **The Great Invocation** ceases to be **The Great Invocation,** and that a proliferation of such preferred versions would confuse and ultimately diminish their power in use. I have therefore agreed to call my own rendering: **Light's Invocation**, in the conviction that it shares the intent (so far as we can know this) of whatever occult phrases may have been revealed, via the **Solar Logos** to our **Planetary Logos,** and passed on for the use of **The Coming One,** to aid humanity's struggle to change itself from a squabbling mass of six billion individuals to coherent cultural groups of enlightened beings, forming perhaps, the **Logos'** heart.

There will always be difference of opinion and therefore preference. The radiant sibling septet have no problem transcending this, via their mastery and their surrender to the energies of the Seven Rays, which, by virtue of their being therein composed, they radiate.

As shall we all.

2
GLOBAL LINKINGS/THE NEW INTERNATIONALIST

String's association with **GL/*Global Linkings*** is based on my own perception of the workings of *The New Internationalist,* with their permission. They request that I describe it as 'loosely based' – perception being always an individual matter, and my having no inside knowledge of its operation, beyond what my **Starter Pack** has given me.

I am glad they feel able in general to accept my account, as I have been a subscriber to **NI** for about fifteen years, and have great faith in the integrity and competence of the members of this Cooperative, who both edit and investigate the themes it covers monthly.

It is also they who distribute the book of aerial photographs of the earth's surface, **Seen from Above,** which holds so much significance for **String.**

3
THE SEVEN RAYS

This formulation of the Seven Rays, taken from the Alice Bailey book, *The Destiny of the Nations*, focuses on ray power in relation to the development of humanity, rather than that of the individual. As the civilising process evolves races into nations, unconscious use of their dominating ray forces may be said to forward chosen purposes.

[The Rays] are called by many names in many different lands, but for our purposes the following seven names will be used:

1 The energy of Will, Purpose or Power, called in Christian lands the energy of the Will of God.

2 The energy of love-Wisdom, called frequently the love of God.

3 The energy of Active Intelligence, called the Mind of God.

4 The energy of Harmony through Conflict, affecting greatly the human family.

5 The energy of Concrete Knowledge or Science, so potent at this time.

6 The energy of Devotion or Idealism, producing the current ideologies.

7 The energy of Ceremonial Order, producing the new forms of civilisation.

This formulation is much briefer than any account in the five volume Ray Treatise, of which the first two books deal explicitly with Psychology, individual as well as esoteric, the third with Esoteric Astrology (thus offering a picture of cosmic causes), and the fourth with Esoteric Healing. All Bailey books are available from Lucis Press Ltd, Suite 54, 3 Whitehall Court, London SW1A 2EF, who hold copyright, and whose permission was granted for these extracts.

174

4 FAMILY TREE

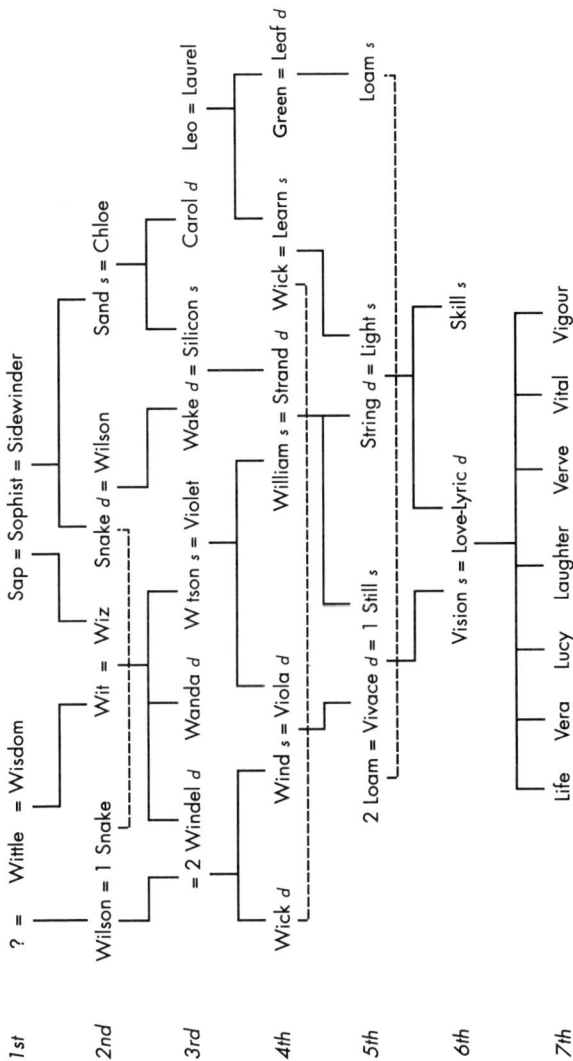